POLICE DEPARTMENT
One Police Plaza
New York, NY 10038

PERSONNEL FILE

Req #: 2014-PL-10945
File #:

TO BE FILLED IN BY IMMEDIATE SUPERIOR:

Detective
MICHAEL BENNETT

6 FOOT 3 INCHES (191CM)   200 POUNDS (91KG)
IRISH AMERICAN

EMPLOYMENT

Bennett joined the police force to uncover the truth
at all costs. He started his career in the Bronx's
49th Precinct. He then transferred to the NYPD's
Major Case Squad and remained there until he moved
to the Manhattan North Homicide Squad.

EDUCATION

Bennett graduated from Regis High School and studied
philosophy at Manhattan College.

FAMILY HISTORY

Bennett was previously married to Maeve, who worked as a
nurse on the trauma ward at Jacobi Hospital in the Bronx.
However, Maeve died tragically young after losing a battle
with cancer in December 2007, leaving Bennett to raise
their ten adopted children: Chrissy, Shawna, Trent, Eddie,
twins Fiona and Bridget, Ricky, Brian, Jane and Juliana.

Following Maeve's death, over time Bennett grew closer to
the children's nanny, Mary Catherine. After years of on-
off romance, Bennett and Mary Catherine decided to commit
to one another, and now happily raise the family together.
Also in the Bennett household is his Irish grandfather,
Seamus, who is a Catholic priest.

PROFILE:

AMENDED REPORT

BENNETT IS AN EXPERT IN HOSTAGE NEGOTIATION,
TERRORISM, HOMICIDE AND ORGANIZED CRIME. HE WILL STOP
AT NOTHING TO GET THE JOB DONE AND PROTECT THE CITY
AND THE PEOPLE HE LOVES, EVEN IF THIS MEANS DISOBEYING
ORDERS AND IGNORING PROTOCOL. DESPITE THESE UNORTHODOX
METHODS, HE IS A RELENTLESS, DETERMINED AND IN MANY
WAYS INCOMPARABLE DETECTIVE.

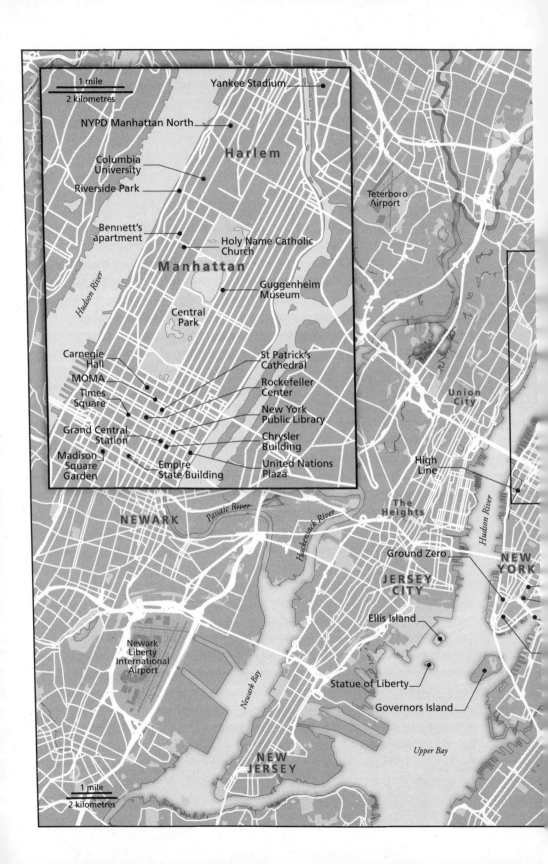

1 mile
2 kilometres

Yankee Stadium

NYPD Manhattan North

Harlem

Columbia University

Riverside Park

Bennett's apartment

Holy Name Catholic Church

Manhattan

Guggenheim Museum

Central Park

Carnegie Hall

MOMA

Times Square

St Patrick's Cathedral

Rockefeller Center

New York Public Library

Grand Central Station

Chrysler Building

Madison Square Garden

Empire State Building

United Nations Plaza

Teterboro Airport

Union City

High Line

The Heights

Hudson River

Passaic River

Hackensack River

NEWARK

Ground Zero

JERSEY CITY

NEW YORK

Newark Liberty International Airport

Ellis Island

Statue of Liberty

Governors Island

Newark Bay

NEW JERSEY

Upper Bay

1 mile
2 kilometres

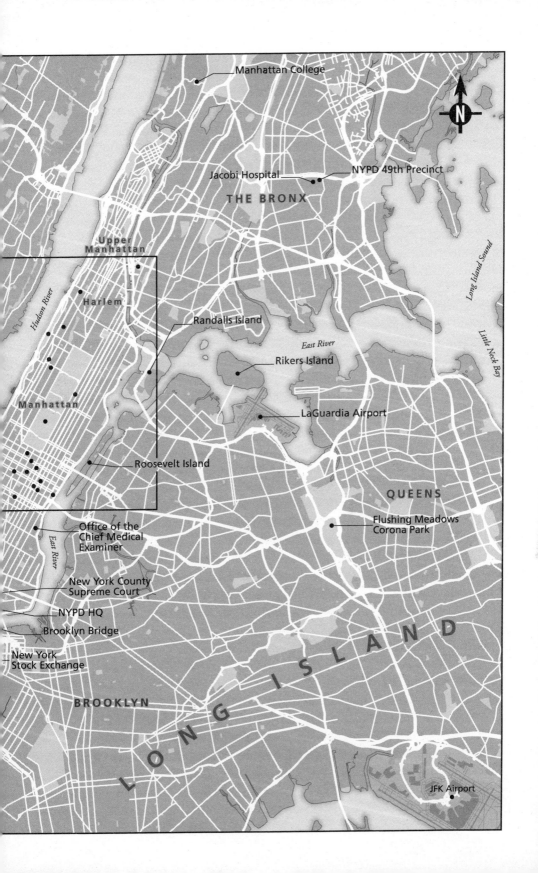

A list of titles by James Patterson appears at the
back of this book

Paranoia

JAMES PATTERSON
& JAMES O. BORN

CENTURY

CENTURY

UK | USA | Canada | Ireland | Australia
India | New Zealand | South Africa

Century is part of the Penguin Random House group of companies
whose addresses can be found at global.penguinrandomhouse.com

Penguin Random House UK,
One Embassy Gardens, 8 Viaduct Gardens, London SW11 7BW

penguin.co.uk
global.penguinrandomhouse.com

First published in the UK by Century 2025
001

Printed and bound in Great Britain by Clays Ltd, Elcograf S.p.A.

The authorised representative in the EEA is Penguin Random House Ireland,
Morrison Chambers, 32 Nassau Street, Dublin D02 YH68

A CIP catalogue record for this book is available from the British Library

ISBN: 978–1–529–13645–6 (hardback)
ISBN: 978–1–529–13646–3 (trade paperback)

Penguin Random House is committed to a sustainable
future for our business, our readers and our planet. This book
is made from Forest Stewardship Council® certified paper.

Paranoia

CHAPTER 1

RALPH STEIN TRIED to swallow. His throat was too dry. He'd been in tight spots before, but nothing like this. He needed to buy time. He wasn't sure what he'd do with it, but the longer he kept this guy's attention, the greater the chance that he might get out of this. Or so he hoped.

Ralph cast a reassuring look over at Gary Halverson. But Gary was past the point of reassurance. Sweat poured down his face, making his thin hair stick to his forehead. The gray stubble on his chin glistened with perspiration.

"This isn't necessary," Ralph said to the guy.

"I agree," the tall man with close-cropped brown hair mumbled. The guy looked pretty calm to Ralph. A real pro.

Ralph tried to keep the fear out of his voice, but it didn't work. "I can get some cash. I can give you more money than whoever's paying you to do this."

"Not about the money." The man checked the two propane tanks he'd placed right in front of Gary and Ralph, and the cord he'd used to secure their hands to kitchen chairs. He showed no emotion and no real interest in chatting with Ralph.

Ralph figured both the cord and the timer were made of some kind of non-synthetic material that would burn away and leave no evidence. He looked around the kitchen. The walls were decorated with photographs and cartoons of sharks. Ralph's favorite was a cartoon of a shark in an NYPD uniform. A street artist had drawn it for him when he was a patrol officer in Times Square. His eyes fell on the crayon portrait that his sister's little granddaughter had drawn for him. She was an absolute doll. Ralph caught the sob before it came out.

"How'd you know about us? Who sent you?" Ralph figured there were plenty of people who could've sent the guy, but why would anyone bother to track him down in Florida now? "C'mon, I can tell by that weird-looking timer you're fixing to those propane tanks that you're no ordinary street hood. You have to know Gary and I were both cops. Doesn't that mean anything to you?"

The man, who looked to be in his late thirties, stopped his work and sighed. He turned and said in a quiet voice, "It *does* mean something. Thank you for your service. Now please stop talking. This is a done deal. You're kinda bumming me out."

Ralph perked up. "You're from Brooklyn, right? I never miss an accent. Especially from back home."

The man continued working, ignoring Ralph.

Ralph kept it up. "Were you in the military? In World War II, Brooklyn led the country in recruits. Not so much these days.

New York has fallen off as a supplier of soldiers." He looked at the man, hoping to spark some conversation. He got nothing.

The man finished adjusting a small green-and-brown device attached to one of the propane tanks. Then he looked up at Ralph and put his finger to his lips, prompting him to keep quiet.

Ralph tried to think things through. The man was probably thirty years younger than him. He was in shape and carried a Beretta 9mm. When he'd knocked on the door of Ralph's little two-bedroom rental house in Hollywood Beach, Ralph had figured him to be a tourist looking to find a bridge back over to town, or maybe the easiest way to get down to Miami. That was his first mistake. He'd lost his edge in his old age.

Gary said, "I already sent the email, Ralph. Considering what the doctors said, I'm no worse off."

One of the first things the man had done after he'd pulled the gun was to make Gary write a good-bye email to his niece. Now Ralph watched as the man pulled the keyboard away from the computer on the kitchen counter and tossed it out the front door.

Ralph mumbled, "What the hell?"

Gary snorted. "It's the difference in assignments. You did most of your time in narcotics, Ralph. I did a stint in homicide. He's got my fingerprints on the keyboard. They'll ID me from that. He tossed it outside like it was blown there by the blast. It's pretty inventive, if I do say so myself."

The man looked up and nodded at Gary. Just a little sign of respect. He pressed a plunger on the little gadget he'd attached to the propane tank on the right. Then he turned the knob on each tank until they could all hear the hiss of the escaping propane.

Then the man was gone. Silently and gracefully ducked out the open door and disappeared.

Ralph prayed the asshole didn't know his sister, Rachel, lived right down the street. She didn't need to be involved in this foolishness. When he thought about it for a moment, he realized *he* hadn't needed to be involved in it either.

CHAPTER 2

RACHEL STEIN CONNORS liked to stroll down the boardwalk on Hollywood Beach in the afternoons with her two grandchildren to visit her big brother, who'd moved into a little house nearby about a year ago. Ralph had spent eight years telling her he was going to retire from the NYPD and move to Florida. Now that he'd finally done it, she made sure to see him every day. Even though he was twelve years older than her, he was a great big brother. He deserved the best retirement in the world.

As Rachel walked, she held the hands of her five-year-old grandson and three-and-a-half-year-old granddaughter. They were both excited to visit Uncle Ralph's house, with all the cool drawings and photos of sharks he had up on his wall.

Suddenly, the little girl froze and scooted behind her grandmother's sundress. Rachel looked up and saw a golden retriever being walked by a young woman. "It's okay, sweetheart, he's on a leash," she said in a soft voice. The little girl had recently conflated things overheard from a news report about a dog who'd mauled a girl in the Broward County town of Miramar, and she'd decided all dogs were dangerous.

The woman paused, realizing that the little girl was scared, and pulled her dog close. She encouraged the children to pet him, reassuring them that her dog was friendly. Rachel went with it, hoping it might be a way to cure her granddaughter's phobia, and was pleasantly surprised when both kids started to pat the dog gently. As the woman leaned down, Rachel spotted her brother's house across state road A1A, over the woman's shoulder.

She saw the flash a moment before she felt the explosion. She heard it too, but the visceral shock to her system was from the blast wave. The entire house seemed to burst at once.

Rachel fell to the sidewalk, still staring at her brother's home, now engulfed in flames. As soon as she gathered her senses, she reached out and grabbed both of her grandchildren. She turned them away from the scene just as she started to feel heat from the quickly spreading fire.

People on the beach were shouting. A blue Mazda, going south on A1A, swerved into an unoccupied bus bench. Everyone seemed to have their phones out, either taking photos or calling 911.

Rachel flinched as more noises came from inside the house. Nothing at all like the initial blast, but loud pops and crackles.

Two thoughts hit her at the same time. Her brother was dead. And if this woman hadn't stopped to let the kids pet her dog, they all would be dead too.

Then she started to cry.

CHAPTER 3

I WASN'T USED to wearing a tie. It was one of those things I didn't have to worry about in my day-to-day life. Unfortunately, I was about to attend a funeral. A cop's funeral. A retired cop who'd died too soon. I guess that's how we feel about anyone we like and respect who passes. Lou Sanvos had spent most of his career as a detective in narcotics. Like a lot of people, I lost touch with Lou after he retired about ten years ago.

The Annunciation Greek Orthodox Church on West 91st looked like something out of a Gothic literary story. Tucked in the middle of Manhattan, the stone walls and tower seemed somewhat out of place. And although I'd passed it about a million times in my life, this was the first time I'd ever been inside. It somehow seemed more solemn than Holy Name, the Catholic church my family attended.

There were about 150 people here, a decent crowd for a guy

who'd retired almost a decade ago. I'd brought my new twenty-four-year-old partner, Rob Trilling, with me. He was having a hard time making contacts within the department, mainly because he was so quiet, and also because he was technically still on temporary assignment to Manhattan North Homicide. He couldn't work a case solo yet. Currently, he was helping Detective Terri Hernandez with an investigation involving a gang responsible for at least two recent homicides. I figured there'd be a few people at this funeral still on the job who I could introduce him to. Besides, I liked having Trilling around. He was entertaining, quirky and unpredictable.

As we slipped into a pew near the rear of the church, I turned to Trilling and said, "You said you were a little weird, and that you like funerals. What do you think of this one so far?"

The young man almost smiled. I'd realized by now that Trilling wasn't as gloomy and brooding as he often seemed. "I don't necessarily *like* funerals, Bennett," Trilling said. "I like the traditions and rituals. Back in Montana, I was in school with some kids from the Blackfeet Nation. When one of their own died, they had four days of mourning. And also cut their hair short to show that they were grieving. That kind of stuff impresses you as a kid."

"After a funeral like this, we usually hold a wake at a bar and tell stories about the departed. That's the NYPD tradition."

Trilling said, "My grandfather always said that going to a funeral is the one thing that you can never expect any repayment for. The deceased can't return the favor and come to *your* funeral. It's sort of an act of good faith and respect. I always thought that was a good way to look at funerals."

We watched silently as an honor guard marched down the center aisle of the church.

Trilling leaned in close and said, "I know Sanvos died in a car accident. What happened?"

I kept my voice low as a decidedly non-Catholic priest started to speak at the pulpit. I said, "Lou retired to White Plains to be near his kids. I heard he lost control of his car somehow and drove right through the front window of a store. The car caught fire. Ironically, the store he crashed into was a fire equipment and safety store."

"It looks like he was popular. I've been to funerals with only three or four people in attendance." Trilling looked around at the turnout.

"Aside from a long career in the NYPD, Lou did a lot for youth groups, especially in the Bronx. He really felt like the key to solving the gun crisis, as well as crime in general, was to provide kids with a safe place to grow up with decent role models. He focused on the worst neighborhoods that got the fewest resources."

Trilling mumbled, "I can see why you two were friends."

That might've been the nicest thing my young partner had ever said to me.

CHAPTER 4

AFTER THE SHORT, official reception at the parish house of the church, I dragged Trilling to the Irish Rose, one of Lou's favorite pubs. As soon as we stepped through the old wooden doorway, it was like entering another universe. The place was absolutely packed. Most of the people who'd attended the funeral were there, plus a bunch of cops just getting off shift, some still in uniform. There was a certain subdued rowdiness that Lou would've appreciated. The Saturday afternoon atmosphere magnified the emotions.

I nodded to half a dozen people as we walked through the crowded pub. Somehow we found a couple of stools at the far end of the bar. Without even asking, a stout bartender with a fancy curled mustache set down two Guinnesses in front of us.

A short, balding Black man with thick glasses crawled up onto a table and started banging a metal tray with a serving spoon. I turned toward Trilling and said, "That's Dave Sharp. One of the truly great guys in the NYPD."

Sharp waited for everyone's attention. "I'll let you get back to drinking soon enough. I just wanted to remind everyone why we're here. Lou Sanvos will never be forgotten in this town. His support for youth centers is unparalleled. Lou's wife, Margaret, tells me she's fine financially and that any money people might want to donate should go to Lou's favorite cause: helping young people.

"I'm going to pass around the bucket, and anyone who feels like it can throw in a few bucks. We'll split it between the two youth centers in the Bronx Lou worked so hard to build."

Someone came up and tugged on Dave Sharp's sleeve. He leaned down, then turned to the crowd and said, "And even though it's not official, let's not forget our own Celeste Cantor, who'll be retiring soon and running for New York City Council. We're hoping that's just a stepping stone to bigger and better things." That comment got a loud round of applause as Inspector Celeste Cantor—an attractive fiftysomething woman dressed in a dark-blue pantsuit and not her usual uniform with more ribbons and medals than a nineteenth-century Bavarian count—stood up and waved to everyone in the bar.

Trilling said, "Cops can run for political office?"

"You have to retire first. If she's half as good a City Council member as she is a cop, we'll all be in better shape soon."

Cantor smiled when she noticed me at the corner of the bar. She pointed directly at me and started marching in my direction, fending off a few people trying to corner her as she approached.

After she gave me a hug, I introduced her to Rob Trilling. Cantor smiled and said, "We've both come a long way from patrol work in the Bronx, haven't we, Mike?"

I turned to Trilling and said, "Inspector Cantor was part of a narcotics squad when she was a lowly sergeant. They called themselves the Land Sharks, after an old *Saturday Night Live* skit. It only took a couple of months before every dealer in the city took notice and worried about 'the Sharks' coming onto their turf. Even the commissioner referred to them as 'the Sharks' during a news conference."

"And now I'm about to be cast out to sea."

"If you're running for City Council, I call that *catching a wave.*"

Cantor laughed. "As tough and dangerous as police work can be, I think I still prefer it to politics."

I raised my glass of Guinness and said, "Hear, hear."

Trilling turned and stared at me, so I quickly said, "Sorry — the Irish pub got in my brain." I turned back to Cantor. "Let me know if there's anything I can do for you."

A crooked smile, the result of a broken jaw from a protester, spread across her face. "As a matter of fact, I do have something you could help me with."

I already regretted making the offer.

CHAPTER 5

KEVIN DOYLE HAD sat almost in the middle of the church during the service. He felt completely anonymous among the waves of cops and family mourning their loved one. He wore a simple blue suit. He could've been a piece of furniture, for all he was noticed. Doyle knew all about their loved one. He'd done his research. Lou Sanvos had gone to Hofstra on the GI Bill after he got out of the Army. After graduating, he'd decided to join the NYPD. It felt like Sanvos had done more for young people in the Bronx than all of the politicians in the whole city. That was a sort of activity Doyle respected. And it was that reputation that had made killing Lou Sanvos so upsetting.

Doyle's dad used to say, "We need to do more for the community because too many people do nothing." Doyle had joined the Army because of his dad's civic sense. And now Doyle had eliminated one of the few people who did more than their share.

Doyle had planned it perfectly. The light traffic up in White Plains had made him feel exposed, but the higher speed limit on the outskirts of town allowed Lou Sanvos to go fast enough for Doyle to tap the front bumper of Sanvos's Lincoln Continental with his stolen Ford. Physics did the rest. After Sanvos's car slammed into some kind of safety supply store, Doyle had been prepared to stop and finish off his target, but when he saw the fire, he knew his job was done.

Doyle remained seated in the church as the service concluded, taking in the architecture and traditions. A young Greek Orthodox priest, dressed in a traditional white cassock for funerals, paused at the end of the aisle and looked at him.

"Are you all right, my son?"

Doyle nodded. He didn't need anyone remembering him. "Just getting ready to light a candle for Lou."

"That's very thoughtful. We're also collecting money for the youth centers Mr. Sanvos helped create. The donation box is up front."

Doyle nodded to the priest as he stood up. The shrapnel in his left knee sent a quick spike of pain through his body. It happened so often he was surprised he still noticed it. Maybe it was judgment. If it was some kind of punishment, it wasn't enough.

The priest said, "Are you in this parish?"

"No, Father, I'm Catholic. Just here for the funeral."

"Are you a police officer?"

Doyle smiled and shook his head. "Not even close."

He turned toward the main entrance to the church, where he stopped and lit a candle for Lou's soul. Then he dug a twenty out of his pocket and slipped it into the donation box the priest had mentioned.

Outside, the fresh air felt good on his face. He looked up at the gathering clouds and decided to head back to his hotel. He'd worry about any messages later. He'd done enough for the cause this week.

CHAPTER 6

CELESTE CANTOR MOVED through the crowd like a great white shark. No pun intended. She was graceful and smooth, and anyone who noticed her got out of the way immediately.

I left Trilling at the bar and followed behind her like a remora. She certainly wasn't cold or menacing. She stopped and talked to a couple of people as we worked our way to an empty table in a corner.

An old-time narcotics detective gave Cantor a hug. He said, "Did you hear about Tabitha Arnold? She died from carbon monoxide after she got drunk and passed out in her kitchen with her car running in the garage."

Cantor nodded. "And I just heard Ralph Stein and Gary Halverson both committed suicide down in Florida."

The retired narcotics detective shook his head and looked down at the floor. "I heard. I knew Gary had advanced lung cancer. I just can't believe they'd use propane tanks to blow them-selves up."

It was a shock to hear from a credible source about the retired detectives, longtime associates who'd started as patrol partners. Police suicides were becoming an epidemic.

Cantor continued to make her way through the crowded pub, graciously accepting congratulations from a half dozen people on her imminent retirement. A few people also wished her luck in her campaign.

It felt like forever, but we finally reached a quiet table in the corner. Cantor sat right next to me and leaned in close so no one would overhear our conversation.

She said, "You heard about Ralph Stein and Gary Halverson. And poor Tabitha Arnold. Now we have Lou Sanvos. We all know the statistics on police deaths. But for four retired cops to die this close together…makes me a little nervous. They were all mem-bers of the Land Sharks. Sooner or later, you start to see a pattern." She reached over and squeezed my arm. "I was hoping you'd come to the wake, Mike. You're one of the few people I really trust."

I saw where she was going but kept my mouth shut. No way I wanted to volunteer for something. I was going to make her say it out loud.

She looked me in the eye and said, "I want you to look at these deaths. But quietly. Just you on it for now. I don't want to start a panic. I can get you a special assignment. You can report only to me. What do you think?"

I didn't want to speak too quickly. I considered several options. Then I said, "I'm not sure why we need to keep it quiet. A little coverage might help flush out information, if there's anything to it."

"That's where personal and public interests overlap. Obviously, it's no secret I'm running for City Council. If these deaths turn out to be something other than what they appear, it'll look bad for me on the campaign trail that I didn't catch it. This is the sort of thing that falls directly under me as an inspector. But if I have you look into things, and if it turns out to be more than random deaths, I look proactive in having recruited you to solve them. You're the best homicide detective out there. Hands down. No one will question me about these deaths if they know I assigned you the investigation."

I appreciated her honesty about how this could affect her campaign. She was also right. These deaths alarmed me and deserved to be investigated.

I slowly nodded. "I've got some time. But I don't need to be reassigned to you. Harry Grissom is on vacation. I'm the acting supervisor on the squad. I should be able to cover this without drawing too much attention."

Cantor patted me on the arm. "I knew I could count on you. As I get closer to my retirement date, I find I have less and less time for real police work. As I said, you're one of the few people I trust to do it for me. I'll get you some reports to read over the weekend so you can get a head start."

Just as I was about to temper her expectations, Cantor stood up to greet a well-wisher. Whether it was official or not, she was already on the campaign trail.

CHAPTER 7

I GOT HOME a little earlier than usual, but I now had on my iPad copies of police reports from White Plains and Hollywood, Florida, along with a report from the Westchester County Medical Examiner. My initial look through the details of these retired cops' deaths told me that the investigating detectives hadn't suspected anything beyond either suicide or accidental causes.

I made it all the way to the kitchen before any of my kids even noticed I was home. Chrissy jumped up from her homework to give me a hug. Jane, who was walking out of the kitchen, gave me a gentle pat on the belly. At least it was better than the stern look my teenager often threw my way these days.

Trent sat at the opposite end of the dining room table, doing his own homework. I leaned in as a concerned parent, willing to offer assistance.

"Whatcha working on?"

"Algebra."

I tried not to recoil too violently. I patted my son on his shoulder, mumbled, "Good luck," and eased my way into the living room. Ricky and Eddie were playing a video game from the couch. The rest of the kids had to be around here somewhere.

I took notice of my wife, Mary Catherine, sitting on a lounge chair on our balcony. She wasn't typically one for "lounging" during the day. In fact, I could easily imagine Mary Catherine calling an Army general too soft for giving his soldiers an hour off during a combat tour. Maybe that's an exaggeration. But maybe it's not.

The flip side was that, as exacting as her standards could be, Mary Catherine was also the kindest and most loving wife and mother imaginable. Though we were technically still newlyweds, for the better part of a decade now she'd been acting as mother to the ten children I'd adopted with my late first wife. And now we were embarking on a brand-new experience for the both of us, being in the early months of expecting an eleventh child after a grueling IVF process.

The more I thought about a new baby around the house, the more terrifying it became. I'd never considered having ten kids a huge challenge. We had fun. We worked well together. And now that a couple of the kids were older, life had gotten a lot easier for me. I didn't know why I kept thinking adding one more would drive me over the edge. I calmed myself down and tried looking at it from a different perspective.

I had to admit the idea of a smiling infant held a lot of appeal. I loved a baby's laughter. I wanted this baby every bit as much as Mary Catherine did. The kids were on board as well.

I went to the balcony and leaned down to kiss her hello, taking a moment to look at her. "Are you feeling okay?"

"Just a little tired. I thought I should get off my feet for a few moments. What about you? How was the funeral?"

I shrugged. That's like asking how someone enjoyed their visit to the dentist. Most people don't like funerals. Unless you're Rob Trilling, who was a little odd. I said, "I might've agreed to do something for Celeste Cantor."

"Something like an investigation, or something like maintenance around her apartment?"

Mary Catherine's Irish accent made most things sound cheerful and funny. Basically, any time she told a joke, I laughed out loud. This time was no exception. I shook my head. "It's not a big deal. I should be able to clear it up before Harry gets back from vacation."

Mary Catherine smiled. "It's hard to think of Lieutenant Harry Grissom actually leaving the job for a few weeks to visit a beach in the Caribbean. I'm glad *you've* always recognized there is a whole world outside of the NYPD. Of course, Harry never had any kids, so he doesn't understand how much time a real family can take."

"He knows how much time a wife can take. He's already experimented with those three times," I said. Then I added, "This vacation might have something to do with Lois Frang, the *Brooklyn Democrat* reporter he met during the sniper investigation. She seems nice."

Mary Catherine giggled and sat up in the lounger. I gave her a hand, helping her to her feet. She used the opportunity to give me a hug. We walked into the living room together.

I saw both Ricky and Eddie immediately set down their

video-game controllers. They never did anything like that when I walked into a room. Mary Catherine was definitely influencing these kids.

As we started toward the dining room, I noticed a hitch in Mary Catherine's step. Then she started to sag. I reached to support her at the elbow, guiding her toward the recliner. Just as Mary Catherine plopped into the chair, she was out. I mean full-out unconscious.

Commotion brewed around me. Jane stepped in from the dining room to see what was going on. She immediately took control of the other children and started barking orders like a Marine Corps gunnery sergeant.

I wasn't sure I'd ever experienced panic like this before.

I had to get Mary Catherine to the hospital. Now.

CHAPTER 8

IT WAS NOT long after dark. Rob Trilling was feeling a little worn-out from the funeral and meeting so many people. But
he still had commitments. He'd been helping Terri Hernandez
out on one of her cases, a series of homicides, including one in
Manhattan North's jurisdiction. Now he sat in the passenger seat
of a city-issued Ford Explorer, looking through binoculars at a
warehouse. Some people called it a "clubhouse." Nice way to
spend a Saturday evening.

From the driver's seat, Terri Hernandez said, "It's getting late.
We'll give it another ten minutes, but I have a birthday party for
my younger sister I'm not going to miss. She's dating a big, goofy
white guy who loves the band Kiss. I don't want to miss his official introduction to my father."

Trilling didn't answer. They'd been watching people come
and go from this building for a couple of hours. Informants said

members of this gang they were currently surveilling were responsible for the deaths of two rival gang members, whose bodies had washed up in the East River.

The gang had turned from street-level drug sales to importing cocaine and heroin. A smart move. Less exposure and higher profits, if more hassle. It looked like the two dead men had been trying to do the same thing.

All he and Hernandez were doing now was figuring out who was a member of the gang and who they did business with. So far, they'd identified seven gang members and five associates. The killer had to be one of the people they'd already identified. Now they just had to figure out which of them it was. Then make a case. Then take it to court. Easy.

Trilling had a special interest—these people were the remnants of one of the gangs Gus Querva used to run. They purposely didn't use a gang name. But that didn't change what they were. Before getting killed by a sniper, Querva had been a drug lord pretending to be a community activist, and Trilling hated what he'd done to the community, and how the media had covered his supposed investments in the neighborhood.

Terri Hernandez seemed agitated. Trilling knew she and Bennett were close, but she was nothing like his talkative senior partner.

"How much younger is your sister than you?" Trilling asked.

"Don't worry about it. You're never going to meet her."

Trilling held back a retort. Instead, after a few seconds, he said, "You don't like me very much, do you?"

"I don't like guys *like* you. Jocks who get moved into homicide after barely any time on patrol."

"I never asked to be moved."

"I did, for years, before I finally got my shot."

"I get that. But I'm not a jock."

"You look like one."

Trilling said, "Looks can be deceiving. For instance, you look like a nice, pleasant person."

Hernandez sighed loudly. "Look, I know you didn't ask to move into homicide. It wasn't right how everyone piled on you when Gus Querva got shot. But it's just frustrating to see someone who's been on the job less than two years already in basically the same position as me, when I've been on eight years."

"We're not in the same position. I'm still on temporary assignment and not even a detective. I'd say you've moved up the ladder well."

"You can say whatever you want, but you've got a lot to prove before I take you seriously."

Trilling nodded. "That sounds fair."

Hernandez groaned in irritation. "What's it take to get you worked up?"

"More than just a reasonable conversation, I guess."

"I can't tell if you're being serious or just messing with me."

Trilling was careful not to answer but let a little smile form, which he knew would drive her crazy.

She groaned again.

That made his smile grow.

CHAPTER 9

THE DRIVE TO Mount Sinai was as terrifying as anything I'd ever faced. Even in my life as a cop. I gripped the wheel of my Chevy Impala tightly so my hands wouldn't shake. Saturday evening traffic was somehow manageable. But I still didn't feel like I was driving fast enough.

Mary Catherine had come into semiconsciousness as we rode down in the elevator. She'd wanted to walk, but I'd insisted on carrying her to the parking garage across the street. Images of Mary Catherine with a baby and a smile on her beautiful face gave me near superhuman stamina as I'd raced to the car with her in my arms. The panic I felt affected my judgment. If I'd been thinking clearly, I would've called for her to be transported in an ambulance. Then again, I would've paced the rug down to threads if we'd had to wait for an ambulance to arrive. Who knew how long that would've taken on a Saturday night. It was pointless to wonder about that now.

Once at Mount Sinai, I felt nothing but frustration. Despite making world-class time to get here, we were then shoved into an exam room and told to wait. A young man in scrubs took some blood and tried to soothe our anxiety by saying someone would be along shortly. Finally, a technician took Mary Catherine for some scans, but half an hour later we were back in the same room, still alone and scared.

Mary Catherine lay sprawled on a narrow examination bed, above the sheets and coarse blanket. I held her hand as she put on a brave face, turning to me and asking, "Michael, what if this isn't meant to be? What if the baby doesn't make it?"

"Let's see what the doctor has to say." It was lame but all I could think of.

"But what…" Mary Catherine started to sob. A truck plowing through the window couldn't have hit me any harder. I felt helpless. One of the worst feelings in the world; one of the reasons I became a cop. I *wanted* to help people. Now I couldn't even help my wife.

I was worried about the baby, but I was more worried about if Mary Catherine was in any kind of danger. At least I was smart enough not to blurt out my concerns. Of course, the whole episode also made me think of my late wife, Maeve. The early days of her cancer diagnosis, the fear, the anger, the feelings of unfairness. *Why us?* I was reliving every one of those agonizing minutes as we waited for a doctor to walk through the door and deliver news. I had to take a breath.

Mary Catherine clutched my hand, and I pulled hers to my

lips and kissed it. I said in a soft voice, "I love you. Whatever happens, we'll get through it together."

"I love you too, Michael." She let out a couple of sobs and managed to add, "I already love this baby, whoever he or she is. I don't care if it's Seamus Bennett or Rose Bennett."

"I'm not sure what's more surprising," I said. "That you've already come up with baby names or that you'd want to name a boy after my grandfather."

"You don't agree?"

"No, I love it. It's just unexpected." I kissed her hand again. "Where did Rose come from?"

She had a hint of a smile as she admitted, *"Titanic."*

That made me smile too. That was all I needed. A moment of relief. A step away from worry.

A young doctor stepped into the room.

I heard Mary Catherine's intake of breath.

The doctor did not have a smile on her face.

CHAPTER 10

ROB TRILLING GRABBED the mail from his box.

"Did you save this city again today, Rob?" his super asked.

Trilling smiled at the comment. "Wasn't able to do much today, George."

"I saw your girl today. That one, she don't say much, does she?"

Rob shook his head as he walked away. "Mostly a language barrier," he mumbled. He trudged up the stairs, feeling the stress of the day and wanting nothing more than to lounge on the couch and watch TV. Provided his roommates accommodated his wish.

Rob looked both ways down the hallway before he opened his front door quickly and slipped into his apartment. He heard the TV on low. When he stepped all the way into the room, he saw it was a rerun of *Sesame Street*. The kids' show had done wonders for his roommates' English skills in a very short span of time. All five of them.

George Kazanjian assumed Rob had a girlfriend living with him. But luckily, the super didn't pay very close attention to who came and went from his apartment. For the last month, Rob had actually been living with five Pakistani women, all of whom he'd rescued from a Bronx warehouse where they'd been trafficked to work in a heroin processing operation, and whom he was now sponsoring to keep them from being housed in an immigration holding facility.

It was true that all five women had relatively similar features. Enough to confuse his super, he guessed. George seemed not to notice their physical differences, other than perhaps hairstyles or different outfits. Rob didn't know what kind of trouble he'd be in if his super figured out there were six people staying in the apartment, but he and his roommates knew to keep as quiet as possible.

After exchanging several hellos and hi's with the women, Rob stepped into his small bedroom, closed the door behind him, and changed into some casual clothes. The women respected the privacy of his bedroom. No one else came in, and they rarely even bothered him when he was inside.

Rob sat on the edge of the bed and dropped his head into his hands. Sometimes everything seemed to catch up with him at once. Coming to New York had been a big move after his stint in the Army. It was nothing like Bozeman, Montana, where he grew up. He tried to get a handle on his emotions and finally realized he was mainly lonely. How could someone with five roommates living in a small apartment in Queens possibly be lonely?

He wondered what his partner, Mike Bennett, was doing about now on a Saturday night. Probably with his wonderful family, enjoying everything he had worked for. Maybe Bennett

was right: He needed to be more open and get out and meet people. But he was always so disappointed by people. They tended to
argue about stupid things, repeat ridiculous rumors, and generally fail to live up to their potential.

Bennett and his family were the exceptions. Rob knew it was a
result of good parenting. He admired Mike Bennett, who displayed a lot of the same traits as Rob's mom. Smart, kind, and
tough as nails.

Before he knew it, Rob found himself stretched out on his bed,
hoping he might actually fall asleep without the aid of the powerful sedative prescription drugs that the VA used to provide for
his PTSD, and that he was trying to wean himself off. He didn't
like how they made him black out. He kept telling himself that all
that was behind him.

It still didn't make sleep any easier.

CHAPTER 11

I SHIFTED MY weight from one foot to the other as we waited for the doctor to look through more reports before discussing Mary Catherine's condition in any detail. I definitely wouldn't have called the doctor warm and fuzzy. She was all business. In a way, it reminded me of Mary Catherine when she was on a mission.

Eventually, the doctor said, "I've reviewed the scans and initial bloodwork. I've consulted with our ob-gyn and neither of us are sure what happened."

"What about the baby?" Mary Catherine interjected.

I didn't like the way the doctor took a moment to let out a sigh. It could've been that she was just tired after a long day. Or it could've been that she was about to give us bad news. I felt Mary Catherine squeeze my hand. Hard.

The doctor cleared her throat and said, "I understand you've been going to a fertility clinic and you're still very early in your first trimester. I would recommend that you consult with your fertility ob-gyn as soon as possible. I see in your chart this is Dr. Christina Ashe. Correct? A brilliant doctor."

Mary Catherine loosened her death grip on my hand and sat up in the bed. "So the baby is fine?" The hope in her voice scared me. It would make the heartbreak all that much worse if things went south.

The doctor took a moment to look at Mary Catherine. "The pregnancy appears to still be viable. But again, I'm sure your ob-gyn can give you more specific insight. Until then, I'm going to put you on strict bed rest for a minimum of two weeks."

I worked up the nerve to ask cautiously, "Is Mary Catherine in any danger?"

"All pregnancies can be dangerous. I think rest, proper diet, and time will maximize outcomes."

She had spoken like a car mechanic talking about a brake job. She never cracked a smile or showed any emotion.

Mary Catherine fidgeted. Telling my beautiful wife that she was going to be laid up for two weeks was like telling a world-class sprinter they could only walk.

"When you say bed rest…" she began.

The doctor didn't let her finish. "Let me make this perfectly clear. I am ordering you, as your current attending physician, to go home immediately, lie down on your bed in comfortable clothes, and only get up to go to the bathroom." She looked up at me like she expected I had something to add. When I didn't say anything, the doctor said pointedly to Mary Catherine, "I'm sure someone can bring you your meals in bed. Perhaps, unless they are complete jerks, they'll even eat a meal or two there with you.

But for the safety of your health and the viability of the pregnancy, you should limit your movements as much as possible. Do you have anyone to help you?"

I chuckled. "We can manage to find someone around the house."

The doctor gave us a few more guidelines, then looked intently at Mary Catherine. "I want you to follow my instructions," the doctor told her. "I do not want you out of that bed for a minimum of two weeks. That is not up for any debate."

For the first time since I'd met Mary Catherine, she had no comeback or comment.

I was at least smart enough to hide the smile that wanted to burst onto my face.

CHAPTER 12

WHEN WE OPENED the apartment door, we were hit with a wave of humanity and a barrage of questions from our kids. Plus my grandfather, who had shown up from his apartment in the Holy Name rectory, just around the block from our building. The only people missing were Shawna and Chrissy. I was hoping my two youngest daughters had already fallen asleep. It was after midnight by now.

I acted like a cop breaking up a crowd. "Move back, move back, give her some air." We'd already called home earlier to give them an update, hoping to avoid this situation.

Juliana had come home from the production of *Godspell* she was performing in, still in stage makeup. The concern on her face told me she must have rushed home as soon as her sister had texted her.

Finally, I held up a hand to keep everyone from speaking at

once. It had the desired effect. I could see why Mary Catherine enjoyed controlling our wild group of kids. There was a certain satisfaction to it.

When everyone's attention was on me, I said, "I'll answer all questions and concerns after we get Mary Catherine to bed." I escorted her toward our bedroom. After a couple of steps, I realized everyone was following us. I turned and said, "Okay, I know I said once *we* get Mary Catherine to bed. What I should've said is once *I* get Mary Catherine to bed. The rest of you wait here and I'll be back out shortly." I ignored the hurt looks I got from some of the kids.

I was still holding Mary Catherine around her waist as we stepped into the bedroom. That's when I found the final two pieces of my puzzle. Chrissy and Shawna lay on our bed, sound asleep on top of the covers. Chrissy's head was at the foot of the bed and Shawna's was hanging off the side. I noticed three glasses on Mary Catherine's nightstand: one of milk, one of water, and one of lemonade. The girls had made sure all of Mary Catherine's favorite beverages were covered. Her pajamas and a robe were also laid out on her side of the bed.

In most circumstances it would have been unbearably cute. But at that moment I had to call in my oldest kids, Brian and Juliana, for some help carrying out their sleeping little sisters.

Mary Catherine quickly changed, brushed her teeth, and got under the covers a few minutes later. I felt like I had accomplished some great feat just by getting her from the hospital to her bed like the surly doctor had ordered.

As soon as I was satisfied that Mary Catherine was comfortable, I told her to rest while I marched back out to the living room to give everyone the details. I made sure the kids all understood that Mary Catherine was not to be aggravated, annoyed, questioned, harassed, or hassled in any way.

Jane immediately gathered the older children to create a schedule so that Mary Catherine would have help over the next two weeks.

My grandfather pulled me out onto the balcony.

"What about you, boyo, how are you holding up?"

I had to think about that for a moment. "Just a little tired." Then I turned it around on him. "What are you doing here at this hour?"

"I couldn't sleep. When Jane called to tell me what was going on, I decided I wanted to spend some time with my great-grandchildren. Guess I'm just getting older."

I said, "Age is just a number."

"That may be so, but when you can divide that number by forty, you're getting up there."

I had to laugh out loud at that one.

CHAPTER 13

I'LL ADMIT TO being a little groggy when I slipped out of bed just after six on Monday morning. Mary Catherine was snoozing comfortably, so I used my best ninja skills to dress quietly and start getting the kids ready. We'd had a calm day on Sunday after Saturday night's excitement, but Mondays were always a little harder than the rest of the week. Kids moved slower. I moved slower. And now I had to stretch my legs to avoid cramps. What the hell was that about?

By the time I made it to the kitchen, I was surprised to see Jane and Juliana preparing breakfast for everyone.

Juliana said, "I'm scheduled to look after Mary Catherine until three this afternoon when Jane gets home. Brian will take over from five until you get home. I'll take the kids to school so you can get ready for your day."

I stood there, speechless. These were the kinds of things

parents usually hallucinate. I knew I had good kids, but this was above and beyond the call.

Mary Catherine was still sleeping by the time I was ready to leave. Brian would stay here in case she woke up and needed anything before Juliana returned from the school run. I was confident Mary Catherine was in good hands.

I was still in a little bit of a fog by the time I walked into the office. The place looked like a ghost town. Since Harry Grissom was on vacation, his office was empty. Only one detective sat at the cluster of desks in the central area. But, of course, our criminal intelligence analyst, Walter Jackson, was working at his desk inside his large office, the largest of them lining the walls, even larger than Harry's office. Like me, Walter keeps early hours.

I popped my head into Walter's office and asked if he'd seen Rob Trilling.

"He worked last night on his gang case with Terri Hernandez. Should be in later."

I sat at my desk and started poring over the reports I'd had since Saturday. I was still distracted, worrying about Mary Catherine. I resisted the urge to call Juliana and see how she was doing.

Four dead retired cops wouldn't usually draw much attention. Taken individually, they all looked like accidents or suicides. People rarely pay attention to problems like suicide among the military and police organizations. The NYPD is larger than most countries' armies, with over thirty-five thousand employees. I hadn't known Ralph Stein, Gary Halverson, or Tabitha Arnold personally. But cops commit suicide on a regular basis. Some obvious. Some not so much.

Even if it was carbon monoxide poisoning that killed her,

Tabitha had been a drinker who'd been drunk when she died. Lou Sanvos had been getting older. Anyone would understand him losing control of his big Lincoln Continental like that.

If there was a connection between these three incidents, it was going to take some real work to find it.

Celeste Cantor had set the whole investigation up well. I appreciated her because she got shit done. She had assured me no one would see any report I wrote except her until the investigation was complete. I knew if I needed other resources, she'd come through for me as she had a hundred times before.

I decided to start the investigation where I start most investigations. Despite Cantor's instructions to limit this whole investigation to my eyes only, I knew I had to talk to Walter Jackson.

CHAPTER 14

KEVIN DOYLE SAT at a table by himself in a little coffee shop on Staten Island. He was reading the two-page intelligence report on his next target. He wished he'd had this kind of detailed intelligence when he was in the service or on some of his other jobs. He figured he'd do some surveillance of the apartment after he finished his coffee and croissant.

Roger Dzoriack had retired from the NYPD nine years ago. Since then, he had not gone to a single function, funeral, reunion, or even a lunch connected to the NYPD. His mini dossier said he lived alone and had virtually no visitors. This all seemed too good to be true.

Doyle intended to follow his usual protocols to make sure there was no way anyone could connect him to the murder. Just as Doyle considered how to do the surveillance, a man came through the coffee shop's front door.

He was probably about fifty and a little overweight. What caught Doyle's attention was the jacket he wore, with patches from the 10th Mountain Division at Fort Drum in upstate New York. The man had a pretty good sway to his walk, like he'd suffered a serious leg injury in the past. His long graying hair hung limply around his shoulders and his beard fanned out in every direction.

The man made a beeline for the rear of the coffee shop, where the restrooms were located. Before he was halfway across the nearly empty shop, one of the baristas shouted, "No, no, no! I told you the bathrooms are just for paying customers." The guy, whose name tag said TONY, came from behind the counter and motioned to someone in the back to also come out.

"Dwight, help me toss this bum out," Tony said to the guy who stepped out of the kitchen. Tony was taller, but Dwight was twice as muscular.

Dwight smiled at the idea.

Before they could reach the man, Doyle said in a loud and clear voice, "He's with me. I'm buying his breakfast. That makes him a paying customer."

The man did a double take and then squinted at Doyle like he was trying to figure out if they knew each other.

Doyle motioned him over. He pushed a chair out for his guest. "Where'd you get the jacket?"

"Kept it when I was discharged."

Doyle smiled and asked, "What's your name?"

"Clint. Clint Fortune, technical sergeant, 10th Mountain Division."

"Order anything you want, Sergeant."

Clint shot a look over at the barista and his friend. Doyle

followed it up with a scowl to make sure there was no more foolishness from Tony and Dwight. This man was a veteran. He deserved respect. He had earned it. Not like these two assholes, who'd probably never spent a minute of their lives trying to help someone else.

Doyle and Clint talked for a few minutes. Clint had been living rough, sleeping outdoors. He'd fallen on hard times after he left the service. Doyle sometimes wondered if he had fallen on hard times too but it just wasn't as obvious.

"What unit were you with?" asked Clint.

"Special forces out of Fort Bragg."

"Green Beret. No shit. I can never talk bad about you guys again."

Doyle grinned. This was turning out to be a pretty good breakfast.

CHAPTER 15

EVERYONE IN THE NYPD seemed to know Walter Jackson. Some might have said it was because of his excellent skill in finding information through the internet and public records. Some people thought it was his pleasant personality and penchant for puns that made him so well-known. I always thought the simple answer was that he stood six foot six and weighed somewhere in the vicinity of three hundred pounds. Someone that size couldn't walk down the hallway without a person asking who he was.

No matter the reason, I was always thankful that Walter worked in my squad. On every case he seemed to save me hours and hours of wasted effort by getting me accurate addresses on witnesses or pointing out flaws in theories because he had records that contradicted the theories. I was almost tired of being amazed by what he could locate on the computer, but he kept surprising me.

I stepped into his office and closed the door behind me. "You got a few minutes?"

Walter closed the reference book he was reading—something about the original neighborhoods of Manhattan—and placed it on the stack of books closest to his desk. The bookshelves behind him were stuffed with pamphlets and other volumes he found interesting. A long table was piled high with more reference materials and old notes. Somehow, within all this organized chaos, Walter always knew exactly where to find the information he needed.

"What can I do for you?" he said. The big man's voice felt like a rumble in the closed-in space.

"I've been given a sensitive assignment that I'm not supposed to speak with anyone about. I'm not sure how strictly I want to adhere to that rule. I intend to talk to you and Trilling about it. But I'd appreciate you not spreading it around to anyone else or using any research avenues that might send up a flag within the department."

I laid out everything I had about the four retired cops' deaths. I also forwarded him the reports I'd gotten from Celeste Cantor and explained he'd have a hard time pulling anything more up on the computer since Inspector Cantor didn't want others to be in the know. As usual, Walter didn't ask a lot of questions. I knew he'd wait until he could read the reports and come up with some ideas in the next few hours.

He brought up on his screen the items I'd just sent him, glanced through them, and nodded solemnly. "This is some serious shit." Without looking, he pulled a dollar out of his pocket and slipped it into a jar on his desk. The jar already had about ten dollars in it.

"I thought that was the jar you had to put a dollar in for your daughters when you made a pun."

"Nope. Now it's a swear jar."

"How did that happen?"

"First of all, I've converted my oldest daughter to puns. Second of all, my wife insisted on the swear jar after my six-year-old called a taxi driver a shithead for speeding down our street."

All parents had been there. It still made me laugh.

Walter said, "Let me tell you one of Nadine's puns."

"I can't wait."

"What concert costs forty-five cents?"

"No idea."

"One with 50 Cent and Nickelback."

I laughed politely.

Walter said, "I couldn't be more proud if she got into the National Honor Society."

I respected his commitment to nerdy humor.

CHAPTER 16

TECHNICAL SERGEANT CLINT Fortune and Kevin Doyle left the café a little happier than when they'd entered. Doyle picked up the bill and even left Tony a tip—an extra quarter, for him to think about how he should treat people in the future.

Doyle slipped Clint a couple of large bills. The former technical sergeant initially declined, but after a little pressure, he stuffed the cash into the pocket of his ratty blue jeans. Doyle waited a moment as Clint got settled in his favorite spot in the alley next to the café.

Clint looked up from the blanket he had pulled around his waist and said, "No one bothers me back here. Unless the guys from the café come out to throw something in the dumpster. Usually, they leave me alone."

Doyle waved and started to walk away when he heard the café

door into the alley open. He paused for a minute, out of sight. When he heard some shouting, he rushed back to the alley entrance.

Clint cowered on the ground with the two morons from the café, Tony and Dwight, standing over him. Doyle didn't need this. Not now and not here. He didn't want any record of him ever being on Staten Island. Frankly, after growing up in Brooklyn, he rarely wanted anything to do with Staten Island anyway. He hesitated, waiting to see if Tony and Dwight were going to get violent. Finally, he couldn't take it anymore.

Doyle stepped into the alley and said, "I thought we'd settled this."

Tony said, "Look, this is none of your business."

"Probably not, but I'm still going to stuff you both into that dumpster over there." Doyle nodded toward the low dumpster with the lid standing up against the wall behind it. "I'm just curious. Why are you hassling him?"

"He won't listen."

"That's a lesson I'm about to teach you. You're not listening either. I thought I made it clear you needed to leave him alone." Doyle paused for a moment and added, "You need to show a little respect for someone who gave so much for the country. Or do you not understand things like that?"

Without warning, the muscular guy, Dwight, swung a big right hand at Doyle's head.

Doyle ducked it easily. Then twisted Dwight and grabbed him by his shoulders, moving him in front of Tony. Just as Tony was throwing his own punch. It caught Dwight right in the mouth, and Doyle could see a spray of blood. Maybe there was a tooth in it as well. He shoved Dwight into Tony. Tony hit his head on the side of the dumpster. Doyle turned to make sure it wasn't too serious. Then he grabbed Tony by the thighs, lifted quickly, and flipped him into the dumpster.

That's when Clint called out from the ground, "Behind you."

Dwight had picked up a broom handle that had been leaning against the wall near the door. Thanks to Clint, Doyle ducked below the swing of the wooden handle. Then Dwight stepped back and pointed the broom handle like it was a spear. He charged Doyle, who shifted his weight slightly, redirected the larger man, and snatched the broomstick right out of his hands.

Doyle looked at the panting man and said, "You're obviously an athlete. But you need to calm down and think things through in a fight like this. Even if you really stuck me, it's just a rounded broom handle. At most it'd give me a bruise." Then Doyle calmly handed the broomstick back to him. "Try again, but make better use of the weapon."

Dwight just stared as he took the broomstick. At first, he held it over his head like he was going to strike straight down. Then he lowered his head and charged forward, knocking Doyle back into the wall.

Dwight smiled and said, "I used to be a linebacker."

Doyle grunted. "I can tell. That was good form."

Tony popped his head over the top of the dumpster and Doyle whipped a quick backfist to knock him down. He turned as Dwight swung the broomstick twice. Missing him both times.

Doyle decided he'd had enough of this. He faked with his left hand and then drove his right knee into the side of Dwight's leg. He was trying to hit a nerve that would essentially give Dwight a "dead leg," which would hurt for a couple of days.

The big man went down on one knee. Doyle delivered an elbow to stun him.

"Easy there," Doyle said, helping the bigger man back up. He led him a couple of feet, then pushed Dwight hard, so he flipped over the edge of the low dumpster and landed on top of his friend.

Doyle looked over the dumpster wall and said, "You guys ever bother Sergeant Fortune again and I'll finish this lesson. Do you understand?"

Both men grunted understanding.

Doyle walked off, satisfied he had solved the issue. He knew these two would never admit that one guy had kicked both their asses at the same time.

CHAPTER 17

IT WAS MIDMORNING and Rob Trilling was riding in the passenger seat of Terri Hernandez's city-issued SUV. The Ford Explorer was reasonably clean, but nowhere near the standards that Trilling held for his vehicles. Everyone assumed it was from his days in the Army, but actually, his grandfather had taught him to always take care of his equipment. Especially his cars.

A body had been discovered in a Bronx stairwell with two .40-caliber slugs in the head. The victim was yet another rival to the gang Trilling and Hernandez were investigating. They wanted to see the scene and talk to a few witnesses, even though the detective in charge was treating it as an unrelated homicide.

Trilling wanted to ask how the party for Hernandez's sister had gone, but after their last exchange, he wasn't sure how she would take the inquiry. He was happy to sit quietly.

Hernandez surprised him, however, by making an effort to ask him a few personal questions herself. Eventually, she got around to: "Do you have a girlfriend?"

Trilling hesitated. Then simply shook his head.

Hernandez said, "Anyone on your radar?"

That was a much tougher question. "I really haven't met a lot of women since I graduated from the academy. I've tried to focus on my job. You know how it is."

"I certainly do. But that doesn't keep me from having a social life. It's important to get out and meet people." She kept digging at the same question from different angles.

Finally, Trilling said, "The last interesting young woman I met was Juliana Bennett."

Hernandez turned her head slowly and said, "As in the daughter of your partner?"

"I didn't say anything happened. I just said she was interesting."

"I know Juliana. She sets the bar awfully high. Beautiful, smart, talented, and way, way out of your league. Besides, Bennett loves those kids so much. If he found out you've become even more interested in Juliana, he might kill you. And he could get away with it. Or, more likely, he'd make your murder obvious as a warning to any potential suitors for his daughters."

Trilling had to smile at that. It was the first intentional joke Terri Hernandez had ever made to him.

They rolled up to the crime scene and saw there were still paramedics on the street.

Trilling said, "I thought the victim was dead when they found him."

"So did I. Let's go see what's going on before these paramedics destroy whatever evidence might be around."

CHAPTER 18

HERNANDEZ HEADED OFF to find the detective in charge of the crime scene. Trilling walked up to the EMS truck and found a young female paramedic dabbing something on an elderly woman's temple. There wasn't much blood, and the woman appeared happy just to be chatting with someone.

The paramedic looked up and smiled at Trilling. She noticed the badge dangling from a chain around his neck. "You're probably here for the dead body, not for a cut on the head." She had a friendly tone, a dark complexion, and a beautiful smile.

Trilling said, "We did wonder why there were paramedics at the scene if the victim was already dead when he was found."

"Ms. Paseo here took a tumble down the stairs in all the excitement. Someone panicked and called 911. Luckily it's not too serious. Won't require stitches." The paramedic looked at the older woman and said, "She refuses to go to the hospital with us."

Ms. Paseo said, "Too many people die in hospitals. It's just a little cut."

The paramedic told Ms. Paseo she was all set. Trilling decided he'd rather wait here and talk to a pretty paramedic until Hernandez had figured out what they were going to do.

Rob Trilling had never been particularly good with women. He just couldn't figure them out. If he had to admit it, women scared him a little bit. But he took a breath and said, "Hi, I'm Rob Trilling."

The paramedic stood up from where she'd been crouching to help Ms. Paseo. She was almost as tall as him. "Nice to meet you, Rob. I'm Mariah Wilson," she said, flashing that beautiful smile again.

They chatted for a few minutes and Trilling was surprised how comfortable he was talking to Mariah. She said she had been on the job for only about six months. "They loved having a Black female in the program. Especially one who could do all the physical training. I thought it was kind of fun."

"That's how I felt about the Army."

They talked some more. At one point, Mariah laughed and put a hand on Trilling's arm.

The next thing he knew, they were exchanging phone numbers. It had happened to Trilling only a couple of times in his whole life.

He almost forgot why he was here. Until Terri Hernandez yelled over to him, "Hey, Super Jock, let's go have a look at the body."

Trilling took a moment to say good-bye to Mariah. He saved her number on his phone as "Mariah Paramedic."

CHAPTER 19

THE CITY PROVIDES me with a car. I appreciate the few quiet moments I spend driving it—today, for example, heading north into the Bronx. The only problem is, today it also gave me time to obsess about Mary Catherine. Almost as soon as I got into the car, I called the apartment. My daughter Juliana answered the phone and treated me like she and my wife were teen girls torturing a boyfriend. Juliana giggled while she said, "Mary Catherine is not available right now." I could hear both of them snickering. "She's resting and won't be accepting calls for some time." In the background, I heard Mary Catherine say, "At least not until we finish the next episode of *Call the Midwife.*"

Frankly, I was relieved to hear Mary Catherine in such a good mood. I couldn't dwell on what *could* happen. I could only work to create the best circumstances for her and the baby. If that meant not bugging her during the day with phone calls, I could live with that.

That left me free to concentrate on some of the information Walter Jackson had found. Like the magician he was, Walter had uncovered tidbits that it wouldn't have occurred to me to look for. Not only had four cops who at some point had all worked narcotics in the Bronx died recently but also at least three convicted drug dealers who'd been arrested by the Land Sharks narcotics team had died in the last month. Two from drug overdoses and one from autoerotic asphyxiation.

Walter had said, when he explained all this to me, "I know a lot of drug dealers die young. I'm not sure this means anything."

"Every death means something."

Walter had said, "You're right. What I meant to say was, I'm not sure these deaths are connected to our retired cops. Although it does look like the victims were all investigated by the Sharks back in the day."

Walter had also pointed me to possibly the biggest suspect the Land Sharks had ever arrested: Richard Deason. His name was on a youth center in the Bronx. I remembered some controversy after he was arrested about leaving his name on the building. I guess, in the long run, it was too much trouble to change it.

Even now, almost twenty years on, it might be hard to find someone in the Bronx willing to talk about Richard Deason. Deason had provided money for several projects in the borough. But he'd also been caught on an FBI wiretap admitting to a homicide. The FBI gave the information to the NYPD, where a smart detective had tracked down the location of the alleged homicide and was able to find several blood spatters with DNA that connected to the victim.

It was one of those cases in which a forensics team used a relative of the victim to determine the origin of the blood through DNA. They'd had to do it that way because the victim had disappeared. No one would've ever known what happened to him if not for an errant comment on this FBI wiretap.

I talked to a couple of my informants. They knew Deason's name but hadn't been active back in the days when he'd ruled the Bronx. I then decided to go outside of my ring of professional informants.

I stopped at a bodega on Van Cortlandt Avenue. The family who ran it made a decent living with a small café that had three tables, in addition to the four aisles of groceries and one of freezers. As soon as I stepped through the door, I heard a woman's voice shout, "Ricardo, look who's come to visit!" An older woman hustled out from behind the counter and wrapped me in a bear hug.

A moment later, her lanky husband, Ricardo, joined in the hug.

Ricardo asked, "What brings you up to the Bronx, Detective Mike?"

His wife, Monica, shushed him and said, "What would you like to eat? We have some delicious pupusas."

I'd met Ricardo and Monica Salazar years ago when I was still involved in hostage negotiation. A gunman had been caught in the middle of an armed robbery and held the couple for almost five hours. It ended when I convinced the gunman that nothing good would come from hurting anyone. When I'd walked up to the front door of the bodega and talked to the guy face-to-face, I'd softened his stance, and he'd released the couple right then. A few minutes later, the gunman surrendered as well. Ever since, the Salazars treated me like one of their family. And I appreciated it.

After I accepted a pupusa to go, I explained I was just looking for some information. Ricardo Salazar got serious and said, "How can we help?"

"Do you remember a guy in the Bronx named Richard Deason? He was—"

"We remember Mr. Deason. I heard he died in jail."

"Yeah, someone shanked him." I noticed the expressions on the Salazars' faces. "Did you know him personally?"

"Yes, Detective Mike, we did."

CHAPTER 20

THE SALAZARS HAD one of their daughters come out to watch the counter as they led me to their tiny back office. Ricardo Salazar shut the flimsy door in the hope they would have more privacy. All three of us crammed into the room. I sat awkwardly with my notebook on my knee.

Ricardo and Monica sat in matching hard metal chairs with straight backs. They looked worried. I tried to put them at ease.

I said, "This is not about Deason. It's a completely separate investigation and won't come back on you at all. There's nothing to worry about." I noticed Monica exhaling in relief. Anyone who'd ever lived in a neighborhood controlled by drug dealers knew the dangers of speaking to the police.

Ricardo said, "What do you need to know, Detective Mike?"

"I don't know much about Deason or his crew. Anything you could tell me about him might be useful."

They started by mentioning a couple of Deason's enforcers. I made note of their names. Then Monica said, "They'd come into the store and take whatever they wanted like we were their private pantry. They never paid. We made our niece stay out of the store because we didn't like the way the men would look at her. It was a terrible time."

"His guys were the problem," Ricardo said. "Mr. Deason wasn't like that. He was always polite and paid for everything. He often left extra money on a table like he was making up for his own people. He liked to eat here. He said he liked the fresh ingredients."

Monica added, "He was always nice. He had an office just down the street, so we saw him almost every day. He'd even come in with his family once in a while."

I asked, "What about his family?"

"Mr. Deason married a beautiful Panamanian woman, Isabel Vega. They had a little boy named Antonio. I'm pretty sure it was Antonio. Cute as could be. You just wanted to pinch his pudgy little cheeks."

Ricardo said, "That's why we were so shocked when we heard on the news about everything he did. We knew the men who worked for him were bad, but we couldn't think of him that way. The news made him sound like a monster."

"Have you seen the wife and son since his arrest?"

Monica shook her head. "No. They got a divorce before the arrest."

"When did he get the divorce?"

Monica bit her lip as she thought. "I don't know. The boy was about eight or ten. So maybe fifteen or twenty years ago."

I did some quick math and estimated the young man would be

in his mid to late twenties by now. I wondered if he was in the business too. I turned back to Ricardo and said, "I see kids still use the Deason Youth Center."

Ricardo said, "Oh, yes. It's busy every day. Even our son, Ricky, used to go there to study before he went to Stony Brook." Then Ricardo leveled his gaze at me. "Did Deason really have all those people murdered?"

I shrugged and said, "It looks like it to me."

"Have you ever met anyone worse than that?"

I thought about it. Then I said, "Yeah, unfortunately I have."

CHAPTER 21

I WAS WHIPPED by the time I got home. I'd run down a number of leads without much success. The obvious lead I had to follow next was Richard Deason's son, who Monica Salazar had thought was named Antonio.

There was no detail too small in a case like this. And I still had other cases I was monitoring. I also had some supervisory duties I was handling for Harry while he was away. Nothing serious. Mainly keeping an eye on some of the younger detectives in the squad. That included Rob Trilling. Pairing him with Terri Hernandez had been a stroke of genius on my part.

I'd held off on calling Mary Catherine again after she and Juliana made fun of me. I realized she was sharp enough to follow the doctor's orders. It was still nerve-racking.

I barely said hello to the kids studying at the dining room table as I barreled through the apartment to check on Mary

Catherine in our bedroom. I froze at the doorway, a smile spreading across my face as I silently took in the scene.

Mary Catherine was sitting up in the bed with her favorite glass — a souvenir from our honeymoon in Ireland — filled with juice. On the nightstand was a plate of fruit, a plate with cheese and crackers, and a bowl of soup. Sitting next to her on the bed were our two youngest, Chrissy and Shawna, playing Go Fish. The smile on Mary Catherine's face was spectacular.

Then Shawna glanced up from her cards and jumped off the bed. Chrissy wasn't far behind. I walked over to the bed with both the girls still hugging me.

Mary Catherine smiled and calmly said, "And how was your day?"

"Usual. How was yours?"

"Since school got out and Brian walked everyone home, we've had a wonderful time. I am about to be crowned Queen of Go Fish."

Chrissy whined, "We've only played three games. A real Go Fish tournament is best of eleven."

I gently kicked the girls out of the bedroom and stretched out on the bed next to Mary Catherine. I said, "How has your day really gone?"

She sighed. The kind of a sigh where you couldn't tell if it was good or bad. It made me nervous. My stomach tightened a little bit. I reached out and grasped her hand. It felt a little sticky. I decided not to make a comment.

Mary Catherine giggled and said, "When the doctor said I had to stay in bed for two weeks, I didn't think it would work. I figured the whole place would go to hell, excuse my French. But these kids have been great. Juliana brought me breakfast after she took the kids to school. She checked on me constantly. Then Brian got out of work early so he could pick up the kids and he brought me donuts from my favorite shop."

I glanced around the room almost involuntarily.

"Sorry. I'm pregnant and we have ten children. There are no donuts left. Besides, I thought cops eating donuts was a stereotype."

I just shrugged. She had me.

Mary Catherine said, "I even like beating the pants off Chrissy and Shawna in Go Fish. So I would say I had a pretty good day."

She leaned over and kissed me on the lips. I realized I was having a pretty good day now as well.

CHAPTER 22

KEVIN DOYLE HAD done his due diligence in his surveillance of his next target. Roger Dzoriack was a retired NYPD detective who lived alone on the third floor of a decent apartment building on Staten Island. Doyle had spent the afternoon learning the streets and alleyways around the building in case it was a problem.

The fact that Roger Dzoriack never left his apartment limited Doyle's options. His plan was simple. Knock on the door. Tell Dzoriack he had something for him from the NYPD. Get himself invited inside. In his pocket, Doyle had a pill bottle of prescription meds crushed into a finely ground powder. He'd been very careful to use widely known pills. There were a few Ambien, nine crushed OxyContin, half a dozen Percocet, and a few Xanax.

Doyle realized there were a lot of challenges in this plan.

Would Dzoriack let him in? How would he get Dzoriack to drink a glass full of water mixed with crushed pills to simulate a suicide? Plus a number of other pitfalls. That was the nature of his occupation. It would be easier to push Dzoriack into traffic or down a flight of stairs. That was his backup plan: pull Dzoriack out of his apartment and throw him down the stairs. There was a lot more risk in that plan.

Doyle had done what he could. He knew exactly where the video surveillance cameras on other buildings were pointed. He made sure there was no video surveillance of this building. He saw there was very little local police presence. Why would there be? Not much happened around here.

He slipped into the building from an alleyway. The lock on the rear door was broken. His wild luck came in when he noticed an empty cake box with a cellophane front lying on the floor near a trash can. There was still cake icing smeared on the sides and the cellophane. It was perfect.

A few minutes later, he rapped on the door of apartment 316. Doyle held the empty cake box in his left hand. He was dressed in nice khaki pants and a button-down shirt with a medium-weight jacket to protect him against the dropping temperatures.

He waited a full minute, then knocked on the door again. He wondered if he'd have to find another way inside if Dzoriack didn't answer. From everything he had read, it was highly unlikely that Dzoriack had left the apartment. Since his retirement, the man had become a virtual recluse who ordered groceries online and had had absolutely no further in-person interactions with any of the people he'd worked with.

Just as Doyle was examining the lock to see how hard it would be to pick, he heard a voice that sounded like a rusty hinge say, "Who the hell is it?"

"John Martin, NYPD. I have something for you, Detective Dzoriack." Doyle was surprised how long he had to wait before anything happened. When the door finally opened a few inches, he noticed not one but two heavy security chains keeping the door from opening any wider.

Then he saw the frowning face of an elderly man. "I don't need shit from the NYPD or anyone else." Then, after a pause, Dzoriack added, "What is it?"

"Cake left over from Lou Sanvos's wake. Everyone thought you would appreciate it."

The door slammed in his face. Doyle wasn't happy about that. Things were about to get much more complicated. Then he heard the sounds of the chains being unhooked. A moment later, the door opened, and he had his first good look at the older man he'd been sent to kill.

CHAPTER 23

AFTER DINNER, WE all crammed into the bedroom with Mary Catherine to watch some show she and Ricky wanted to see. My grandfather had magically appeared about thirty minutes ago, specifically requesting that we watch the show as well. It didn't surprise me to find out it was a cooking show. Some of the other kids suggested shows on Disney+ or Netflix. Frankly, I thought any of the other suggestions sounded better.

The cooking show was hosted by a guy from Brooklyn who looked like he ate more of the food he made than served it. The show was called *Rising Chefs*. The host's named was Gino Carmelli, and he leaned into his character hard. He carried most of his extra seventy-five pounds right around his waist. His black hair was slicked back and the ring on his left pinky finger looked like it weighed two pounds.

His Brooklyn Italian accent was so thick I thought it sounded fake. There were a lot of phrases that felt lifted from *Goodfellas* or *The Sopranos*.

Jane said, "I heard they just picked up this show on the network to counter the Gordon Ramsay show. This guy even tries to act like Ramsay. He's loud, he's got a foul mouth, and he makes the worst jokes you could possibly imagine."

I said, "Really? I start most days off with a barrage of puns from Walter Jackson. Can this be worse than that?"

Trent said, "*I* think Mr. Jackson is hysterical. He looks like he played football at Ohio State, but he's as smart as someone who went to Michigan."

I did a double take. "Did you just make a joke about the rivalry between Ohio State and Michigan?"

Trent just grinned. That boy was sneaky smart and very funny. I might have to keep an eye on him as he got older.

My grandfather said, "I thought it'd be a nice change from watching the Kardashians or playing video games."

Mary Catherine turned to my grandfather and quickly said, "No one in this house watches the Kardashians."

I caught the glances and smiles that passed between my fourteen-year-old twins, Bridget and Fiona, and my oldest daughter, Juliana. I had wondered what they were doing in Juliana's room in the evenings. Now I had a pretty good idea. I didn't have to guess who Seamus was talking about concerning the video games. All the males in this house, myself excluded, played a lot of Call of Duty or The Last of Us.

I noticed Ricky was silent during the conversation about what we should watch and not watch. I realized he, my grandfather, and Mary Catherine were part of some sort of conspiracy. It was almost like reading an Agatha Christie novel. I just sat back and took in the experience until their actual motive was exposed.

We all turned our attention to the TV as the heavyset man wearing a chef's hat came on and started to introduce teenagers as contestants on his show. That's when I realized this was a *kids'* cooking show.

Now it was starting to make sense.

CHAPTER 24

KEVIN DOYLE QUICKLY set down the cake box on the kitchen counter, away from Roger Dzoriack.

The elderly man stood in the middle of his tiny living room and mumbled, "Lou Sanvos was a good man."

Doyle said, "I agree."

That made Dzoriack look up and acknowledge Doyle's existence in his apartment. He said, "Where are you stationed?"

"The Bronx."

"What precinct?"

Immediately, Doyle realized his error. He hadn't thought this through.

Roger Dzoriack said, "Cat got your tongue? I asked you where you're stationed. What are you, some kind of moron?"

Doyle said, "Look, I'm really sorry about this." He pulled his Beretta out from under his jacket.

"What the shit is this? Who the hell are you? Did some bastard I once arrested send you?" Dzoriack shook his head in disgust. "You look too clean-cut to be a killer for a dope dealer. Those are the only criminals I arrested with enough money to hire someone like you." Then in a softer voice, he said, "Doesn't matter. I sit in this shithole bored and depressed. I don't have the balls to end it all. Now a cocksucker like you shows up. Looks like *you* have the balls to shoot me."

Doyle was dumbfounded. This had never happened before. Not in private jobs or government ones. He wasn't sure what to say. "I…I…um." He had to pause for a moment. "You *want* me to kill you?"

"Yes, I do. If you're not a pussy."

Doyle didn't want to waste this fantastic opportunity. "Can I get you to write a note?"

"A suicide note? Shit yeah. Can I keep it short and sweet?"

"Anything you want."

As Dzoriack snatched a yellow Post-it note and pen, Doyle pulled out his pill bottle with the crushed meds inside. He stepped into the kitchen, opened a couple of cabinets until he found a glass. He filled the glass with water from the leaky faucet—took some work to get it to shut off completely—and mixed in the crushed pills.

Doyle stepped back into the living room, handed the glass to Dzoriack, and politely asked him to drink it.

Dzoriack stared at the glass, then at Doyle. "I thought you were going to shoot me. I could have taken pills myself."

"What if I tell you I'll shoot you if you don't drink it?"

Dzoriack shrugged, then took the glass and gulped most of it down. He looked up at Doyle and said, "I just thought of a better note." He stepped over to the counter and grabbed another Post-it note. Then he smacked his lips and said, "That shit you had me drink is nasty. Like a Russian whore."

The old man talked like a crusty Marine. Doyle helped Dzoriack to his bedroom, where a Michael Connelly hardcover Harry Bosch novel lay open on the nightstand. *Echo Park.* Doyle made a mental note to get a copy.

He wiped his prints from the glass, then took Dzoriack's left wrist and said in a soft voice, "Can you close your hand around the glass?"

Dzoriack slurred a response but reached out and closed his left hand around the glass once. He barely had the energy to bring the hand back to his side on the bed. Doyle carefully placed the glass on the nightstand next to the book.

It wasn't long before the old man was out cold. A few minutes later, Doyle checked his pulse. There was none. He had completed another assignment flawlessly.

He twisted the lock on the handle of the front door. He wanted to make sure the place was secure for whoever found Roger Dzoriack. Doyle caught himself smiling as he closed up the apartment. It would look like a suicide inside a locked apartment. *Perfect.*

Just as Doyle turned toward the staircase, the door to the apartment next door opened. A woman, about thirty, with very long, straight black hair looked out and smiled.

She said, "I'm so glad Roger had a visitor. Are you a relative?"

All Doyle could think was *Oh, shit.*

CHAPTER 25

NO FATHER IS unhappy when his whole family is doing something together. I didn't really care about a cooking show, but I enjoyed having the kids around me. I was happy Mary Catherine was engaged and not alone in bed. But I still had a sense there was something else at work here.

Then it became clear to me.

My grandfather, sitting in a chair Brian had dragged in for him, called to Ricky, who was sitting on the floor in front of the bed with the other boys. Seamus said, "Ricky, this looks like a show you should try out for. Based on that guy's accent, I bet it's gotta be filmed somewhere in New York."

Ricky was quick to answer. "It's filmed in Brooklyn. Some of it in a studio and some of it at his restaurant."

I held back my smile at Ricky's instant response and robotic delivery. This was clearly something the two of them had planned and practiced. I said, "Getting to Brooklyn's tough sometimes. I'm glad none of us has to deal with going all the way down there from here on the Upper West Side."

Ricky was quick to say, "They do a lot of filming on the weekend, so it doesn't interrupt the kids' school schedules. I read that Mr. Carmelli, the host, says he never wants his show to interfere with education."

"If he cares so much about the kids, why is he yelling at them?"

"Because he wants to make them better chefs."

I'd had enough fun. I said, "Ricky, would you like to try out for the show?"

His smile told me he'd already applied.

CHAPTER 26

BEFORE KEVIN DOYLE could even think, Roger Dzoriack's pretty neighbor had introduced herself as Elaine. When she invited him into her apartment, Doyle accepted. She'd already seen him. He needed to figure out how to contain this.

There was a bag of groceries sitting on her kitchen counter. A quick glance told him she was a fitness buff. And she ate healthy. He could've probably figured that out just by looking at her.

All he could think about was how this perfect assignment had gone off the rails at the last possible moment. He gave her his NYPD cover story.

Elaine said, "I try to keep an eye on Roger, but he doesn't like to be looked after."

"I got that impression."

"Can I get you something to drink?"

"No thank you. I really have to be going."

Elaine touched his arm with her right hand and said, "I'm sorry to hear that. I hope you come by to visit Roger again soon."

Doyle tried to think of something to say, but he knew what had to be done. He really didn't have a choice. He couldn't leave a witness who'd seen him so clearly. There was no sense in delaying it. He leaned forward like he was going to say something. He moved his right and left hands at almost the same time, his left reaching behind Elaine's head and gripping her neck and hair, his right moving to her chin. He didn't hesitate. He used his weight, leverage, and strength to rotate her head quickly.

Elaine never had a chance. He heard her neck pop like it was a champagne cork. She went limp immediately. When he released his grip, Elaine tumbled into his arms, her startled brown eyes staring right at him.

Doyle gazed down at her for a moment. Elaine's open eyes felt like an accusation. Now he had a new problem. What to do with her body? He couldn't just leave it in the apartment. It would throw Roger Dzoriack's "suicide" into question.

Doyle pushed Elaine into a sitting position on the couch. He dug his burner phone out of his pocket and dialed a number in Manhattan. As soon as someone answered, Doyle said, "I need to speak to Amir."

"Hold one second."

After a short wait, a voice Doyle recognized came on the line. "Who is this?"

"Your friend who gives you business now and then."

"What do you got?"

"Pickup and disposal."

"Where and when?"

"Staten Island and right now."

"It's going to be expensive."

"I know. I'll come by later in the week and settle up."

"How big is the package?"

"Maybe five foot six and one hundred thirty pounds."

"Be there in less than an hour. Text me the address."

Forty-five minutes later, two men with a dolly and a washing machine box were at the apartment door. Amir nodded to Doyle but didn't say anything.

Amir and his partner walked directly to where Doyle had left Elaine on the couch. They gently lifted her, more from a need to be quiet than out of respect for the body, and slipped her into the box. Doyle felt awful about this one. But he told himself it had been unavoidable.

He watched the men roll the dolly back to the stairway and carefully lower it one stair at a time. He waited ten more minutes, then slipped out of the building himself.

Doyle was no longer in a good mood.

CHAPTER 27

I WAS IN the office and settled fairly early. Mary Catherine had plenty of help and I was happy she had still been snoozing quietly when I'd left. Of course, Rob Trilling and Walter Jackson had beat me into the office. When I'd walked in, they were both at their desks, hard at work. I was no longer the office early bird. I didn't mind. It happens.

I had greeted both of them quickly, then scooted to my desk. A case like this requires a great deal of reading. Not just scanning through useless documents but looking for details hidden deep in the reports.

I found the reports from the New York Department of Corrections on the death of Richard Deason, seven years ago. There wasn't a lot of detail to get from the short report, but they had included a number of black-and-white photos that were plenty gruesome even without color. The narrative of the report simply said Deason was repeatedly stabbed with an edged weapon in the face and neck. The accompanying photo showed a toothbrush handle sharpened to a point.

The autopsy photo showed ten holes in Deason's face and three more in his neck. His right eye was punctured. Nasty stuff. The report noted that the killer claimed his motive for the murder was because Deason had disrespected 1980s star Mr. T. Apparently, Deason had infuriated his killer by claiming Mr. T, his hero, was just an actor and not an athlete.

I was still shaking my head when Trilling walked up. He parked himself in the seat next to my desk.

"What's going on with the case you and Terri Hernandez are working?" I asked.

He shrugged and said, "We keep finding bodies who are rivals of our group. We're still trying to identify who does business with them. They could be involved in the murders as well."

"You look beat."

"I'm okay."

I felt responsible for this young man. I couldn't let this one slide. "Talk to me. Honestly. We've been through too much to have any secrets."

Trilling smiled. I think he appreciated that I didn't mention his recent suspension. It had turned out to be a well-orchestrated frame-up. Trilling had handled the suspension and aftermath extremely well. The young man had impressed me.

But I noticed he still didn't tell me why he looked so exhausted.

I decided to take a different tack. "What do you have going on Sunday for dinner?"

"I thought Mary Catherine was on bed rest. I don't want to be any trouble."

"You forget we have Ricky."

Now Trilling gave me a wide smile. "Can I bring anything?"

"Nope. But you can bring some*one* if you want."

Trilling blushed. I didn't comment about it. Then my phone rang. It was Celeste Cantor.

She said, "Retired detective Roger Dzoriack was just found in his Staten Island apartment. Another former member of the Land Sharks. It looks like he committed suicide."

"Give me the address and I'll be there shortly." I wrote down the address, then looked up at Rob Trilling. It was time for me to bring him in on this whole Land Sharks business. "Let's go."

CHAPTER 28

THE APARTMENT BUILDING was a nice-looking four-story walk-up off Clove Road in the Sunnyside neighborhood of Staten Island. A white van with a blue stripe identifying its crew as New York medical examiners was parked directly in front of the building. There were two patrol cars as well.

Trilling said, "I thought there'd be more cars out front."

"Not for a death inside an apartment. Usually, the meat wagon gets here right toward the end of any investigation. They've probably already written this off as a suicide."

"You call the medical examiners' van a 'meat wagon'?"

"Sorry. It's an old habit. We're not supposed to call it that anymore, and I agree with that sentiment. It's just that's what homicide detectives called it for so long."

As soon as we were out of my car, I saw the M.E. technician move to the rear of the van and pull out a gurney.

I mumbled, "Oh, shit."

Trilling asked, "What's wrong?"

A woman in her forties with dyed blond hair and a tight-fitting uniform shirt yanked the gurney onto the asphalt with practiced ease.

She shook her head when she noticed us. "What are you here for? This is not Manhattan North. Are there no homicides in Manhattan? Surely some cop has shot someone today in your jurisdiction." Her Russian accent—or, more precisely, Belarusian accent—was obvious from the first syllable.

"Hello, Alina. Nice to see you too. I thought you worked the night shift."

"I had to stay after. This my last pickup. I don't have cushy job like detective. In Minsk, I was pediatric nurse. Here, all I do is pick up dead people."

"Everyone from Belarus or Russia I have ever met had some important job back home. There's nothing wrong with working for the New York medical examiner's office. And we both know being a detective is not a cushy job."

Alina said, "What time did you start today?"

"I got in the office a little after seven."

"And did you have dinner with your family last night?"

I nodded. I knew where this was going, but I didn't want to rob her of a victory.

Alina said, "That sound cushy to me." She looked at Trilling but didn't say anything. Then she said, "Why are you out here on a suicide? Did you know the man?"

"He was a retired NYPD detective. Just checking up on a few things. Have you seen the apartment?"

"Nice apartment. Old man had very few guests. Building's

super needing to check something. He found old man." She looked around to make sure we were alone. "The patrol officer point out suicide note. All it say was 'Had enough, bottoms up.'"

"That's about the most coplike suicide note I've ever heard."

Alina added, "Looks like he drink a glass of water and some crushed pills. There's a glass by his nightstand with something in it. Maybe he drink it, then lie down on the bed. Very peaceful scene. Not like what we usually see."

I said, "Thanks, Alina. Hope you can get some rest today."

She cut her eyes toward me. "You call me lazy?"

"No, no." I realized it was a losing battle. Some people can never be satisfied. I just waved to her and headed to the stairs.

As soon as we were out of earshot, Trilling looked at me and said, "What's her story?"

"We used to date."

Trilling stopped on the staircase halfway between the first and second floor. Finally, he said, "Are you kidding?"

"Yes, Rob, I'm kidding. She's got something against cops. Someone told me it has to do with an encounter in Minsk. Today was actually about the nicest she's ever spoken to me."

"Why do you put up with that?"

"I don't want to make her distrust the police any worse. And if you listen to what she says, she has an excellent eye for details. She also overhears patrol officers' gossip and often tells me if they've disturbed anything. You just have to get past the surly exterior." I let out a laugh.

Trilling said, "What's so funny?"

"That's pretty much how I describe you to people too."

CHAPTER 29

A UNIFORMED PATROL officer stood by the open apartment door. The young officer was making some notes just inside. She looked almost as young as Trilling. When she turned and saw the badge around my neck, she nodded. When she noticed Trilling, a smile spread across her face.

The patrol officer gave me basically the same rundown Alina had, with less sarcasm. We walked through the apartment. I saw the suicide note on the nightstand. I noticed the glass with the cloudy water. And I saw Roger Dzoriack looking like he was taking a nap on top of the covers of his bed. I said a quick prayer over his body. It's something I always do when I come across the dead, as a show of respect.

Trilling and I looked through the apartment, but the only thing we found of interest was another Post-it note in the garbage with a longer message. It said, "You can all kiss my ass and I don't care if anyone comes to my funeral." I guessed he had a change of heart right at the end, left a slightly less aggressive note.

Trilling and I stood in the cramped kitchen and looked around at the apartment. Over the years, I have found this to be a good way to get an overview and maybe pick up some detail I missed initially.

Alina and another technician came through the apartment with the gurney. I stepped into the bedroom and watched her methodically prepare to move Roger Dzoriack's body onto the gurney. Alina might have been a little crude and abusive, but she was a professional. She snapped orders at her young assistant and was ready to move the covered body in about half the time it took most M.E. techs.

When they faltered at the top of the stairs, Trilling didn't hesitate to rush out and help them. Maybe it was my joke comparing him to Alina. To be fair, my new partner genuinely tried to help people. All people. I appreciated that and hoped it wouldn't wear off after a few years on the job.

A pudgy man in his fifties wearing a blue shirt with the name "Mario" embroidered on the chest peeked around the corner from the end of the hallway. I motioned him over and he identified himself as the building's superintendent, the one who'd found the body. He told me he'd been trying to locate a leak on a lower floor and had knocked on Roger Dzoriack's door. He hadn't had to force the door to get into the apartment; the door was locked but neither of the dead bolts had been thrown, so he'd been able to use a master key.

The super told me he'd been hesitant to use his key. "Mr. Dzoriack once told me he'd cut my dick off if I ever walked into his apartment unannounced."

I tried to hide my smile. That certainly seemed in keeping with Roger Dzoriack's personality.

Mario answered a few more questions for me. I asked him if Dzoriack was friendly with anyone in the building.

"Elaine, next door, tried to check on him a few times a week. The woman at the end of the hallway, Lesa, she's a retired librarian, and she'd bring him books. Mr. Dzoriack wasn't the friendliest guy in the world. Those two women should be considered saints."

The heavyset man looked nervous, but that's common when someone is talking to the police. He fidgeted and moved from foot to foot.

I finally asked if he was okay.

"It's not you. I like cops. My brother's on the force out in Nassau County. Thing is, I got a urinary tract infection and I gotta keep moving so as not to think about it."

I didn't respond. I was afraid he might really open up to me.

I stepped back into the apartment. I made sure the patrol officers in from the local precinct packaged the glass and note for evidence. I picked out a few other things to take into evidence. A death like this didn't warrant a crime-scene tech. The patrol officer looked like she knew what she was doing. The last thing I pointed out was the other suicide note we had taken from the garbage and laid on the kitchen counter.

The super had been helpful but really hadn't given me much information I could use. I had to admit, on the surface, this did look like a suicide. And frankly, Roger Dzoriack looked like exactly how I would picture someone who committed suicide. But it was one more retired cop added to the list that seemed to be growing.

CHAPTER 30

I LET ROB TRILLING catch a ride back to Manhattan with a patrol officer headed to One Police Plaza. He needed to do some more work on his case with Terri Hernandez.

I decided to talk to a couple of Roger Dzoriack's neighbors but waited for the medical examiners to leave with the body before I knocked on any doors. I started with the woman the super had pointed out to me, the retired librarian named Lesa Holstine, who used to leave books for Roger Dzoriack to read.

I was greeted by a charming smile and welcomed inside. As soon as I stepped into Ms. Holstine's apartment, I noticed the cats on either side of the entryway, standing like guardians.

"They're rescues," she told me. "I try to keep it to four or fewer cats. A police friend of mine said any time he enters a house with more than four cats he just assumes the resident is crazy."

I laughed politely but didn't refute it.

She led me into her living room and then brought me a cup of tea before we sat on a comfortable floral-print couch next to a coffee table piled with books and crossword puzzles. I knew from talking to the super that Ms. Holstine was a retired librarian, but even if he hadn't mentioned it to me, the stacks of books would have clued me in.

She noticed me glancing at the crossword puzzles and said, "I prefer to work those out on paper. The only one I do on the computer is Wordle because you can't really do it on paper."

"I'd hate to play you in Scrabble."

Her shy smile told me she was too modest to confirm my statement. It also told me she'd rip me to shreds in any word game.

I took a sip of tea and asked her a very open-ended question about her interactions with Roger Dzoriack.

She said, "I heard the commotion this morning and knew immediately something had happened to Roger. I've lived on the same floor as him for eleven years and have almost never seen him outside the apartment."

"Ever seen anyone visit him?"

Lesa Holstine shook her head and looked down at the coffee table. "Not many. He would barely let me and our neighbor Elaine inside the apartment. Even then it was clear he didn't necessarily want to engage in conversation. He loved to read, though, so I often brought him books I thought he'd enjoy."

"Do you know if your neighbor Elaine had any deeper conversations with him?"

"Not that I'm aware of. The best I could say is that Roger tolerated how she kept trying to get him to engage with the world.

But she is a wonderful and beautiful young woman. Most men of any age would be thrilled to have someone like that pay so much attention to them."

"Is there anything else you can tell me about Roger Dzoriack that I haven't asked?"

Ms. Holstine shook her head slowly. "He may have been gruff, but he was also kind. He donated money to some youth center up in the Bronx. He gave cash when the superintendent's wife was going through chemo. The only reason I know that is because Roger asked me to slip it under Mario's door but made me swear never to tell the super who it was from. The envelope was thick with cash. Really thick. No one will probably admit it, but the world isn't quite as nice without Roger Dzoriack in it."

After I finished the interview and thanked Ms. Holstine for the tea, I walked down the hallway to the other neighbor who had interacted with Dzoriack. In the back of my mind, I wished Rob Trilling was with me — not because I needed help with the interview but because I wanted Trilling to see the value of interacting with one's neighbors. I didn't want Trilling to end up like Roger Dzoriack. All alone in an apartment.

I smiled when I remembered that Trilling was hardly alone in his apartment these days. He had five Pakistani women as roommates until he could find a place for them to live safely. Considering how introverted he was, Trilling would probably appreciate some solo time in his apartment about now.

I knocked on the door to neighbor Elaine's apartment. I waited but got no answer. I wedged my business card into the seam around her door, making a note to myself to come back and speak with her if I needed more information.

CHAPTER 31

KEVIN DOYLE SAT in the third row of pews at the Church of St. Agnes on East 43rd Street in Manhattan. He preferred the smaller parish church to the huge St. Patrick's Cathedral over by Rockefeller Center, but his father had appreciated the architecture and would tell him wonderful stories of how Irish workers helped build some of the greatest structures in New York, such as the cathedral. Doyle wasn't sure if his father had known what he was talking about, but Doyle certainly had liked the stories. His father's pride in the accomplishments of the Irish and his interest in community service were some of the reasons Doyle had gone into the Army in the first place. He didn't like to think how far he had drifted from his original ideals.

He'd been coming to St. Agnes on and off for over a decade. That's why he recognized a couple of the priests as they walked past and nodded a greeting.

One stopped and said, "Haven't seen you in a while."

"I've been traveling. I hope to come to mass on Sunday."

The priest patted him on the shoulder. As he walked away, the priest said, "I'll keep an eye out for you."

There was something about the priest's manner that made Doyle smile. Those were the kinds of interactions he'd had growing up. Comfortable and friendly.

Doyle couldn't run away from the fact that he had some serious questions about his life. He regretted taking on a job that required him to kill retired cops. To him it was as distasteful as killing retired veterans. Anyone who had given so much for their country shouldn't be repaid with murder. And Doyle was starting to doubt whether he was the one who should be doing it.

He waited until there was an opening at the confessional. He knew there were ways to schedule appointments, and Doyle had heard some churches even allowed confession via Zoom. He figured he was traditional enough to actually come to a church and speak to a living, breathing priest—but at a booth with a privacy grill, not face-to-face as many preferred nowadays.

He slipped into the confessional. When the priest slid back the old-fashioned wooden panel so they could speak through the ornate grill, Doyle said, "Forgive me, Father, for I have sinned. I have not treated people correctly and I regret it."

It was an older priest with a deep and comforting voice. "Would you like to be more specific, my son?"

Doyle simply said, "No, no, I would not."

"I usually get some specifics."

"And I usually don't talk to people. So let's meet halfway."

The priest was a little more tentative. "Did you hurt someone?"

"You could say that from one perspective."

"What about from another perspective?"

"I'm helping someone else."

The priest was clearly frustrated but after a brief further interaction gave Doyle a penance far too light for his sins.

Doyle didn't feel any better as he walked away from the confessional toward the front door. His penance was nothing compared to his horrendous actions recently. He reached into his pocket and pulled out his leather wallet with FORT BRAGG inscribed in black. He pulled out all of his cash, about three hundred bucks, and stuffed it into the donation box next to the exit.

CHAPTER 32

ROB TRILLING FELT nervous. He took a moment to check himself in the rearview mirror of his car. He smoothed out the cowlick on the left side of his head and wished he had a little more fashion sense. Pretty much his only system was a simple one his grandfather had taught him. If he wore tan pants, he matched them with a dark shirt. If he wore blue pants, he matched them with a light shirt. His sister tried to update his wardrobe occasionally, but Rob always fell back on his grandfather's color schemes.

He slipped out of the car and walked two blocks to the café. He'd driven past it once to make sure he knew exactly where it was. He didn't want to make any mistakes or be late. He checked his watch for about the tenth time, then turned the corner.

Rob took a deep breath and marched directly to a table on the sidewalk in front of the café. He smiled and said, "Hope I'm not late."

Mariah Wilson, the pretty paramedic he'd met yesterday, smiled back and said, "Right on time. I don't know why when someone's late, everyone at the fire department likes to say they're on 'NYPD time.'"

He liked that she felt she could joke with him. He sat across from her and ordered a Diet Coke when the waiter came by.

She held the stem of her glass of white wine. "I'm not on duty today. I can drink at lunch."

Her smile captivated him. And made him more nervous. He'd been thrilled to get her lunch invitation, but he still wasn't sure if he should be treating this as a first date or a friendly meal. Either way, he intended to use all of his limited interpersonal skills.

They immediately bonded over the fact that they were both relatively new city employees. Unlike Rob, however, Mariah had grown up in New York, on Staten Island. Her father was an administrator for the city's public works department. She had been a paramedic for only ten months.

Mariah said, "I'm glad you could meet me."

"I needed a break. Trust me, I was looking forward to this all morning."

"I generally work one day on, two days off. That gives me more time to spend with my parents and little sister. Are you close with your family?"

"Some of them. My sister lives north of the city in Putnam County and I get to visit her quite a bit. Right now my mom and grandfather are over from Bozeman, Montana, visiting her. I'll try to get up and see all of them together as much as I can while they're here."

"Are you close with your dad too?"

Rob hesitated. He *knew* the answer. He hadn't really seen his father since he was a child. He just wasn't clear on what he should say. He settled on "Not as close as I should be." That was the truth.

As Rob paid the lunch bill, he noticed something behind him catch Mariah's attention. Her eyes flickered up and then she did a double take. He looked over his shoulder to see a muscle-bound guy in his early twenties walking toward them.

Mariah mumbled, "Shit."

"What's wrong?"

"My ex-boyfriend."

Now Rob Trilling was starting to remember all the problems involved in dating.

CHAPTER 33

I'D DONE ALL I could do at Roger Dzoriack's apartment. Now I was back at the office, poring over anything I could find on philanthropic Bronx criminal Richard Deason's family. Walter Jackson had been able to find the records of marriage and the birth of the son. The divorce decree was harder to find, but everything was in order.

Walter came out from his office and plopped into the chair next to my desk. Sometimes I cringed when he did that. I didn't have faith in that wooden chair holding up to someone Walter's size dropping into it so heavily.

Walter said, "I found everything on Deason's ex-wife. She died of cervical cancer in Miami about six years ago."

Ever since my own wife passed away from cancer, I always flinch on the inside when someone tells me about a cancer death. Immediately, I wondered about the son, who would've still been a teenager at that time. I saw firsthand what the trauma of losing a mother could do to children. And I was right there with them the whole time. What did this kid do with his father already dead?

Walter said, "I found some records on the son, Antonio. I couldn't find any photographs anywhere. It looks like he was at the University of Miami and was renting an apartment in Coral Gables until about five years ago. Since then there's almost no record of the young man. It's a pretty good mystery."

"A mystery I think we should unravel if we're going to dig deeper into this case. These retired cops were connected to the Land Sharks and working in the Bronx. Plus, you said a couple of Deason's thugs also died recently. That can't be a coincidence."

"You think it might be some kind of revenge?"

"Who knows? Could just be some kind of business arrangement that someone needs to expand their territory." I paused and considered other options. "We've seen crazier motives. This one might have an almost cinematic quality. A son waits for years to get back at the cops who put his father in prison? Sounds like a movie I might watch."

Walter said, "Not me. After experiencing all these bloody homicides up close by working here with you guys, I only like comedies and musicals. And I'm happy to sit through most Disney movies with the girls. Except *The Little Mermaid.*"

"What's wrong with *The Little Mermaid*?"

The big man shrugged. "I don't know. She just gives me the creeps. What's the difference between a sea creature on land and an alien from outer space? It just freaks me out. It always has. Every time we have a body wash up in the Hudson, I get a little nervous. Who knows what a crazy-ass mermaid might do."

I had no answer for that.

CHAPTER 34

ROB TRILLING TRIED not to be obvious when he turned in his seat to get a view of Mariah's ex-boyfriend, but he didn't want to give the guy the chance to smack him in the head when he wasn't looking. Mariah's eyes stayed on the ex as he stopped right next to their table. He wore an expensive-looking sport coat over a T-shirt and jeans. Rob wondered if he was trying to dress up the casual clothes or dress down the sport coat.

The ex eyed Rob a little longer than necessary. Then he put on a fake smile and said, "Hey, Mariah. What's going on?"

"Hi, Timmy. This is Rob."

Timmy didn't say anything, so Rob stood up and offered his hand. Timmy took it hesitantly. He mumbled, "Nice to meet you." He was a couple of inches taller than Rob, maybe six foot two, and a good thirty pounds heavier. All of it muscle. Timmy started to squeeze Rob's hand a little tighter in a show of dominance.

Just as the pressure started to get intense, Rob subtly twisted his hand, so he didn't have to jerk it away in pain. He didn't like where this confrontation was going.

Timmy said, "What do you do, Rob?" Something about his tone hit Rob wrong.

He said, "I'm a trust-fund baby." That seemed to take Timmy by surprise.

"That must suit Mariah fine." Timmy took some time to assess him. For his part, Rob had stepped away from his chair just in case he needed to use his fists or feet.

Then Timmy looked down at Mariah but kept speaking to Rob. "I hope she treats you better than she treated me."

Without thinking, Rob said, "I hope I treat her so well she doesn't need to treat me badly."

Mariah said, "Timmy's a bouncer at the Sixth Floor Club." It was an awkward warning. Rob had already realized this guy would be a handful.

"Never heard of it," he said.

Timmy said, "Maybe you should get out more. But not with her." He tried to stare Rob down. When that didn't work, Timmy made a show of removing his coat.

Before he had the coat off his shoulders, Rob tripped him and shoved him into a chair. He took another chair, slipped it off the ground, and wedged it down Timmy's back so he could neither get the coat off nor remove the chair. He floundered like a turtle on his back.

Rob looked at Mariah and said, "We should go."

As they hurried down the sidewalk together, they could hear Timmy yelling, "You mother…"

Rob had to laugh out loud. Mariah was giggling as well.

Mariah said, "You have a nice laugh."

"I don't think I've ever been told that before." As he said it, Rob realized it was because not many people had ever even heard him laugh.

CHAPTER 35

I WAS BACK home by a reasonable hour. That's not always possible on my job. I'm not whining about it. There's nothing to whine about. Duty sometimes dictates that I stay much later than I've expected. For all of his crazy antics, my grandfather, Seamus, taught me the importance of duty. "Feeling passionate about something that helps society." That's how he used to explain duty to me. We have a duty to our families, to our friends, and usually to our jobs. Certainly, not everyone agreed with me.

It was still daylight, but just barely, when I walked through the front door. Most of my crew was sitting at the dining room table doing homework. They were almost lined up according to age. Chrissy, Shawna, Bridget, Fiona, and Ricky were all on one side of the table. Trent and Eddie sat on the other side. Jane walked around the back of each kid like a proctor during a test.

But she would stop and help when she saw someone with a problem. It was good to have a brainiac in the family.

Everyone looked up and said some form of "Hey, Dad," in unison. I didn't want to destroy the atmosphere, so I walked around the table and kissed each of the seated kids on the top of his or her head. Then I gave Jane a kiss on her cheek.

I stepped into the kitchen, where Juliana was preparing some kind of casserole. It smelled delicious.

"Hey, Dad. Mary Catherine is doing great. But she keeps trying to get up to do things. Jane and I wrestled her back to bed, but we think you need to talk to her."

It had been only a couple of days, but it felt like my whole world had been turned upside down. Usually it was Mary Catherine telling me I needed to talk to one of the kids. Now the kids were telling me that I needed to keep Mary Catherine in line. It was going to take me some time to get used to this new dynamic.

Juliana stopped what she was doing to face me. "Mary Catherine also tells me that you invited Rob Trilling to come over for dinner Sunday night."

"I did, and he surprised me by accepting my offer." I studied my oldest daughter's face a little more closely. "It's not a problem, is it? You keep telling me you guys are just friends."

Juliana avoided my eyes but said, "It's no problem. I just needed to know the head count. I was going to have Ricky make pasta. He thinks working on an Italian dish might help his chances of getting on that crazy cooking show."

"Sounds great. We'll have the whole crowd, and I'm sure my grandfather will show up as well."

On cue, Seamus walked through the front door. I noticed he

got a slightly more enthusiastic greeting than I had. Several of the kids jumped up from the dining room table to give him hugs. I could see why he liked coming over as often as he did.

He declared, in his best Irish brogue, "I thought I was coming over to drag order out of chaos. Instead, I find each of my great-grandchildren doing exactly what they are supposed to do. What a blessing."

He posed each kid a specific question. He asked Fiona how she was doing on the basketball team. He asked Ricky about the status of his application to the TV show. When Seamus stepped into the kitchen, he even asked Juliana how her audition had gone this morning. Something I wasn't even aware of. My grandfather had a better line on the kids than I did sometimes.

Juliana looked at me in the kitchen and said, "You've got enough to worry about. This was just for an understudy role in an upcoming play."

"How do you think you did?"

A sly smile slid across her face. "I crushed it."

Seamus saw Juliana's confidence and said, "I tell you what, these kids are all superstars. I can't wait to see Juliana on the screen, Jane in the operating room, Brian running his own air-conditioning company. I think I've done a great job with these kids."

I chuckled and said, "I'm sure Mary Catherine and I had no part in it."

"Don't be so hard on yourself, my boy. You provide them with a roof over their heads and three meals a day. I'm happy you've been able to manage that."

His smile made him look like an evil, taller leprechaun. And I loved him for it.

CHAPTER 36

AFTER OUR DINNER of beef casserole and fresh green beans, which we all ate while perched around the bedroom, we settled in to watch TV with Mary Catherine. Somehow, even with all the kids and my grandfather stuffed into the bedroom, it didn't feel crowded. It felt comfortable. I loved it. I could tell by my grandfather's face that he loved it too.

The boys were serious about making him relaxed. Ricky, Trent, and Eddie somehow managed to muscle one of the recliners from the living room to the doorway of the bedroom. Even though he was half in and half out of the bedroom, Seamus looked completely at ease, stretched out in the leather recliner.

Everyone was excited to watch another episode of *Rising Chefs,* the show Ricky had applied to be on. Ricky sat right in the middle of the crowd of kids at the foot of our bed. He was enjoying being the center of attention at home, for however long it lasted.

Ricky got up and began to mimic the host, Gino Carmelli. He did a pretty good imitation of the man's gesticulating arms and heavy Brooklyn Italian accent. "Yo, if you wanna make the perfect lasagna, you havta soak the noodles beforehand. My dear nonna, God rest her soul, taught me this when I was only eight months old. But the lesson, it stuck with me."

I wasn't sure I'd ever seen Ricky quite so animated in front of everyone. I got an even bigger surprise when my oldest son, Brian, stood up.

He went right into the accent as well. "Then, when I was two years old, my mamma taught me the secrets of a great gravy. You need fresh tomatoes. If someone tries to tell you to use canned, stewed tomatoes you just tell them fuggetabouit."

He had all the syllables just right. Mary Catherine started to laugh so hard as she drank, some water came out of her nose. Even then she was laughing too hard to completely hide it.

Then we actually watched the show for a while. The chef had six young teens and tweens who looked to be middle schoolers or maybe freshmen in high school, and all of the contestants were from the New York City area. Each had a cutaway in which they talked about their lives and their interest in cooking. I found those stories much more compelling than the main part of the show.

A teenage girl from Yonkers said she just liked being in the kitchen. She couldn't explain it. But a kid from the Bronx said that he saw cooking as his chance to get out of the cycle of crime and drugs many of the people in his neighborhood suffered from. I took this to heart. I'd heard many athletes say the same thing about football or boxing being their ticket out. I liked hearing kids talk about other avenues to pursue.

One thing I didn't like was the way the chef talked to the kids. He made jokes at their expense, he raised his voice, and in one case he threw a young man's garlic bread onto the floor because the boy hadn't followed directions.

I sat up in bed and looked over to the crowd sitting on the floor. "Ricky, are you sure you want to put up with this kind of abuse? I think I like the English guy better."

Ricky didn't hesitate. "I think Mr. Carmelli can make me a better chef. If it's what I really want to do in life, I need to see what it's like in a big kitchen."

Unfortunately, Ricky made perfect sense. Even I knew that professional kitchens weren't the most calm and easygoing of places. The problem was, I had a feeling this TV chef was more interested in ratings than in actually helping any of the kids. But I wasn't going to say anything. I didn't want to dampen Ricky's enthusiasm in any way.

I tried to lie back and enjoy having the family around me. Then I noticed my grandfather had dozed off in the recliner, blocking the doorway. That was going to be an issue when everyone had to go to bed.

CHAPTER 37

THE NEXT MORNING, I decided to go directly to the chief medical examiner's office instead of my office. I knew my good friend Aurora Jones would be on duty. I'd left a message on her phone the previous night asking if she could conduct an autopsy on Roger Dzoriack.

Generally, the medical examiner's office gave priority to violent crimes and other incidents that might require legal proceedings. Suicides were pretty far down on their list. Especially the suicide of a reclusive sixty-seven-year-old man.

I met Aurora in her office. Surprisingly, she'd already conducted the autopsy and an initial drug screen.

Aurora was eating a cherry yogurt with her feet up on her messy desk.

I sat down across from her, after moving a couple of files from the chair onto a credenza overflowing with medical journals and other files. I also tossed an old sandwich wrapper into the garbage can.

"Bennett, what are you doing on a suicide?" Aurora asked, her Jamaican accent making the question sound like the start of a joke. "Don't you have enough to do?"

"You saw he was a retired cop."

"A lot of retired cops commit suicide. I don't usually have the city's top homicide investigator leaving me a message asking me to look at it carefully."

"Did you find anything of interest?"

She smiled. Aurora started speaking slowly, choosing her words carefully. "You are one of the few people I think could handle some of my insights. Because they are not all just from scientific review."

"This isn't a court hearing. You can say whatever you want, and it'll stay between us. I doubt you could insult me."

Aurora smiled again. The glasses hanging around her neck had sparkles glued to the frames. It matched her personality. "First of all, I called in a favor and had NYPD forensics take a sample of the water from the glass next to Mr. Dzoriack's bed and run it through a spectrometer. There were four different prescription drugs crushed up in the water. I did some checking and found out Mr. Dzoriack had a prescription for only one of them. Ambien. I read in the report that no one found any other bottles of prescriptions in the apartment."

I realized what she was saying and I saw where she was headed. If he never left his apartment, how did he get all the other pills? It was a good question.

I started to make notes. Perhaps we'd left the crime scene too early. I needed to look through Roger Dzoriack's apartment again.

Aurora said, "Now I'm going to move out of my lane, as the kids say, and tell you something else I picked up from the forensics report."

"I'm listening."

"The glass by the side of the bed that had the water and crushed-up pills looks suspicious to me."

"More than just because it held a deadly concoction of prescription drugs? How so?"

"There were only four fingers and one thumbprint on the glass."

"Were they in a pattern as if he were holding a glass and drinking?"

"Yes, that's exactly how they were placed. But those are the *only* prints on the glass. Are you telling me this man only held the glass one time, while he poured water and crushed pills into it? Did he really never set it down even once before he drank from it? Typically, you would pick up and put down a glass a few times. There should be dozens of sets of prints on it from all that handling. Yet this glass looked like it was wiped clean—except for a single set of Mr. Dzoriack's fingerprints. It just doesn't feel right to me."

Aurora was onto something. The entire situation didn't feel right. I had more work to do on the Roger Dzoriack investigation. That meant I had more work to do on this whole case.

CHAPTER 38

KEVIN DOYLE DIDN'T know the Bronx like he did Manhattan and Brooklyn, and even Staten Island. The Bronx seemed more alien to him. It was harder for him to blend in and keep a low profile here. Plus the neighborhood people tended to know one another and were wary of strangers.

Doyle still couldn't stop thinking about Elaine, the pretty neighbor he'd killed when she saw him coming out of Roger Dzoriack's apartment. He'd barely slept in the two days since. The image of her lifeless eyes staring up at him after he broke her neck kept returning to his mind and weighing on him.

The retired cops he had killed recently were bad enough. At least he understood the reasons behind the orders. But poor Elaine was just being nice. She was checking on an elderly neighbor. Did she have a boyfriend? What would her parents do? Doyle tried not to think about her loved ones. Especially because of the fact they would never have any idea what happened to her. No closure at all. She was just collateral damage on one of his assignments. Amir and his friends would dispose of the body so that there would be no trace of Elaine left.

Even when he'd been posted to Afghanistan, he'd felt regret for some of the lives he had taken. At least there it was him or them.

He could even justify some of the CIA contract work. He recalled the guy in Morocco who'd released the names of four locals who had been working with the Agency. They were commonly called informants but were really just sources of intelligence. One of them, a twenty-one-year-old seamstress, had been raped before her throat was cut. She had been left in the streets of Rabat as a message to anyone else thinking of working with the CIA.

Doyle had put a bullet in the head of the asshole who'd killed her. From three feet away. Then he'd left the man in the street as a message to others to *not* bother CIA informants.

Even though killing Elaine still bothered him, he pushed those thoughts out of his head. He was back on his assignment. At least this time it wasn't a former cop. In fact, the guy he was looking at right now, José Silbas, looked like a cancer on society. Just judging from the intelligence sheet he had on the target, Doyle realized he wouldn't have many qualms about killing this guy.

Silbas was fifty-four years old. He'd been born in New York and arrested nine times. Some of them were drug offenses. There was also one for aggravated assault, another for attempted murder, and the last one for kidnapping. He had pleaded guilty three times and was sentenced to probation each time. He went to trial on the attempted murder charge. Apparently, he had choked his ex-wife unconscious. If a Marine on leave hadn't intervened, it would've definitely been a murder. Silbas spent six years at Groveland Correctional. His ex-wife mysteriously "disappeared" while he was upstate. Doyle suspected Silbas's criminal friends.

Doyle parked today's stolen car, a Honda this time, down the street from Silbas's apartment building. He used his pair of Tasco mini binoculars to count three windows over and one window up from the main entrance. He was looking directly into an apartment but couldn't see anyone. He was pretty sure it was the right apartment.

Doyle wasn't trying to make this complicated. He had a tool he'd bought from a hardware store in Queens. It was used in carpet installation. Heavy and straight with a deadly sharp point to it, it would be perfect. All he had to do was catch Silbas in the open and he'd be done. No one cared about making drug dealers' murders look like suicides. These guys met violent deaths all the time. The two he'd already handled were easy enough. He'd made one look like autoerotic asphyxiation, where the guy choked himself to death in a sex game gone wrong. The second one he'd made look like a heroin overdose. There was another name on that list, but that guy had coincidentally died of an overdose on his own, weeks before Doyle arrived in New York. Go figure.

Doyle noticed a couple walking down the street. They weren't so much a couple as a male and female walking together. He'd been around long enough to recognize a couple of NYPD plainclothes detectives. They went up the stairs and into the building. *Shit*.

He brought his binoculars up to the apartment he was looking into before. He could make out someone walking into Silbas's apartment.

Doyle didn't know what the cops wanted with Silbas. He didn't care, but he couldn't do anything right now.

He would wait to act.

CHAPTER 39

ROB TRILLING ATTEMPTED to read a file on his phone as he kept pace alongside Terri Hernandez. He wanted to mention to her that she could have given him the file ahead of time. But he decided things were already tense enough. So he was trying to fill in the blanks before they talked to a drug dealer named José Silbas. The man had done six years at Groveland Correctional but didn't appear to have caused any problems in the three years since his release. He worked for a shipping company on the night shift. Unless that was some kind of cover.

Hernandez stopped right in front of the apartment building. She turned to Trilling. "This shouldn't take too long. Then I thought we could check the warehouse to see who's coming and going. Do you have anything going on tonight?"

Trilling said, "I have dinner plans."

Hernandez let a smile slip out. "Really? Good for you."

She took the steps up to the building without another word. Hernandez rolled her eyes at him when Trilling held open the front door. That was how he was raised. It was hard to break life-long habits. To be fair, Trilling tried to hold the door for anyone walking into a building with him.

As they walked down the second-floor corridor toward the apartment, Hernandez turned to Trilling and said, "Just a reminder. This is *my* case. You're assisting me. I'll ask the questions. You keep your eyes open for any threat. Got it?"

Trilling nodded.

Hernandez knocked on the door firmly. Even the way she knocked sounded official. A few seconds later, a bleary-eyed man wearing a white undershirt and shorts answered the door. He was balding but kept his hair long and wild on the sides. A stubbly gray beard grew in patches across his chin. He stared at Trilling and Hernandez but didn't say anything.

Hernandez held up her ID and said, "Mr. Silbas, I'm Detective Hernandez and this is Detective Trilling with the NYPD. We need to ask you some questions about the death of James Reyes."

Silbas looked more interested when he heard the name Reyes. "Why do you want to talk to me?" His voice had a rough edge to it, like he had smoked most of his life.

Hernandez said, "We're not trying to make a case on you. Reyes's mother said you were his godfather. We just want to find out who shot and killed your godson."

"You and me both. But if *I* find out who it is, there won't need to be a trial."

Trilling noticed that Hernandez let Silbas's threat of a potential felony slide completely. Silbas turned and motioned them into his apartment. Trilling stifled a cough from the smell of stale cigarettes and beer.

All three of them sat at a small round table next to a window in the living room.

Silbas looked between the two partners and said, "Who do I talk to?"

Hernandez said, "I'm going to ask you some questions."

"What if I don't want to talk to a woman?"

"Then we're that much further away from catching the man who shot your godson. We really don't have time for bullshit, Mr. Silbas. Do you want to talk to us?"

"How do I know you're tough enough to catch Jimmy's killer?"

Hernandez kept perfectly calm. "If you want, after we're finished speaking, I'll kick your ass. Is that fair?"

Silbas smiled. "You're a mean one. I like that. What if we just arm wrestle to see if I'll help?"

Trilling didn't like the look on Hernandez's face. He hoped she wasn't about to put him in an awkward position. Internal Affairs already knew his name.

CHAPTER 40

ROB TRILLING'S EYES involuntarily darted between Terri Hernandez and José Silbas. He noticed her left hand ball into a fist. Trilling had to admit that he'd enjoy seeing Hernandez smack the smirk off Silbas's face. He was also a little relieved when she started to speak in a reasonable tone.

"Help us now, and I'll arm wrestle you before we leave."

Silbas shrugged and said, "What do you need to know?"

"Any idea who put two .40-caliber slugs into your godson's head?"

"None at all. I don't understand any part of it. I used to work in that business."

Hernandez gave him a hard stare and said, "The narcotics business?"

"Why else would you even be here talking to me? But I didn't want Jimmy to get into it."

"Why do you think he started in it, then?"

Silbas dropped his head. "The same reason we all start deal-ing. The money. It's a different time now, though."

"How so?"

Silbas gathered his thoughts. "Back before I did my time, it was just business. I worked for a guy named Richard Deason. He managed to keep a lid on things. There was none of this random violence."

Hernandez said, "Just focused violence."

Silbas shrugged again. "That's the business."

Trilling picked up on the name Deason. Just once, their infor-mant in the gang he and Hernandez were surveilling had let slip the name of a contact. They'd called him "Little D." He wasn't a member of the gang, but he definitely wanted to meet with them. D for Deason?

Or was he just grasping for leads now?

Hernandez asked more questions. Silbas couldn't provide any useful information. He'd been out of the business so long he didn't even know who the players were anymore. But he'd clearly been fond of his godson and seemed like he was trying to help.

Silbas went on a little more of a rant about how good things were years ago. He ended by saying, "I guess cops change too. Back then I might've been shaken down for some money or got-ten my ass kicked for no reason. I guess some things get better and some things get worse."

Hernandez closed her notebook as a signal they were done.

Trilling started to stand but noticed Hernandez didn't move. Then she said, "Do I still have to arm wrestle you?"

Silbas said, "You said you would."

Hernandez didn't hesitate to put her right elbow down on the table and hold up her hand. Silbas smiled. Trilling wondered if he intended to try to hurt her. He figured that wouldn't work out for anyone.

Silbas planted his right elbow and grasped Hernandez's hand around her thumb.

Hernandez said quickly, "Ready, go." She slammed his hand against the flimsy tabletop. The sound echoed through the apartment. Silbas grunted and pulled his hand away, shaking it in the air like he had touched something hot.

He said, "That ain't nice."

Hernandez said, "Neither was choking your wife."

"I already went to prison for that."

"But what happened to her while you were in prison?"

Silbas didn't reply.

Hernandez stood up from the table and marched out of the apartment without another word.

CHAPTER 41

KEVIN DOYLE WATCHED the two detectives leave José Silbas's apartment building. He stayed put in his stolen Honda. Doyle had an eye for detail, and the detail he noticed was that neither of the cops looked too excited. They'd probably just been in there asking Silbas some routine questions.

Still, Doyle wasn't sure he wanted to act right away. Then he saw Silbas pop his head out the front door of the apartment building and look around as if checking to see if anyone was hanging around, looking for him. He'd never spot Doyle in the car, way down the street.

Ten minutes later, Silbas stepped out onto the sidewalk dressed in what looked like a company uniform, blue khakis and a beige jacket, and stood next to the street. A Toyota Camry stopped in front of him. Doyle saw the Uber emblem on the windshield.

Doyle decided to follow. He was curious to see what had

gotten Silbas out of his apartment before his evening shift at the shipping company where he worked. Doyle had thought about doing something at Silbas's job. But maybe he'd get a better opportunity now, since he wasn't sure how many people would be around the business later.

The Uber headed west toward the Hudson River. Doyle stayed back a block or so as he followed the car. He didn't know the streets well enough to do the surveillance on a parallel street. That was the right way to conduct a surveillance like this.

The Uber let Silbas out next to the Hudson about a mile south of Columbia University. The Hudson River Greenway had a few different walking trails, but no one was around. Somehow Doyle managed to find an open spot to park his stolen Honda. Then he got out and followed on foot as Silbas continued to walk toward the south along the river. He walked nearly half a mile. He was trying to hide his tracks as well. He didn't want any kind of record to show exactly where he was going. Was he planning to kill someone? Silbas paused several times along the river to check all around him. It was pretty good counter-surveillance. Then he stopped near where an older man in an overcoat sat on a bench among several others along the river, next to a statue. There were a few more people around here. But not many, and they soon moved along.

Doyle hung back while Silbas spoke to the older man.

He waited, trying not to seem obvious as he looked out over the river, occasionally glancing over his shoulder at the two men. Doyle could feel the weight of his heavy, sharp carpet tool secured inside his jacket. He also had his Beretta 9mm shoved in his belt holster. There was no such thing as being too prepared.

Doyle eased closer. The current dreary weather kept most

people out of open spaces like this. Plus the breeze off the water could be brutal.

Silbas raised his voice. The two men seemed to be arguing. Even at a distance, Doyle caught some of the conversation. "It's not right," Silbas repeated several times. He was seriously pissed off about something having to do with someone named Jimmy.

The older man told him to "cool down." He said something about looking into it. Doyle couldn't catch it all. Then it was over. The older man stood, then turned and started to stride away quickly. Silbas stayed looking out over the water, closer now to the railing above the seawall.

Doyle made a split-second decision. He started walking toward the benches, pretending to be interested in the historical plaque mounted below the statue. It didn't really matter. Silbas wasn't paying any attention to his surroundings. Maybe he'd been out of the business too long to stay alert all the time.

Doyle moved quietly between two benches to stand directly behind Silbas. He already had the carpet tool in his hand. He used his left hand to grab Silbas across the mouth and his right to reach around and shove the razor-sharp tool deep into Silbas's chest. He felt the man's entire body stiffen as the spike plunged through and then skipped off a rib. It was just like a job he'd done in Berlin. He knew it was going to take more than one stab with the weapon. He just started moving his arm like a piston. He struck three, four, then five times. He paused for a moment, then thrust the tool into Silbas three more times for good measure.

Silbas's beige jacket showed a pattern of spreading blood. Doyle was amazed the man was still standing. Silbas wheezed a couple of times, then his knees started to give out. Doyle gave him a shove over the railing and let him tumble into the river. He barely made a sound. He must've sunk immediately. When Doyle looked over the railing, there was nothing but dark, choppy water.

Doyle gave a quick glance around the area. No one was nearby. No one could've seen anything. And there was no trace of Silbas anywhere.

Doyle quickly stalked away, back toward his stolen car. About five hundred yards north of where Silbas had gone into the water, Doyle tossed the carpet tool into the river as well.

For the first time today, Kevin Doyle smiled.

CHAPTER 42

MY MEETING WITH Assistant Medical Examiner Aurora Jones this morning had left me contemplating the apparent suicide of Roger Dzoriack. I'd studied philosophy when I attended Manhattan College. That included several classes on logic. I often joked that the only thing logic classes did for me was keep me out of discussions of politics. Logic and politics do not mix well. But in police work, logic often comes in handy. And logic dictated that if Roger Dzoriack's suicide was actually a murder, then the other suicides I'd been investigating might also be murders.

That meant I needed to make a trip to Florida and take a closer look into the deaths of Ralph Stein and Gary Halverson. I had the reports, but although it was clear that their deaths were considered suicides, I'd never really considered the use of propane tanks as a method of suicide. After I did a little research, however, I discovered that wasn't as suspicious as it had originally seemed to me—apparently propane explosions had been used several times in suicides. There had even been another case in Palm Beach County, just north of where the two retired NYPD detectives had lived in Hollywood Beach, Florida. Maybe that's where they'd gotten the idea.

It would seem a simple matter to fly from New York City to Fort Lauderdale, Florida, on one of the dozens of flights from LaGuardia every day. That wasn't my holdup. It was the unending bureaucracy of the NYPD. I couldn't approve my own travel even though I was the acting supervisor of my squad.

I took Celeste Cantor at her word that I could drop by anytime. I wanted to propose this trip in person. It would be no big deal for her to approve it. Which is how I found myself at One Police Plaza, the single place in the greater New York City area I actively avoided. And why, three minutes after I entered Cantor's office on the second floor of the building, I stood in shock, hearing her deny my request.

"I can't approve a trip to Florida on this case," she told me. "We're trying to keep it quiet, and any kind of expense will draw attention. If not now, in the future. I sent you all of the reports from the explosion that killed Ralph and Gary. Why do you feel you have to go down there in person anyway?"

"You know as well as I do that reports don't tell the whole story, Celeste. If you really want me to get to the bottom of this, I need to go to Florida."

Cantor's assistant tapped on the door, then stuck his head in and said in a soft voice, "Everyone's waiting for you in the conference room."

Cantor nodded impatiently. "Tell them I'll be right there, Chuck." She turned toward me and said, "Don't we have enough of these suspicious NYPD deaths here in New York for you to find out everything you need to know? Or is it in every New Yorker's DNA to go to Florida at some point?" She smiled at her weak joke.

I said, "I hear what you're saying. I even understand it on one level. But now I'm in too deep on this case. I can't just walk away. I wouldn't think you'd *want* me to walk away."

Cantor said, "You're a really bright guy, Mike. I have every confidence you'll figure this out." She started walking toward the door. Just as she slipped out of the office, Cantor looked over her shoulder and said, "Keep me in the loop on anything you find out."

I didn't want to risk saying something I might regret. I took a breath and nodded. Then I followed her out the door and found myself alone and unprotected.

As I headed to the elevator, I heard a voice yell out, "Bennett, what are you doing here?"

I turned to see Internal Affairs Detective Sergeant Dennis Wu walking toward me. This visit had just gone from bad to awful.

Wu said, "You supervising that madhouse while Grissom is on vacation?"

I nodded.

"Still working with that crazy Army vet, Rob Trilling?"

"Are you deliberately trying to insult a young man who's done nothing but public service his entire adult life?"

"No, I'm deliberately trying to insult you. Mainly because you're an asshole."

"At least we feel the same way about each other. Excuse me, Detective Sergeant, I have real police work to do."

Wu couldn't let that little jab slide. As the elevator doors closed, he said, "And I'll be keeping an eye on you while you do it."

CHAPTER 43

BROODING AT MY desk in Manhattan North Homicide after my meeting at headquarters, I had to admit I saw Celeste Cantor's point. But she was the one who'd brought this case to me, and now it looked like the real deal. Not just a rumor or conspiracy theory.

In the meantime, I had work to do as the acting supervisor, which took me away from my own cases. It also reminded me why I'd never been interested in being promoted. I was sick of reading and approving other people's boring reports. I wanted to focus on my own boring reports.

I scrutinized the information Walter Jackson had provided. It looked like Richard Deason had run the most multiethnic crew to ever operate in New York. His list of associates included males and females, whites, Hispanics, and Black people. Deason had used a legitimate CPA for his personal finances, who claimed that his client told him he was a "venture capitalist." I always thought every drug dealer was some form of venture capitalist.

No matter what else I was discovering about Deason, I always circled back around to his son, Antonio. My imagination ran a little wild when I envisioned what he would look like now. I assumed he'd be a tough-looking, muscle-bound thug. In reality, his Florida driver's license and his identification card from the University of Miami both showed a good-looking, smiling young man with longish hair. But both were at least five years old. I had almost no up-to-date information on him.

Walter Jackson shuffled over to my desk. The way he sat in the chair told me he had something important he wanted to talk about. When he didn't come up with a pun right away, I knew it had to be serious.

I said, "What's troubling you, big guy?"

"I've been helping Rob on the case he's working with Terri Hernandez. Most of the reports and info have been going through Terri first. I saw something unusual and looked up the case file."

"Please don't tell me Trilling did something to screw up one of Terri's cases. He'd have a better chance of survival if he told the commissioner to kiss his butt."

Walter chuckled. "No, nothing like that. They've been doing surveillance of that gang up in the Bronx. Looks like someone in the group is good for a couple of homicides at least."

"So what's got you worked up?"

"They have an informant inside the group who gives them pretty good intelligence about who comes and goes from the warehouse they call their headquarters, any outsiders they're setting up a meet with."

"Okay. So they should be able to figure out who's good for the homicides by looking at the members of the gang and their associates, right?"

"That's exactly what I was thinking. So I ran thorough backgrounds on everyone mentioned in their reports." He paused and looked at me.

"Why am I starting to feel this has something to do with me?"

Walter continued. "There's a guy the informant mentioned, someone Trilling hasn't heard him talk about before. I can't find background on the name at all. The informant called him Little D." Walter shrugged his broad shoulders. "He's a potential new supplier—meeting with the gang tomorrow to talk business. Trilling and Hernandez are planning to convince the informant to wear a transmitter."

"Little D…as in little Deason? Antonio Deason?"

"Informant said he moved up here not too long ago. From Miami."

CHAPTER 44

WALTER SENT TRILLING our meager stock of two outdated images of Antonio Deason, just in case he and Terri spotted him tomorrow, while I brought Trilling up to speed on what else we'd been doing on Celeste Cantor's behalf. The frustrations of bureaucracy consumed me for the rest of the day, and I was the last one to leave the office. I wondered how Harry Grissom maintained his calm while dealing with bureaucracy *and* supervising the squad. He never seemed to have a problem finding funding for investigations. It felt like he won every argument with the bosses at One Police Plaza. If anything, my admiration for the man had grown in the last week.

I felt exhausted as I stepped through the front door of our apartment on the Upper West Side. I pushed all my thoughts about the case out of my head. Between working late and Mary Catherine being in bed, I halfway expected anarchy to reign in our house. I was not far off. To the naked eye, things may have seemed calm—there was no shouting or broken furniture—but a cardinal rule of our home was being openly flaunted: Brian, Jane, Trent, Bridget, Fiona, and Shawna were all eating dinner in the living room rather than in the dining room. As far as Mary Catherine was concerned, that was a mortal sin. Even worse, the kids were watching TV as they ate their hamburgers.

Even as I recognized the hypocrisy of our doing almost the same thing by eating and watching TV in the master bedroom these last few days, that had felt like a special circumstance. I suspected seeing it happen out in the open like this would have made my wife's head explode.

I stood at the edge of the living room and said, "What if Mary Catherine sees you if she gets up to use the bathroom?"

Bridget snickered. "She's dead asleep. Plus Chrissy's in the bedroom too, so she can be our early warning system."

"Who are you, NORAD?"

Bridget smiled. "Actually, we're studying the Cold War in history class. Did you know that Father Francis was in Havana for some of it? He really makes it interesting."

"It *is* interesting."

Bridget just shrugged.

I glanced around the room. Every kid had a hamburger and some potato chips. Not my first choice for a healthy dinner, but at least they were all eating.

I said, "What are you watching?"

Brian said, "Right now we're watching a rerun of *Seinfeld* until Ricky finishes his homework. Then we're going to watch more episodes of his cooking show. We want to help him prepare for his audition."

When I checked the crowd, I noticed another missing child. "Where's Eddie? Don't tell me he's yet another picket in your early warning system."

Brian shook his head. "He's working on the same project as Ricky."

I wandered down the hallway toward the entrance to the boys' room. Along the way, I peeked into our bedroom. The kids' early warning system had a glitch. Chrissy was lying on the bed, fast asleep next to Mary Catherine. A half-eaten hamburger lay on a plate next to her on the bed. It was picture-perfect. I softly closed the door to the bedroom.

When I got to the boys' room, they were both on the floor using a laptop to search Google. I said, "What's all this?"

"We both have the same project due in social studies. We have to find articles to support a position we hold."

"What's your position?"

Ricky said, "That fast food is dangerous. It's the root cause of the obesity epidemic in the US."

I nodded. That was a good topic. I turned to Eddie. "What are you trying to support?"

"Why the Jets won't win a playoff game in the next decade."

"That can't be too hard to support."

My son just smiled.

Ricky said, "I need to finish quick so I can watch *Rising Chefs*. My application was accepted, and my audition is a week from Saturday. Nothing's more important."

I said, "Except school. I don't want you guys using any of those artificial intelligence programs either."

Eddie snapped his fingers and said, "We didn't even think of that. Thanks."

I just shook my head. I know it's a stereotype, but having four boys and six girls has taught me that boys never prepare ahead of time. This little stunt didn't even throw me for a loop. I remembered having to help Brian years ago with a report on Benjamin Franklin because it was due later that same day. Jane, on the other hand, would always prioritize her homework, ever forgoing fun activities in order to complete a project as soon as it was assigned.

I heard the sound of Mary Catherine stirring, so I stepped into our bedroom. I had made up my mind about something I needed to tell her. I sat down next to the sleeping lump that was my daughter Chrissy. She didn't stir at all.

I said to Mary Catherine, "I really need to go to Florida on a case. I think I can do it all in one day. But I want to make sure it's okay with you."

"Of course. I have all the help I could need here. But that day trip sounds taxing."

"Not as taxing as being away from you guys."

"When do you plan to go?"

"I'm going to look for a ticket right now. I'd like to go tomorrow morning."

Mary Catherine patted my arm.

I threw in, "And I'm paying for it out of my own pocket." She didn't even ask me to explain. She trusted me and my judgment. That is the best kind of life partner.

CHAPTER 45

I BOOKED AN early Thursday morning JetBlue flight out of LaGuardia and tried to make use of my three-hour travel time to Fort Lauderdale. Flying out before the sun rose had been a little on the stressful side. But now I was safely tucked into a middle seat, between an older man in the window seat, who fell fast asleep as soon as the jet took off, and a woman on the aisle loaded down with bags of tchotchkes she'd clearly collected during a tourist trip to the Big Apple.

I discouraged any conversation by gluing my eyes to my iPad and reviewing the many files Walter Jackson had sent me. Most of the documents contained information I knew already. Some of them were just background. All of them revolved around Richard Deason.

Say what you want about Deason, he created an effective organization. I have always wondered what would happen if guys like him decided to work for the government instead. If it hadn't been for the Land Sharks, Deason and his gang might've still been operating in the Bronx.

Reading the old narcotics reports was like stepping back in time. The Sharks had been in three different shoot-outs with Deason's people. I remembered one of them at a Midtown bar. It was an undercover operation that had gone wrong. Two of Deason's goons shot the place up in an effort to cover their escape. Celeste Cantor herself had been one of the cops to stand her ground and save a lot of lives.

There were also two instances in which witnesses against Deason and his people had been murdered. One of them was a US Customs case—one of Deason's people had been caught trying to bring a kilo of heroin in through the port system. The guy agreed to cooperate and three days later was found dead in his cell from a knife wound. Another inmate was charged with the crime but never admitted to anything.

It turned out that the man who committed the murder in the federal holding cell had owed Deason a ton of money. The theory was that Deason forgave the debt and set up the man's family for life while also sending a message to others who thought about cooperating with the government against Richard Deason.

Walter Jackson had also sent along everything he could find on Richard Deason's son, Antonio. It wasn't much. He'd found Antonio Deason's signature on some kind of form from Con Edison, then traced it back to an apartment owned by a holding company. It looked like Antonio was living in SoHo. It also looked like he had made a mistake by signing the ConEd form. But that's where Walter's information ended.

Using some contacts, I was able to get ahold of a Florida Department of Law Enforcement special agent who was aware of the explosion that had killed Ralph Stein and Gary Halverson. FDLE generally didn't get involved in cases like this. They were supposed to go after criminal organizations and public corruption. Luckily, I had reached someone willing not only to help but also to meet me at the airport.

It was midmorning when we landed. I hadn't even had a chance to dig my phone out of my pocket after disembarking when a tall woman with short brown hair stepped in front of me and said, "Michael Bennett?"

I nodded.

She stuck out her hand and said, "I'm Carol Frederick. I'm with FDLE. I've got a lot to do today so let's get a move on." She turned and started walking quickly.

I liked her. A lot.

CHAPTER 46

FDLE SPECIAL AGENT Carol Frederick drove us down to the town of Hollywood to take the causeway over to Hollywood Beach. She drove like a New Yorker, cutting in and out of traffic with just a quick wave or an occasional middle finger.

To make conversation, I said, "I was curious to come down here and see some of the infamous 'Florida Man' activities. Anything weird or unusual would be fine with me. An alligator thrown through a Wendy's drive-through or a man who uses a python for autoerotic stimulation."

Frederick gave me a mercy laugh. Then she said, "The only problem with all those Florida Man stories is the media never mentions that the dumbass doing something stupid is almost always originally from somewhere else. There is a reason *Jersey Shore* was filmed in Jersey."

I laughed too. "It's true. I guess we definitely have our share of morons in the greater New York and New Jersey area. And it's no secret that tons of New Yorkers move to Florida. I'll keep that in mind next time I read a story about something crazy going on in Florida—whatever it was might've been caused by one of our own." That seemed to satisfy her.

As she drove, Special Agent Frederick said, "After we spoke, I did a little research into you. Why's a big-deal homicide detective like you coming down to look at a double suicide?"

"It could be part of a bigger case." The fact that she'd researched who I was told me she was pretty sharp. I decided to turn things around on her. "I've got a question for you."

She smiled like it was a game. "Ask away."

"Why's a big-deal special agent with the chief law enforcement agency for Florida looking at a double suicide?"

"Touché. I deserved that."

She smiled again. She had one of those smiles that could disarm you just before she eviscerated you. I could tell she knew what she was doing, and she appreciated challenges.

Finally, she said, "I'm on the Joint Terrorism Task Force. We look at any kind of explosion or serious fire just in case it's not what it seems. In this case, the Hollywood cops did a good job and examined all aspects of the incident. They even picked up a computer keyboard that had been blown out of the house. One of the men who died, Gary Halverson, had written a good-bye note to his niece. Apparently, he had advanced lung cancer. His fingerprints were still on the keyboard."

We headed south on state road A1A into Hollywood Beach. Traffic was lighter. I focused on the surroundings. Everything here was greener and brighter and warmer than New York.

After a couple of quick turns, we came up to the shell of a

small house. Not only were the windows and doors blown out; the heat from the fire had even melted the plastic siding, making the house look like something out of a horror movie.

Special Agent Frederick and I exited her car and walked around examining the house. I didn't really know what I was looking for. Maybe I just needed to tell myself I had gone to the scene in person and done everything I could.

I shook my head and said, "Who uses propane tanks to commit suicide?"

"It happened up in Palm Beach County."

"I know. I read the story online about the deputy US marshal who used propane tanks to commit suicide. But it seems like an outlier."

Frederick shrugged. "Everything is an outlier until it's not. Maybe this is a new trend. If you have any doubts about the suicide or any information, I'm all ears."

It was refreshing to see someone with such an open mind. There was no pretext. She was interested in getting things right. I wished I saw more of that from government employees.

I eased off the topic by saying, "I guess I've never seen it in New York because not many people have propane-powered barbecue grills."

"Well, you can't blame Florida Man when this was done by two retired cops from New York."

She had a point. I smiled and said, "Touché."

CHAPTER 47

WE SPENT A little while longer looking around at the burned-out remains of the small house. I knew from the reports that Ralph Stein's sister had witnessed the explosion while walking nearby with her two grandchildren. The sister had already given several statements, but Special Agent Carol Frederick had managed to schedule us another interview with her for later in the day just to be on the safe side. She'd taken the initiative and set that up on her own, on short notice. I appreciated the effort.

Frederick stood next to me as I poked around the house and said, "Clearly, you think there's more to this case."

"What do you think?"

"I looked through the reports and I did a couple of interviews. Everyone said the same thing. Stein and Halverson were perfectly nice neighbors who mostly kept to themselves. A few people noted that they were pretty heavy drinkers. Sounds like a lot of people I know, especially retirees. We're still waiting on the toxicology report, but my guess is they were pretty loaded at the time of the incident."

"Are there any bars close by?"

Special Agent Frederick thought about it and said, "There's a little place called Hollywood Squares less than a mile up the road."

"Hollywood Squares? Really? Like the old TV game show?"

"Been there a long time. I guess they're just trying to capitalize on the city's name. It's not a spring break kind of place. You can get a burger, but it's mostly alcohol sales to older, serious drinkers. Most of them live on this side of the Intercoastal."

Every community had bars like this. And every bar had a bartender who was much more observant than people thought. "Could you stand a hamburger?"

"You think we should talk to the bartender."

I just smiled. Carol Frederick reminded me of Terri Hernandez. Always thinking and usually a step ahead of me.

Hollywood Squares was exactly as I'd imagined it. A one-story cinder-block building with few windows and a flat roof. There were two cars in the gravel parking lot. An old pickup truck and a Ford Escort with cardboard where the rear passenger window should be. Painted on the front, around a single window and door, was a mural with manatees and dolphins swimming around the words "Hollywood Squares." A caricature of the famously campy 1960s game show panelist and comedian Paul Lynde poked out from the *H* in "Hollywood."

We opened the front door, stepped inside, and I was surprised to find the place not nearly as dark and dingy as I'd expected. There were two TVs, both playing ESPN. Two men sat at the bar. One was eating a hamburger and drinking a beer. The other was just drinking a Budweiser from the can. Neither bothered to turn around to see who had just entered the bar.

The bartender was a woman in her fifties with dyed blond hair and a pretty face. We ordered hamburgers and beers, then Special Agent Frederick took a moment to chat with the bartender and ease her into a few questions. The bartender's name was Leslie Hodge. She'd been the manager of this place for more than twenty years.

Frederick laid a few photographs of Ralph Stein and Gary Halverson down on the bar.

The bartender cut her eyes at us and said, "I figured you two for cops as soon as you walked in. We get a fair number of cops in here. I was sorry to hear about Ralph and Gary. They were all anyone talked about for a couple of days after the explosion."

Leslie told us the two retired cops used to come into the bar almost every afternoon. "They usually left about seven, when they'd walk home. More like staggered. They were good customers, tipped well. Everyone liked them."

It wasn't anything specific the bartender said, but something about the way she talked about the two men made me suddenly realize: Gary and Ralph hadn't just been friends—they'd been a couple. I felt like an idiot for not putting the pieces together sooner. I mean, they *lived* together. I didn't care one way or the other and didn't know anyone who would. It was their choice to keep things on the quiet side. I just couldn't believe I'd overlooked something so obvious.

Leslie said, "Gary introduced backgammon night on Tuesdays. We're going to call it Gary's Backgammon Night from now on. Ralph used to work in the kitchen when we were shorthanded. He refused any pay. Sometimes he'd ask us to donate to some environmental fund. Cops must have pretty good retirements. They never seemed to worry about money. Gary and Ralph just liked helping people. We're gonna miss those guys."

After lunch, Frederick and I spoke to Ralph Stein's sister, Rachel. She was still grieving the loss of her brother but told us about how Ralph had been a grandfather figure to her grandchildren. How he had enjoyed their company and had displayed their artwork on his refrigerator. Then she broke down and started to sob uncontrollably.

Later, when Special Agent Frederick was driving me back to the airport, she turned to me unprompted and said, "You may be onto something. Those two don't seem like candidates for suicide."

All I could say was "I'll keep you in the loop."

CHAPTER 48

ROB TRILLING SAT quietly with Terri Hernandez. They were on surveillance in the Bronx, listening in on a conversation going on inside the warehouse. Their informant, Jaime Nantes, was working off a serious assault charge that included the use of a Colt .45, and he had agreed to cooperate in exchange for a chance to avoid a lengthy stay upstate.

Nantes had reluctantly worn a transmitter that would relay whatever he heard inside the warehouse. They hoped it would help them piece together a case and figure out who'd been killing the dopers they'd been looking at the last few months.

Hernandez said, "Just keep your eyes and ears open, Super Jock. This isn't like any police work you learned about in the academy or working homicide cases. There's an art to dealing with informants. You have to remember to never trust them."

"If we can't trust them, why do we use them?"

"Because we're not trying to arrest Boy Scouts. The people who mix with the criminals we're looking at are generally criminals themselves. All he's doing is picking up conversations. We just have to hope he's more afraid of going to prison for five to seven years than he is of being found out."

"Couldn't we just send him in with a recorder?"

"At least you're starting to ask the right questions. In case he gets in trouble, since he's under our instructions, we need to be ready to go in and rescue him. Not that I think anything's gonna happen. But with these other players coming in to talk to the group today, I wanted to make sure we were erring on the side of caution." She adjusted the controls on the receiver linked to the transmitter hidden in the informant's baseball cap. Then she looked at Trilling and said, "All you really have to do is sit there and look pretty. I know you're good at that."

At least she acknowledged his existence now and again. Though Trilling wasn't sure if he liked it better when she ignored him or when she actively insulted him.

When they first arrived at this particular surveillance spot, Trilling had noticed and photographed an electric Porsche Taycan sitting at the far end of the block. It had to belong to someone inside. The tag came back with a company Trilling was willing to bet didn't really do much. He'd give all the information to Walter Jackson later. He also had a couple of new puns he wanted to try out on the jovial criminal intelligence analyst.

Several voices could be heard over the receiver, but the problem was the transmission faded in and out. Hernandez had said she thought it had something to do with the building and the metal in the columns. All Trilling could tell from the conversation was that some men who were not part of the group were inside.

Hernandez said, "It's a little unusual that they're all speaking English. I think at least one of the outsiders doesn't speak good Spanish. They're talking about some kind of business. It sounds a little tense."

"Something we should worry about?"

Hernandez kept listening. She didn't answer, which told Trilling the answer was yes, they should be worried.

Trilling wished he knew who the gang was talking to. Based on the voices he heard, he figured there were three people in there talking with one outsider, and there was a guy with the outsider who stayed silent much of the time. This was in addition to Nantes, who also had remained relatively quiet through the whole conversation so far.

Suddenly, the transmitter came in clearly. Someone said, "We run a tight ship. We don't include a lot of people in our business. It's not like the old days, when your dad…" The transmission faded out. Trilling couldn't hear what was being said, but he now got the same sense as Hernandez. The discussion was tense.

The conversation resumed when the outsider, sounding younger than everyone else, said, "I don't care how things used to be done. I just want a stable distributor who can handle my business. As long as we can stay quiet and under the radar, we'll all make money. Lots of money. That was the problem in the old days. Everyone wanted to be famous one way or another. *Por la fama y la infamia.* Whether it was being the biggest gangster in town or getting their names on buildings. Everyone was a showoff."

Another voice said, "What do you know about the old days? You talk good, but we ain't seen nothing from you yet. It don't matter who you're related to. We need to see some product that we can move on the streets."

"I don't do auditions."

"Then we don't have no use for you."

There was silence. The outsider said, "Put that goddamn knife away. This is a business meeting."

Trilling turned to open the car door. They couldn't stand by and let a murder happen.

CHAPTER 49

TERRI HERNANDEZ HELD her hand out to stop Rob Trilling from jumping out of the car. She said, "Hang on. They're just trying to scare him."

A blue Tahoe came barreling down the side street, fast.

Over the receiver they heard the other newcomer, clearly the younger man's muscle. "Put that knife away before I shove it up your ass."

There were some chuckles, then the main man said, "Stop fooling around, Nestor. We've got a lot to talk about with these guys."

Trilling was still on edge. But when the blue Tahoe drove right past the warehouse, it showed Trilling how much his imagination was playing tricks on him. He wished he could stay as calm as Terri Hernandez.

The same man said, "We need to see something from you other than nice clothes and a fancy car."

The outsider said, "What's that supposed to mean?"

"It means you may think you're a hotshot, but we know the streets. We don't do business like we used to do. We need each other."

The conversation was getting tense again. How many times could someone make snotty comments without some kind of retribution?

Hernandez shifted in her seat and reached back to make sure her holster was secure.

Over the wire, they heard the outsider say, "Watch how you talk to me. I don't like the disrespect I'm hearing. We'll do business when I say." There was a garbled transmission and it sounded like people were moving around.

Hernandez said, "I hope they're not getting ready for some kind of fight. We're not interested in the drug deal. We just want to know who committed the homicides. I wish they'd talk about that."

Trilling said, "Would they discuss that kind of stuff in a group? I don't know. I'm new to all this."

"I think the killer is someone in that warehouse. I could be wrong. As homicide detectives, we make a lot of assumptions, but in this case it feels right to me. They're all involved in criminal activity. Drug dealers aren't known for their discretion. Maybe we should go back and talk to that asshole José Silbas again and see what else he knows."

"We didn't leave on the best of terms with him."

Hernandez frowned and said, "I'm sorry I lost my cool at the end of that interview. But it seems clear to me that Silbas had his wife murdered while he was in prison. Pissed me off."

"And Jaime Nantes tried to shoot someone over a drug debt.

But we're still using him as an informant. Like you said, none of them are Boy Scouts."

Hernandez said, "Don't use my own words against me. That just confuses things." She gave him a little smile.

Trilling felt like he had just crossed some kind of threshold. It was the most pleasant thing she'd ever said to him. Then the transmission came in clearly again. The voices were still raised and tense. Trilling's stomach tightened. He'd already been in one gunfight inside a warehouse. He wasn't interested in doing it again if it could be avoided.

The outsider said, "I've got to make a few connections, then I'll get back in touch. You guys keep your shit together and don't draw any attention."

The main man said, "Don't think you're some kind of gangster. Don't tell us what we need to do. We're not even sure we're going to work with you."

The door at the far end of the warehouse opened and two people stepped out into the dull sunlight. The clouds cast an eerie patchwork of shadows over that end of the street. Hernandez picked up a camera with a telephoto lens from the console. She snapped photos of the two men as they walked from the warehouse, one bulkier than the other. Trilling glanced again at the two outdated images Walter Jackson had sent him of Antonio Deason. It was impossible at this distance and in this light to make an ID, plus the more slender man of the two kept his head down. He was dressed in a button-down shirt and nice slacks. It wasn't professional enough to work on Wall Street, but it was too formal for a meeting with drug dealers in the Bronx. Trilling wasn't surprised when he stopped at the Porsche. Hernandez snapped a few more photos as both men slipped in, then the Taycan shot down the street.

Hernandez and Trilling listened to the receiver and heard normal conversation in the warehouse, most of it in Spanish.

Hernandez explained to Trilling that they were all mumbling about what a slick asshole their visitor was. But it sounded like he could make them some money, so they were inclined to do business with him anyway.

Trilling said, "What's that mean for our case?"

Hernandez shook her head and said, "I have no idea."

CHAPTER 50

ROB TRILLING WAS glad the surveillance had gone as well as it had, despite not making a firm ID of "Little D." He was anxious to take a few moments to call Mariah, the paramedic. He'd talked to her a couple of times since their lunch. She definitely seemed interested. She had texted him a couple of times from the fire station where she worked. On one of the texts, she'd added at the end: Be careful out on the streets. It was nice. And the first time a woman other than his mom and sister had ever shown concern about his safety.

Before Trilling could get out of the SUV with Terri Hernandez, though, she wanted to go over what they'd learned.

Hernandez said, "We found out a few things today. This group is doing business with outsiders, and the dead men we're investigating all seemed to have been associated with them, either working together or as rivals. We need to find what they had in common. How does this new outsider figure in? Were they in favor of or against doing business with him? Did the victims all know something that someone else needed to keep quiet? Was there some financial aspect to their murders? Was there an emotional reason these men were targeted? Those are the main reasons homicides are committed: passion, money, or silencing someone."

Trilling almost felt like he should be taking notes. Hernandez may have been rough and stern with him, but she definitely knew what she was talking about. He was learning a lot. He couldn't wait to get back to the office to talk all of this over with Michael Bennett. He found his senior partner always had a way of putting things in perspective. Plus, who knew if any of what they'd heard today could be of help in Bennett's investigation.

As they sat in the SUV, he and Hernandez noticed an elderly woman with a walker start to cross the street alongside a little girl who was probably seven or eight. The little girl held on to one side of the walker as the woman slowly made progress from one sidewalk to the other.

Hernandez said, "Let's see if we can track down our informant and debrief him. Maybe he can fill in the blanks of what we missed and identify the outsider more clearly."

Trilling nodded. Their standard method for talking with Nantes was to drive around in Hernandez's car so no one saw them sitting and talking somewhere, like at a restaurant. Hernandez would have Trilling sit in the back seat, directly behind the informant, in case he did something unexpected and the situation turned bad quickly. Trilling understood her concerns. He hadn't dealt with a lot of informants, but none of them seemed particularly stable or trustworthy.

Trilling got out of the front seat and went to open the rear passenger door so he could slip into the back of the SUV. When he opened the door, the wind caused several papers to blow out onto the sidewalk and he had to chase down a couple of the sheets. As he recovered them, he noticed the elderly woman and the little girl about halfway across the street—and a delivery van rounding the corner way too fast. Acting quickly, Trilling darted into the street and managed to grab the woman around the waist and the little girl under her arm, pulling them out of the way of the speeding van. The three of them basically fell onto the street, a few feet away from where the van swerved, missing the pedestrians but clipping the walker, sending it flying through the air.

The van slowed for a moment, then the driver hit the gas and fled the scene. The woman on the ground started to speak in Spanish. From her tone, Trilling thought she was scolding him.

Hernandez hopped out of the SUV and reached them in a couple of steps. She started speaking to the woman in Spanish as she helped her to her feet. Trilling still had the little girl in his arms. After they had all made it safely to the sidewalk, Trilling recovered the mangled walker, then turned to Hernandez and said, "I'm not sure what she's so angry at me about."

Hernandez laughed. "Why do you think she's angry?"

"Her tone and how loud she is."

"She's excited. She's saying God sent an angel down to protect her and her granddaughter."

The little girl hugged Trilling around his leg. Then the old woman stepped over and gave him a hug as well. It confused him. He wasn't sure what to do. The elderly woman motioned him to bend down. She kissed him on the cheek and said something else.

Hernandez smiled and said, "She wants you to come to dinner Sunday night."

Trilling couldn't hide the grin that swept across his face. He said, "I wish I could, but I've already got an invitation to Sunday dinner."

The detectives stayed with the woman, helping her and the little girl make it to an apartment half a block up from where they'd almost been killed by the delivery van. Once the woman and the girl were inside, Hernandez turned to Trilling and said, "You just turned the term Super Jock from an insult into a compliment. I've never seen reflexes like that. If you hadn't been here, that little girl and her grandmother would've been dead meat. The way that delivery guy took off, he probably would've fled even if he'd hit them. I'd say you've earned the rest of the day off."

Trilling smiled. All he really wanted was time to call Mariah.

CHAPTER 51

IT WAS PRETTY late by the time I got back to my apartment on the Upper West Side. The early morning flight and investigation in Florida, followed by a two-hour flight delay out of Fort Lauderdale, had really taken it out of me. The only thing I could think about was sprawling on the bed next to Mary Catherine and being unconscious for as long as the kids would let me.

I'd been turning over the case in my mind for hours. Each of the retired cops' deaths had some odd aspect to it. Even FDLE Special Agent Carol Frederick had agreed that Ralph Stein and Gary Halverson weren't candidates for committing suicide. But the one thing they all had in common was a connection to the old Richard Deason case.

I entered the apartment like I was a second-story man. I was quiet and deliberate. I managed to open, close, and relock the front door without waking anyone. I stood in the darkness of the entryway and listened for a moment. It was one of the few times in the last decade I could remember the apartment being this silent.

I was hungry. But more tired. I padded back to our bedroom, still working hard not to disturb anyone's sleep. I quietly eased open the door to the master bedroom, hoping to avoid any of the usual creaks. As I turned in the dark after closing the door softly, a voice startled me.

"I was starting to worry about you."

Mary Catherine flicked on the light next to the bed. I was about to apologize when I noticed the three extra bodies strewn across the bed like it was a war zone. Shawna and Chrissy were lying sideways near the foot of the bed, and Trent was sprawled with his head resting on Chrissy's leg and his feet on my pillow. They all snoozed peacefully. I gave Mary Catherine a look.

She shrugged and said, "I'm a soft touch. When they come in and want to spend a few minutes with me, I can't say no."

"What are you doing awake so late?"

"Are you kidding? I sleep all day. At some point my body rebels and makes me stay awake. It's okay. I've done about two hundred sudokus and found a Wordle archive online. It keeps my mind active."

I eased onto the bed next to her on the opposite side from Trent and ran my fingers through her hair. Then I leaned down and kissed her on the forehead. "How do you feel?"

She let out a long sigh. "I really don't know. It's only been a few days, but I feel like I've been stuck in this bed for months. I feel useless. Worse, the kids have gotten by just fine without me. No one's been late to school, and either Jane, Brian, or Juliana has gotten everyone to all their activities. Ricky supervises the kitchen and meals. While I just sit here like a big lump."

"Don't be silly. You're not all that big." She punched me in the arm as I grinned. "Now be serious with me. How do you feel physically?"

Mary Catherine bit her lower lip. It was one of her easy "tells" for when she's anxious. "I don't know how to answer that. I don't feel lightheaded or faint like I did the other day. I'm just so worried about the baby. We went through so much just for me to get pregnant."

I stroked her hair as I tried to word my next comment as carefully as possible. "We might need to be prepared for the worst. We can try again and again. But your health is the most important thing to me."

"Prepared for the worst? Failure's not an option."

I chuckled and Mary Catherine wrapped her arms around me. She scooted over a bit and had me lie down next to her without shooing away the children. I popped off my shoes but kept all my clothes on. I was so tired, I felt like I was falling into a cloud.

She said softly, "Tell me about your Florida trip."

I was going to tell her about the FDLE agent. I was going to explain how helpful Special Agent Frederick had been and how much she reminded me of Terri Hernandez. Before I began, I decided to take a moment to rest my eyes.

The next thing I knew, the kids were scurrying around, getting ready for school. I was still in my clothes and lying on the wrong side of the bed next to Mary Catherine.

CHAPTER 52

ROB TRILLING WAS seated at his desk when I walked into the office. In fact, everyone was seated at their desks. It was after nine o'clock. I had been slow to start this morning. Juliana had wrangled all the kids off to school and I took advantage of a few quiet moments with Mary Catherine. I had wanted to make sure she felt okay both physically and emotionally.

And I had needed another hour's worth of sleep.

From his office, Walter Jackson walked over to where Trilling and I sat. He casually said, "My daughter saw a deer on the way to school."

Without hesitation, Trilling said, "How did she know it was going to school?"

Walter let loose with a belly laugh. "I can't believe you beat me to the punch line." He looked at me and said, "This young man is going places."

"If we don't solve this case, the only place Celeste Cantor is going to have us going is back to patrol."

That put a damper on the jovial mood. Everyone focused. Walter took out his tablet.

I noticed a patch of road rash on Trilling's left elbow. "What happened?" I said, pointing toward the rough patch of scab.

He looked down at his elbow and the injury about the size of a drink coaster. "Nothing, really. Just fell in the road."

If he wasn't bothered by it, neither was I. After looking over a few notes, I filled in Rob Trilling and Walter Jackson on my time in Florida. Everything I'd learned was reinforcing my gut feeling that these deaths had been orchestrated, not just accidents or suicides. And that they were all involved in the case against Richard Deason years ago.

Trilling waited patiently while I told them about my trip. As soon as I finished, he looked like a kid ready to burst from not telling a secret.

Trilling fidgeted in his seat. "Terri and I had an interesting day yesterday."

"Tell me about it."

"We saw Antonio Deason."

"Are you certain?"

"Terri took some pictures, and his head is down in most of them. But I'd say it's the same man as in the images Walter sent us. Our informant confirmed that 'Little D' was the son of a big-time trafficker who was working the city almost twenty years ago. Deason was talking to our group in the Bronx. We didn't get a great transmission, but the informant says he's talking about moving a couple of kilos of heroin a week through them."

This *was* interesting news.

Trilling said, "Antonio sounded young but pretty tough. He was there with one other guy who probably was his backup—a bigger guy—but Antonio stood up to the gang himself. He told them they needed him if they wanted to make any real money. Then the two of them came out, jumped into an electric Porsche, and took off. We could not risk following them."

"Sounds like progress to me. I saw in the docs Walter sent me that Antonio signed a ConEd agreement for an apartment in lower Manhattan. I say we do this the easy way and go talk to him at his apartment."

Then Walter said, "I've done a little more digging and there's something else we might need to look into."

From the way he'd said it, I could tell it meant we had a lot more work to do.

CHAPTER 53

WALTER JACKSON LOOKED at his tablet like he was a sports reporter about to run through some stats on the Yankees. Trilling and I both leaned forward in anticipation of whatever he was about to tell us.

The big man made the wooden chair creak as he shifted his weight. He waited a few moments, then let out a sigh.

I had to say, "C'mon, Walter, is this for dramatic effect? What's so important?"

"My mom always says to make sure we have everything straight when trying to explain something. You sound like my daughters, always rushing me."

"Now, that's a shocker. I couldn't imagine why anyone would want to rush you." I smiled to let him know I was just joking. "Seriously, what have you found?"

Walter got to the point. "In all the research I've done on

Richard Deason and now Antonio Deason, I kind of neglected the wife's background."

Trilling said, "Didn't she die, like, six years ago?"

"She did. Richard Deason's wife, Isabel, died at age forty-seven of complications from cervical cancer at Jackson Memorial Hospital in Miami. Antonio went to college there to be close to family."

I snapped my fingers and said, "It's about *her* family, right?"

"And that's why I like working here. I'm surrounded by smart people. Yes, it's about the wife's family. This is what I needed to tell you."

Sometimes Walter liked to put on a show to earn a little extra praise for his extraordinary efforts. I wasn't against it. He constantly amazed me with his ability to dig out small details that sometimes made a big difference in a case. This time, as he looked down at his tablet, he said, "She was from a wealthy Panamanian family. I mean superrich. Rockefeller rich."

"We got it."

He smiled, showing me he was intentionally annoying me. "Her family name is Vega. Isabel graduated from the University of Panama with a degree in economics. She had three brothers. One took over the family importation business bringing in raw materials used for construction and the government. It's one of the top companies completely owned by Panamanian nationals.

"Another brother is a surgeon in Panama City. There are a ton of news articles about him. And even though the Google translation is a little rough, it looks like he's also considered one of the most outstanding surgeons in the country."

I glanced at Trilling, just as he looked at me. I could tell we were both wondering what this was about.

Then Walter said, "It's the third brother who might be con-nected. He was in the military when the US invaded Panama to get rid of Noriega. He fled Panama shortly after that and is known to be a 'military consultant,' or mercenary. His name is men-tioned in several articles about fighting in various locations around the world."

I blurted out, "You think he could be the one orchestrating these deaths? Maybe in some way to avenge his brother-in-law or help his nephew?"

Walter shrugged. "I don't necessarily think he's a viable suspect. Although I have all of his vitals and as many pictures as I could find of him. But he does run in circles that I suspect might be able to hire someone to do something like this. Maybe an American. Someone who would blend into the fabric of New York."

Trilling chimed in. "Everyone blends into the fabric of New York."

Walter nodded, then added, "But what about the fabric of Hollywood Beach, Florida. Or Westchester County? I think it's an avenue we might want to consider."

I reached over and nabbed Walter's tablet from him to scroll through what he had on the new suspect. The brother's name was Gonzalo Vega. There was a picture of him as a twenty-one-year-old lieutenant in the Panama Defense Forces. There was also a picture of the whole family from a newspaper. His sister, Isabel, was a few years younger than him. It also spoke to the wealth and power of the family. Who gets a family photograph in the main newspaper of their country? The last photo of him was from about four years ago. He would've been about fifty then, but he still had the look of an active military member. Lean and fit with short, dark hair.

I handed the tablet to Trilling. He scrolled through the files as well. I was wondering where we went next. Trilling answered when he said, "When do you want to go talk to Antonio Deason?"

I had to like that can-do attitude from my new partner.

CHAPTER 54

KEVIN DOYLE SAT in a diner on the Brooklyn side of the Brooklyn Bridge. He was reading a number of newsfeeds on his iPad. He had connections with military suppliers and former government operatives all over the Western world. He used to be sent on important missions that the people who hired him said were a matter of national security. Now he was stuck in New York, killing old men and women, and he wasn't clear on the reasons. He'd been told why he had to do it. He just wasn't as certain as his employer that it was necessary work.

Doyle liked the diner. This was his fourth time here this week. It wasn't anything fancy. When you ordered coffee, your choices were black or with cream and sugar. He appreciated the simplicity of ordering coffee without having to go through a list of what he wanted or didn't want. Best of all, the same friendly waitress had been there every morning. Her name was Tammy, and she'd told him that she was training for an IRONMAN tri-athlon. She'd also shared that her uncle owned the diner, though he was a horrible boss who treated both her and her mother terribly. At least she got to pick what shifts she wanted to work, so she could fit in her training.

He always sat at the far end of the counter so that if Tammy had a few free moments, she could come over and chat with him without anyone else too close. Today he was in a little later than usual, after the breakfast rush. There was one person at a small table near the front door and two others at the other end of the counter. Tammy came down with a fresh pot of coffee. He could tell by her biceps that she was an athlete. But she also had a pretty smile.

Doyle asked, "What's your workout for today?"

Tammy said, "It's an easy jog. I thought I might even take the subway and run in Central Park. Just for a change of scenery." She poured some coffee into his cup, then said, "You look like you're in pretty good shape. Wanna go for a run with me?"

Doyle couldn't hide his smile. The only problem was he needed to keep a low profile while he was here in New York. He remembered an unfortunate situation in Berlin when a girl he'd had a one-night stand with almost gave him away to the police. It was after he'd eliminated a right-wing extremist who was becoming too popular for some people's tastes.

Doyle had been afraid for a little while he might have to eliminate the young German woman too, but he'd managed to get out of the country without doing anything drastic. He was still distressed about killing Elaine and didn't want to make the same mistake here. Then he looked up at Tammy's bright smile and couldn't help himself. "That sounds like fun, as long as you don't run me into the ground."

She giggled and said, "Six miles, then we'll do a little ab work. That's it."

"Yeah, but at what pace?"

"I'll let you set the pace."

He realized this girl really did want to spend some time with him. They made a plan to meet later, then she rushed off to help other customers. Doyle laid down twice the amount of the bill and gave her a quick wave as he headed out the door.

He left the diner in the best mood he'd been in since arriving in New York.

CHAPTER 55

ONE OF THE things I liked most about working with Rob Trilling was that he was not a procrastinator. He didn't find other things to do when we had an interview or some other casework to complete. We wasted very little time between making the decision to talk to Antonio Deason face-to-face and actually arriving on Greene Street in SoHo, looking for his building.

We found the building quickly. It's pretty easy to find things down in SoHo. This was a typical six-story redbrick building with a clothing store on the first floor and the building's entrance a little farther down. We walked past the recessed entry quickly to see how secure the door was. There was no doorman, but the door had a good security system.

The building was by no means flashy. I would call it nice. Maybe even trendy. But there were plenty of more luxurious buildings a big-time dope dealer who drove a Porsche could live in. I wasn't worried about his housing tastes at the moment. All I wanted to do was get inside the building without having to buzz Antonio Deason's apartment.

Surprise is often the key to a good interview. If we tried to buzz our way into the building, he could simply refuse to let us in. But if we knocked on his door, he'd be more likely to open the door, assuming we were the super or a neighbor. Then we might get a chance to talk.

Trilling said, "I don't see his Porsche parked anywhere on the street."

"I doubt he'd want to park on the street. He probably has a garage somewhere nearby where he keeps it."

Trilling and I were both dressed casually, and we blended in with the crowds strolling along the street. I said, "Let's take a stroll around the block and see if we can find a better way to get into the building."

We fell into an easy conversation as we ambled down the sidewalk and pretended to window-shop. It was a minor respite in what had been a busy week, and really my first chance in days to talk with Trilling one-on-one.

As we walked, Trilling turned to me and said, "You ever get tired of this?"

"What? Walking around lower Manhattan or investigations?" Trilling gave me one of his looks and I knew exactly what he meant. I said, "Sure. Everyone gets a little tired of something they've done for so long. But then I get a note from someone I helped years ago, or we catch a killer before he can kill again, and I'm back to being excited about my work. I don't know how many people can say that."

As usual, Trilling didn't say anything else right away. After we walked around the corner, I said to him, "What about you? Is the job wearing you down already?"

"No, not really. You and Terri keep me busy enough that I don't even think about getting bored or complacent."

"Is Terri still tough on you?"

"I've had tougher in the military."

"I bet. It always takes Terri a while to warm up to someone. She barely spoke to me the first few cases we worked together."

It was one of the most comfortable conversations I'd had with the young former Army Ranger. I said, "You still coming to dinner Sunday evening?"

"Are you sure it's no imposition with Mary Catherine laid up?"

"Ricky's in charge of the food. All the kids have really stepped up and made sure the apartment looks good. Maybe not quite to Mary Catherine's standards, but as Eddie said, 'She's stuck in bed. She'll never see it.' You gotta love that kid's practical view of the world."

Trilling said, "I'm looking forward to a nice meal."

We found an alley behind the building. Unfortunately, the rear door was as secure as the front. As we walked back around to the recessed entrance to the building, a deliveryman in a uniform was coming out of the door.

I said, "Hey, Chuck."

The man looked at me and said, "It's Bill."

I edged past him through the open door and said, "Sorry. You look like my friend Chuck."

The deliveryman just kept walking. But now Trilling and I were inside Antonio Deason's building.

CHAPTER 56

ROB TRILLING AND I wasted no time in rushing up the stairs to the fourth-floor apartment listed on Antonio Deason's ConEd statement. There was always a chance he didn't really live in the apartment. This is what slows down police work—leads that don't go anywhere. But it is all part of the job.

We didn't run into any other residents as we wandered down the fourth-floor hallway, looking for apartment 406. We found the door, knocked, then automatically moved to flank it. Tactical thinking isn't something you can turn on and off. Even for an interview like this, there is always a risk. Too many cops had been shot through doors for me to spend any time in front of one after I knocked.

The door opened almost immediately. The young man in front of us was tall and handsome. I immediately recognized him from his driver's license as Antonio Deason. His hair was cut in a trendy fashion, and he wore a button-down shirt and nice slacks. He looked more like he was ready to go out for the night instead of lounging around his apartment.

Clearly, we had taken him by surprise. He looked at both of us and said, "May I help you?"

I wasted no time. "I'm Michael Bennett. This is Rob Trilling." I stuck out my hand to see if he'd shake it. He didn't hesitate. He looked me in the eye and gave me a firm grip.

Then Deason asked, "And you are…?"

"With the NYPD. We were wondering if you had a few minutes to talk with us."

He looked at each of us again. "How did you get into the building?"

I didn't want to give him time to think. "Can we come inside and talk?"

"I have nothing to say."

"You don't even know what we want to talk about."

"Doesn't matter."

I said, "We're just trying to clear something up. We were hoping you might be able to help."

Deason folded his arms. "Am I under arrest or am I free to go back into my apartment?"

"No, Mr. Deason, you're not under arrest."

"Good." He shut the door, and I could hear the dead bolt slide into place as soon as it closed.

I looked at Trilling and said, "I guess the easy option is off the table."

CHAPTER 57

KEVIN DOYLE ARRIVED early to his meeting in Central Park. He wanted to make sure he could warm up and stretch a little before he saw Tammy. Although he tried to stay in shape and exercised a couple of times a week, Tammy was serious about it. She was also a little younger than him. He didn't want to embarrass himself.

It was cool outside, so he wore a sweatshirt he'd bought from a sidewalk vendor over an old Army T-shirt. The gaudy I ♥ NEW YORK on the front made him smile. He didn't know why. Maybe because it was so unlike his usual drab clothes.

Doyle strolled to the front of Belvedere Castle, where Tammy had said she'd meet him. He soon saw her jogging toward the castle as he stood waiting for her.

Her smile immediately lifted his spirits. This was one of the best decisions he'd made since coming back to New York. Tammy surprised him by coming right up and giving him a kiss on the cheek.

Then she said, "Let's go!" And took off in an easy sprint toward the interior of the park. The overcast sky and the fact that it was a weekday meant they didn't have to dodge many people.

Doyle caught up with Tammy and they started to chat as they jogged along. Doyle kept up a decent pace despite the shrapnel in his left knee. It was like being on a first date. He guessed it *was* kind of a first date. He learned that she had her AA degree in biology and was enrolled in City College to finish her BA. He told her about his time in the Army but left his post-military career vague, referring to himself as a consultant who traveled quite a bit. Which wasn't entirely a lie.

Tammy surprised him by occasionally stopping to do push-ups and a couple of times even pull-ups on the low branches of trees. It was nothing he hadn't done a thousand times before, but it felt like she was evaluating him. His competitiveness kicked in and he made sure to show perfect form when he did his own push-ups or pull-ups.

Finally, they ended up back in front of Belvedere Castle. They went through a few stretches as Doyle tried to figure out the best way to invite her to dinner. She certainly seemed interested in him. He even wondered if his hotel room was clean enough to bring her back. That was something he should have thought of before he came to the park.

After a few minutes, Tammy said, "I knew you were in good shape, but that was very impressive. Especially for a guy who has to hold down a job. And I think I can figure out what kind of job you have."

"I'm not sure what you mean."

"A guy with your background doesn't stay in shape like you are unless he's still doing physical work. There was just something about the way you came into the diner every morning. I could tell you weren't like other guys I knew. I've been wanting to ask you a question for the last few days. Now that I've gotten to know you better, I feel like I can finally ask it."

"Okay, you've got my attention. What's the big question?" Doyle's mind raced with possibilities.

Tammy stood up from her stretch and turned to face Doyle. She moved closer and reached out to take hold of his right hand. She glanced around to make sure no one was near them.

His heart started to beat a little faster.

She leaned in close and whispered in his ear, "My uncle has ruined my life. He's basically holding me in servitude. If something happened to him, I'd be free to do whatever I wanted."

Doyle stepped back and said, "What?"

"Would you kill my uncle for me?"

CHAPTER 58

YEARS AGO, WHEN I was assigned to a robbery task force, my sergeant told me, "After four in the afternoon you should be done with your work or out on the street for an investigation. Never be sitting at your desk after four." It was the sergeant's way of saying work hard but don't neglect your family. It's too bad a lot of cops fall into the trap of endless hours, which often leads to the trap of endless divorces.

Unfortunately, by late afternoon I was back at my desk. And still in the damn office. But at least the office was quiet. I appreciated the peace. I was questioning my decision to rush out and interview Antonio Deason earlier. Maybe we had jumped the gun. I was not sure what I'd been expecting to accomplish. A confession? No way. I suppose all I really had wanted was to get a decent read on the guy. Was he a copy of his badass father? Was he smart? Was he just a street thug? I hadn't gotten an answer to any of those questions, and now I felt like an idiot. An idiot sitting alone in Manhattan North Homicide's office late in the afternoon. Maybe I was just a dumbass.

Terri Hernandez had said she had a date tonight and there was no surveillance scheduled, so I'd sent Trilling home an hour ago. He needed some time off. I worried about him. Not just because he was new to a dangerous job or because he was a long way from home. Although he had filled me in generally about his mental health treatment from the VA, I worried about putting too much pressure on the young man. I knew he was still talking to his VA counselor, but Trilling didn't share any specifics. And I didn't ask.

I also wanted him to spend a little more time away from the job. God knew what kind of effort he had to put in at his apartment to keep those five roommates of his comfortable and fed.

I leaned back in my chair and stretched. That quick trip to Florida had really taken it out of me. I felt like I could put my head down on the desk and sleep. I decided it was time to go home. But before I could finish up and hit the road, I heard the main door to our offices click open. Someone had slid their security pass across the lock. I looked up and muttered, "Oh, shit," a little too loudly.

"What's wrong, Bennett, not happy to see me?" Detective Sergeant Dennis Wu, from Internal Affairs, glided through the workspace. He glanced at each desk as he went by to see if anyone had left any sensitive material out in the open. He may not have said that's what he was doing, but I knew.

I tried to take the high road. "What do you need, Wu?" Then I heard the tone in my voice and quickly added, "How can I help you?"

Wu sat down at Trilling's desk next to mine, and wiggled in the chair to find a comfortable position. Then he faux-casually said, "Had a few questions that no one at One Police Plaza could answer."

"What sort of questions? No one's falsifying any time sheets here." It was a minor dig about some of the petty bullshit Internal Affairs usually looks into. I had to admit, I felt a butterfly in my stomach wondering what he was up to. I knew how this guy operated. Wu never came directly at you. It was always an oblique attack.

He put his overly polished Bruno Magli shoes up on Trilling's desk. "That's funny, Bennett. You know I don't handle any issues like that. I'm more interested in why you submitted a Flying Armed form to the TSA."

"What?"

"I saw you had Lieutenant Stiorra Stasha sign your form to fly to Fort Lauderdale. But I didn't see any travel documents or how it was related to a case. What's the story, Bennett? You go down there to scare an old boyfriend of your wife's?"

"No, I thought I could visit your mom and heard she lived in a rough neighborhood."

"You're full of jokes today, aren't you?"

"Look, Dennis, I'm trying to wrap things up here and get home. I don't really understand why an Internal Affairs detective sergeant stationed at headquarters would come all the way uptown just to harass me."

He chuckled and said, "It's kind of a hobby of mine. Besides, Harry told me to keep an eye on the squad."

That made me laugh out loud.

Detective Sergeant Wu said, "What the hell's so funny?"

I leaned forward in my chair and said, "I don't really know algebra. I don't understand European politics. But I know for a fact that Harry Grissom would never ask you for anything."

Now Wu was all business. "Why'd you go to Florida?"

"A case."

"What case?"

I could drop Celeste Cantor's name and this would be over. But I had to admit I was having fun. I kept going. "A classified case. I couldn't wait for travel approval, so I paid for it myself. Stasha approved a legit Flying Armed request. So don't give her any shit."

"What if you explain this case to me."

I nodded. Then I stood up. "Okay, we'll do it the easy way. Follow me. This will explain everything."

To his credit, Dennis Wu didn't ask any more questions. He just followed me out the main office entrance and down the corridor to an unmarked door.

I stood next to the door until he caught up to me. I didn't say anything. I just opened the door and gestured, like all of his answers were on the other side. He stepped through the doorway. I heard him say, "Hey, this is just—" as I let the self-locking door slam shut.

I gathered up my stuff and headed out for the night in a damn fine mood.

CHAPTER 59

KEVIN DOYLE FELT like he was wandering the streets of Manhattan aimlessly. In truth, he knew exactly where he was going. He'd been there half a dozen times in the past. It was just that Tammy's plea for him to murder her uncle had thrown him for such a loop, he was in a fog. Sure, it was his job. But he'd never had anyone ask him to do it as a favor. And he'd never had anyone not already in the know just figure out exactly what he did. It made him question whether he was getting sloppy.

Doyle had considered Tammy's unusual request, but only for a few seconds. He realized that the pretty triathlete probably wouldn't have given him the time of day if she didn't think she could get something from him. At least that's what he kept telling himself. There was a moment, just a moment, after she'd asked him to meet her in the park when he'd envisioned a life with her. What would it be like to live somewhere warm and comfortable?

He could move to Florida, like his parents. He liked the sunshine. No one would notice another New Yorker crossing the border down I-95. And he appreciated the fact that he could blend into a big and diverse state like Florida.

All that was over now. He was back to business. That's why he walked through the doors of a particular camera shop among the scores of camera and electronics stores along the streets of touristy Manhattan.

As soon as he walked through the door and stood there for a moment, the skinny teenager who'd been sitting on a stool reading a graphic novel sprang up and ducked into the back room. A few seconds later, Doyle saw Ari Shaver stick his head out from behind the door. A smile spread across his face, and he beckoned Doyle into the back with a quick flick of his hand.

Doyle followed him through a cluttered office, then through a second, more secure door into a windowless storeroom. Two fluorescent lights across the ceiling made the place look like a new-car showroom. But it smelled like a basement with a leaky water heater.

Doyle said, "Should I call you Ari or Amir when we are all the way back here?"

The man said, "Any time we're talking about business other than the cameras or electronics that I sell in the store, you call me Amir. Out there, call me Ari. That way there's never any confusion. It also lets me know exactly why someone is here."

Doyle nodded. "I settled up on the disposal job you did for me on Staten Island. Now I just need a few supplies and to ask about a quote for another disposal job."

Amir said, "Not a last-minute, super-rush job?"

"No. I'll schedule it and make it convenient."

"How big is the package?"

"About the same size as the last one."

"Another woman? It's not like you at all."

Doyle looked down at his feet. "It may not be necessary. I have to think it through. I figured it was best to talk to you when I was here anyway."

Amir looked like he was doing some math in his head. "You're a reliable customer. I'll give you a good break for anything like that. Especially if you can do it next to one of my vans and we can just shove her in the back." Then he clapped his hands and said, "You said you needed some supplies as well?"

"I could use more of that same cord you gave me before, two disposable trackers, and a decent monocular that could fit in a jacket pocket. The binoculars I have are too bulky for most of the stuff I need to do here in the city. In fact, I'll give them to you in case you can sell them up front."

"You have the original box?"

Doyle nodded. Above all else, Amir was a businessman. He had a family to feed.

The young man from the front called back, "Ari, can you come out here?"

"You'd probably rather be in here while I deal with customers. I'll be back in a minute," Amir said.

Doyle looked through some of the shelves that held a few weapons and other tools someone like him might need. He spotted a box on which someone had written "C-4." His first impulse was to doubt it contained actual explosives. Then he remembered where he was and realized that was exactly what would be in the box. He could hear Ari out in the showroom chatting with a customer and laughing at some lame joke. Two minutes later, the wiry Israeli was back in the storeroom.

Amir grabbed what Doyle had asked for. Doyle handed over cash to cover his supplies. They stepped into the camera shop in the front and suddenly Amir became Ari again. He told the young man to go get something to eat while things were slow.

When they were alone, Ari turned to Doyle and said, "It's a lot different working on your own than working with the Agency, huh?"

"You can say that again."

"The Agency usually handles stuff like this, but they have a lot of rules. I hate rules."

Doyle nodded. "Me too."

Ari said, "I follow only one business rule now. The customer is always right." He started to cackle.

For some reason, Ari's nonchalance and humor made Doyle smile too. He was glad that he'd never given Tammy his last name and had always paid cash at the diner. As long as he never went back, there was no way she could ever identify him.

Still, he hated any loose ends.

CHAPTER 60

AFTER A LONG week, I needed some time with my family. Even if it meant mixing work and family on a Saturday morning. Perhaps the only drawback I find of having ten children is not getting enough time to spend with each one of them individually. I usually spend a little more time with the younger kids. The older ones always seem so independent. Especially my second oldest daughter, Jane. She's so smart and carries herself so well, sometimes I forget she really is still just a teenage kid.

"Isn't me riding in your work car against the rules?" Jane asked me now. "It feels weird."

"I like to think of it as more of a serious guideline. A guideline in that *if* I get caught, I *might* be in trouble," I said. "For me the weird thing was taking the Brooklyn Bridge over the river. It's way too close to One Police Plaza. I probably wouldn't have gone this way if it was a weekday."

I had decided to take Jane with me in my city-issued Impala to visit Celeste Cantor at her campaign office in Brooklyn. I figured a Saturday morning was about the only time I could catch up with the inspector without dozens of eyes on us. "Besides, I thought you might like to see what a campaign headquarters looks like."

"I've seen plenty of them on TV shows. I'm guessing it'll be hectic, with a bunch of young, attractive people racing around," Jane said with a grin. "It's still nice to do something just the two of us."

I don't care if you're a parent or not, when a young person says something like that to you, it means something. I said, "I have no idea what these offices look like. It's for a City Council election, not the US Senate."

Jane said, "Does this have something to do with your trip to Florida?"

"Sort of. It's all part of a case that Celeste Cantor is very interested in."

"Is the case dangerous?"

I took my eyes off the road for a moment to look at my beautiful daughter. I could read her concern even in my quick glance. Every cop has to deal with questions like this occasionally. It's a fine line to walk between being honest and trying not to frighten your own children. It took me a moment to express myself properly.

"I don't feel like it's at all dangerous for me. I'm just looking into some deaths that occurred. It's not like I'm on patrol and having to pull over a suspicious car in the middle of the night. Most people don't realize how incredibly dangerous that kind of situation can be. By comparison, being a homicide detective is a walk in the park."

"That's good to hear. With the baby on the way, you shouldn't be taking any chances."

I smiled. If I hadn't been driving, I would have given her a hug.

The building we were looking for was ahead on the right. It didn't exactly look like something out of a shiny TV show. The closer we got, the less fancy it looked. It was a one-story building with wide windows, like it might have once been used as some kind of showroom. Amazingly, I was able to pull into a parking spot right in front of the building.

Jane said almost exactly what I was thinking. "This place is kind of run-down, isn't it?"

"Like I said, she's not running for US Senate." The atmosphere didn't get any better as we walked through the glass front door. The place had a vaguely unsettling odor. Maybe, rather than a showroom, it had once been a produce market and they never quite got the smell of rotten fruit out of the ventilation system.

No one paid our entrance much attention. Looking around as we stood by the front door, I recognized a few retired cops among the dozen or so people working at desks. A few were making phone calls while others went through lists of some kind, maybe of potential donors.

Finally, Celeste Cantor came out of the back. She immediately made a big show of welcoming us, then did a double take when she recognized Jane. "I can't believe what a beautiful young woman you've grown into." Then she looked at me and said, "My God, if Jane looks like this, how old is Juliana?"

"Enrolled at City College."

Cantor jokingly grabbed a chair to steady herself. "It's been too long since our families have gotten together. I may have gotten custody of Chuck, Mary, and Joseph in the divorce, but I hardly see them now that they're in college. Plus they're not that crazy about David."

It was the first time I'd heard Cantor speak seriously about her second marriage, to David Stone, a big-shot realtor. Normally, she'd just joke about how she did the good Irish Catholic girl thing and married a firefighter. Then she did the smart thing and married a rich real-estate mogul.

She said, "David was able to get us this storefront for nothing. It used to be some kind of health-food restaurant."

I thought, *That explains the smell.*

Cantor continued. "Of course I'm not officially running, but between cops who want to help, cousins, and a few friends, we're starting to draw up a decent battle plan. If you love the city, you can't just walk away even after you retire from the NYPD."

She graciously took Jane around the whole operation. I pretended to show interest, but really I was just here to talk over the case. Finally, when Jane became distracted by hearing all about a computer program they were using, I pulled Cantor aside.

She led me all the way into a back room. "I know you didn't come down here on a Saturday to see how my campaign machine is running," she said.

"Last night Dennis Wu came by my office—"

"Don't give that pocket-squared nerd the time of day. I'll deal with Dennis Wu. What the hell did that asshole want anyway?"

"He was asking about my trip to Florida."

"What trip? I thought we decided it wasn't worth it."

"Actually, you said that you didn't want to spend any money on it. I paid for it myself. Wu saw my paperwork to fly armed and came uptown to ask me a few questions." I had a hard time reading the expression on Cantor's face.

"What'd you learn in Florida?"

"That Ralph Stein and Gary Halverson were not candidates for suicide. None of the deaths I've looked into have seemed suicidal, natural, or accidental. I think we should open an official homicide investigation."

"No, no, no. We don't want to draw that kind of attention yet. We need more."

"What more do we need?"

"Maybe a decent suspect?"

I filled her in on everything I'd found on Antonio Deason. I even mentioned the thwarted attempt to interview him.

"You think he could be good for these deaths?"

"Possibly. He has connections to not only the cops but also similar killings in his father's old drug gang."

Cantor thought for a moment. "Keep looking at Antonio Deason, but keep it quiet. Use your new partner, the good-looking young guy who was tied up in that sniper investigation. But don't bring in anyone else."

Great. That's not exactly how I like to work cases. Using as few resources as possible makes it harder to catch an actual killer. But Celeste Cantor didn't need to know I'd already gotten Rob Trilling as well as Walter Jackson involved in the case.

CHAPTER 61

KEVIN DOYLE DROVE up to East Harlem in an older Toyota he'd located in Brooklyn. He'd originally thought he'd need to hot-wire the car, but he'd found a key stashed under the floor mat. His plan was to return the Toyota to the same spot in Brooklyn when he was done. His conscience had been nagging at him. He didn't like the idea of taking other people's stuff. Especially a car like this, which was probably all the owner could afford. Maybe he'd even stuff a couple of twenties in the console. The owner would probably think they had lost the cash at some point. It would make their day.

In East Harlem, Doyle drove between two different bars that had been identified as hangouts for two of his targets. Both targets were in the drug trade. Both were in their fifties. And both had horrendous criminal records.

One of them, Carlos Rios, had done nine years for manslaughter after stabbing a man in the throat with a broken bottle at a bar. The other was Oscar Tass. His criminal record read more like a guy who went along with the crowd, no matter how stupid the idea. He'd been arrested four different times for being involved in attacks. Always in a group. Never alone. He ended up doing four years upstate for the last attack, in which he and three buddies beat a homeless Navy vet so badly the man lost an eye and had a collapsed lung.

Doyle had no elaborate plans for these two hits, but he was hoping his targets would be together. It would be deeply satisfying to handle two of these scumbags at once.

There was no need to disguise anything with these guys. He didn't have to set up any elaborate scenario to confuse the cops. People in the drug trade being killed by gunfire was not going to attract undue attention or speculation. Doyle's only goal was not to be identified. He had a Mets baseball cap and superwide sunglasses he planned to use to cover his face. It wasn't perfect, but he had learned that during a shooting, people tended to panic and not pick up on details.

As Doyle drove, he couldn't help but think about Tammy. He fantasized about what life would be like with her. Really, with any woman. One word he always came back to was "peaceful." That is what he longed for. Peace and quiet. He had traveled enough and taken plenty of risks. Doyle felt he had earned a quiet retirement. Maybe after he was done with this job. At least that's what he hoped. *Why did she have to screw everything up with her crazy idea that I kill her uncle?*

About the fifth time he drove past the bar known as Caballo Loco, a.k.a. Crazy Horse, Doyle thought he spotted one of his targets through the window. The guy was just over six feet tall, with dark, neat hair and a trimmed goatee. Yep, it was definitely Carlos Rios.

Doyle scanned the area, then parked on the next block. He walked through an alley that came up alongside the bar. He came around a giant dumpster and froze. Rios was in the alley, standing not thirty feet in front of him. Doyle slipped back behind the dumpster and tried to get a surreptitious look.

Through the dappled light from the bar, Doyle realized that Rios was urinating against the wall of the building next door. And there was someone else with him, but it wasn't Oscar Tass. It was a woman.

Doyle shook his head. Even though he'd lived in barracks with dozens of other men, he still hated to have anyone near him when he went to the bathroom. He couldn't imagine carrying on a conversation while he peed.

Doyle kept peering around the dumpster, judging how long it would take him to sprint back to his stolen Toyota. He weighed the options. If he opened fire from here, he'd risk not only hitting the woman but also having a witness walking around.

As Doyle hesitated, the woman looked up and noticed him. In a loud voice, she said, "Hey, what are you doing, you pervert?"

Rios turned quickly. He reached behind his back and pulled out a pistol. When Doyle looked closer, he saw the woman had a gun too. *What the hell?*

Then a bullet pinged off the dumpster just above his head.

CHAPTER 62

AN ACTUAL GUNFIGHT next to a crowded bar was not what Doyle considered low-key. But now that it had started, he didn't panic. He never panicked. This was his specialty. The government had spent hundreds of thousands of dollars to train him in the use of several weapons. But his favorite was the M9, his 9mm Beretta.

He drew his Beretta from his belt holster, where it had been well concealed. He didn't even look. He popped the gun into his left hand and reached around the dumpster. He fired two quick rounds just to get everyone's attention and make them lower their heads.

That's when Rios shouted to him. It made Doyle freeze.

Rios yelled, "You the cat who killed my friends? We been expecting you to show up again. Now we can settle this like men."

Doyle knew he couldn't waste time chatting with this asshole.

He was relieved to realize no one in the bar had heard the gun-shots and there was no panic or rush for the door.

Rios yelled again. "You not going to answer me, *pendejo?*"

This guy was going to talk until one of his friends came out to help him. It was a smart move. But Doyle knew what to do. As soon as he heard Rios start to shout again, he didn't hesitate. He peeked around the corner of the dumpster with his pistol up and fired three times. He was already moving forward when he saw Rios drop to the ground. Doyle was certain he'd hit him twice in the chest and once in the face.

The woman got off one quick shot that went wide to the right. Doyle didn't stop moving forward as he fired three more quick shots. Same as Rios. Two hollow-point bullets hit the woman in the chest and one in her face. She went down onto the filthy sur-face of the alley right next to him.

Instinctively, Doyle switched out magazines, giving himself an additional fifteen shots if something were to happen or some-one came out of the bar.

He scanned the street and realized there was no one outside. He had just been lucky to see Rios. He was disappointed not to find Oscar Tass at the same time, but he had to be satisfied with one of them.

Doyle slipped the pistol back into his belt holster, covered it with his shirt, and hustled in the opposite direction of the alley. He turned the corner and was in his stolen Toyota less than thirty seconds later. He didn't race away from the scene. That would attract attention. He pulled from the curb slowly and put on his left turn signal at the next intersection.

There was not a soul on the street. He was one step closer to being finished.

CHAPTER 63

I LOUNGED ON the bed next to Mary Catherine. Her spirits still seemed to be pretty good. A lot of that had to do with the kids keeping her entertained. She and I had just finished a game of back-gammon. Before I came in, she had played a series of card games with Chrissy and Shawna. This wasn't our usual kind of Sunday afternoon activity. We often tried to go as a family to the park and do something physical. Sometimes it was flag football; other times it was just shooting baskets or kicking a ball around an open field. Eddie liked to call that soccer. I called it exhausting and low-scoring.

My grandfather was already here in anticipation of Ricky's Sunday meal. Some of the kids were finishing up homework assignments they had put off or watching an old war movie on TV, and I got to spend some time with my beautiful Mary Catherine. I appreciated the quiet moments we could spend together. With so many kids in the house, it was a rare opportunity.

The doorbell rang and Mary Catherine jumped. "My, Rob Trilling is a stickler for being on time, isn't he?"

I checked my phone and saw it was 6 p.m. on the nose. "Yes, he is. It wouldn't surprise me if he got here early and has been waiting quietly in the hallway until the clock struck six." I kissed Mary Catherine on the forehead and went out to greet my partner.

Some of the kids headed to the door as well. Trent and Juliana stood next to me as I opened the door. They knew who it was but liked Rob so much they wanted to greet him right at the door.

As the door opened, I saw Rob holding a bouquet of flowers and a bottle of red wine. Classy. The young man from Bozeman, Montana, had decent manners. He was even smiling, something that still took me by surprise, I saw it so infrequently.

Juliana stepped forward with a big smile on her own face.

Then Rob said, "This is Mariah."

That's when a tall, gorgeous young woman stepped into the doorway. Her dark complexion set off her spectacular smile. She immediately extended her right hand to me and said, "Nice to meet you."

Rob said, "You told me I could bring someone if I wanted."

"Of course! Are you kidding? We've got enough food to feed a football squad. Both offense and defense." I ushered them into the apartment. I also noticed that Ricky, Eddie, and Brian immediately sprang up to greet Rob's attractive date. I was afraid I was going to have to turn a hose on them the way they were all gawking at her. But Jane stepped in to rescue me. She led Mariah into the living room to introduce her to my grandfather.

Juliana said, "I'm going to check on Mary Catherine." She hurried down the hallway to our bedroom.

As Rob stepped into the dining room with me, I said, "Anything new?"

"There was a double homicide in East Harlem last night. A drug dealer and his girlfriend. I talked to Terri, who said she was monitoring it but thought it was probably a domestic or some kind of love triangle because of the woman. She's letting the local precinct detectives handle it. I told her I'd pass the info on to you."

"I'll look into it at the office in the morning." I glanced into the living room, where Mariah was chatting with Seamus. She had a little crowd around her like she was a celebrity.

I said, "Where did you meet Mariah? At a photo shoot?"

"Ha. Is that your way of saying you think she's out of my league?"

To be honest, that was *exactly* what I was thinking.

CHAPTER 64

KEVIN DOYLE SAT in the dark. He could hear all kinds of sounds in the empty apartment. People talking in the hallway. Kids running in the apartment upstairs. A rat or something in the wall. He thought of it as a tiny little universe of its own. That was just one of the games he played to keep his mind alert and stay engaged.

He had slipped into Oscar Tass's apartment just after dark. He knew the drug dealer was out, a few blocks away with his gang. They were probably discussing what had happened to Carlos Rios the night before. Doyle had decided to come deal with Tass in his apartment. He tried to clear his head as he waited for Tass to return.

Doyle carried his Beretta as well as a garrote with strong nylon rope and a folding knife with a half-serrated four-inch blade. He was prepared for hiccups in his plan. That's why he

even carried an extra magazine of 9mm bullets. But his preference was to do this silently.

Doyle had never dreamed he'd be waiting so long. It had been
hours and was now full-on evening. The hallway noises had
calmed down and he figured most of the residents were eating
dinner. Something he missed from his childhood: Sunday dinners with the whole family. Sometimes even his cousins would
come over to their house in Brooklyn. His sisters would try to be
included in the older boys' games. Good times. At least a lot better than sitting in a dark apartment that stunk of marijuana.

He leaned forward in the chair he was lounging on when he
heard a noise. A heavy footstep on the stairwell two doors down.
Then he heard a man's voice. This was it. Doyle quietly stood up
from the chair and retrieved his garrote from his jacket pocket.
He went over his plan in his head. As soon as Oscar Tass stepped
into the apartment and shut the door, Doyle would step from
the shadows and loop the garrote over his head, then pull him to
the floor as he choked him.

Doyle had loosened the light bulb that came on with the
switch next to the door. They'd be in complete darkness. It would
take under two minutes. No one would notice anything for a day
or two. Then Tass would start to stink. Someone would call the
cops. By then it'd be a stale homicide.

Doyle flexed his hands and gripped the handles of his garrote.
A key slipped into the door. Then there was a pause. Doyle heard
Tass say something.

Then a woman's voice answered with a laugh.

Shit.

The target was not alone.

CHAPTER 65

THE KIDS GAVE Mariah a little space. My grandfather was almost as taken with the striking paramedic as my boys were. Why not? She was engaging and bright. Mary Catherine got her introduction over FaceTime, via an iPad linked to Mary Catherine's phone in the master bedroom. Mary Catherine held off on her usual grilling of a visitor. The FaceTime showed only her face. Earlier, she had seemed touchy about having a guest come see her in the bedroom. I understood. Everyone wants to be seen at their best.

Fiona stepped into the living room and announced that dinner was served. I smiled at her attempt to lower the pitch of her voice and sound formal. When I looked toward the dining table, I was shocked. Somehow, while we chatted only a room away, Bridget, Fiona, and Trent had managed to set a beautiful table. There were plates, two glasses, and the correct silverware at each seat except two. The iPad sat on the table so Mary Catherine and Juliana could eat with us. Juliana had insisted that Mary Catherine not be left alone for a family dinner.

Rob Trilling sat to my right with Mariah next to him. I leaned in close and asked, "Does Mariah know about your roommates?"

He turned to me and whispered, "No."

"She going to find out anytime soon?"

He just shrugged.

Then Ricky stepped out of the kitchen dressed in a chef's uniform, including hat and white jacket.

I blurted out, "Where'd you get that outfit?"

Ricky said, "Juliana got it from the prop department of the playhouse where she's working. She has to get it back tomorrow." He motioned toward the kitchen. Trent and the twins marched out with serving bowls, set them on the table, and all three stayed in line as they went back for more.

Ricky made a show of uncovering each dish. The manicotti smelled divine. I realized he was mimicking what they did on *Rising Chefs*. He was practicing.

Mariah asked him, "Did you make this all yourself?"

Ricky beamed. "Everything."

Trent added, "I set the table."

Eddie said, "I sliced some onions."

Even Brian said, "I took Ricky to the store to buy everything."

I smiled as I caught Jane rolling her eyes at her brothers.

Dinner proceeded like most of our Sunday dinners. Loud conversation. A lot of people talking over one another. And excellent food. Everyone had a glass of water, and the adults had wine. The younger kids settled for grape juice and pretended. My grandfather seemed to drink their share of the wine.

Mary Catherine occasionally chimed in from the bedroom.

I enjoyed seeing Rob Trilling out of our usual element and with a pretty girl. Mariah was social enough to cover some of his shyness.

After a while, she offered, "I'm from a big family too. But nothing like this. Just a sister and three brothers. But we don't work as well together as you guys."

Seamus said, "Family is a blessing. They can be a lot of work too, but mainly a blessing. With God's help, we'll have another blessing soon."

From the iPad, Mary Catherine said, "Amen."

Mariah looked at the iPad and said, "Juliana, I understand you're an actress. What play are you in now?"

Juliana's face came partially onto the screen. "Nothing really. Just an amateur production of *Godspell*."

Mary Catherine said, "Don't be so modest. She's super in the play. Juliana's going to be a star."

Mary Catherine's supportive tone finally made me realize why Juliana had fled to the bedroom when Rob Trilling and Mariah arrived. Damn, I can be slow on the uptake sometimes. I knew that in the past Juliana had had some kind of feelings for Trilling, but they both claimed to be just friends. Now I guessed some other feelings had bubbled up.

While I was still mulling this over, Ricky and Fiona brought out a dessert of tiramisù on one of our silver serving platters. After a couple of pieces were sent to the bedroom and we all finished our portions, Mary Catherine declared it the "best dinner ever."

Chrissy said, "Ricky is going to win that show. I want to go with him."

Ricky said, "Only two people can come with me, and one has to be a parent or guardian."

I said, "I'll be there."

The night continued to be a success. As we said our good-byes, I realized I had to face reality tomorrow morning.

CHAPTER 66

DOYLE MADE A split-second decision and retreated to the small kitchen. He slid between the refrigerator and the wall. There was just enough room to fit and be completely out of sight from the entryway. He felt like he should hold his breath but gave up on that idea when the door opened and all he could hear was the booming voice of Oscar Tass.

The woman was much quieter.

Tass flipped the light switch. Nothing. He cursed, then wiggled the switch with no results.

The couple moved into the living room, still chatting in the dark. Doyle couldn't make out what they were saying.

Doyle heard the couch creak. It had made the same noise earlier when he had sat on it. Doyle felt a wave of disappointment. He didn't want to kill another female witness. There was no need for it. But he wondered how long he could stay hidden, crammed against the wall and the old humming refrigerator.

The conversation died off. The couch creaked some more. Doyle realized the couple was getting romantic. How long would this take? Would the woman leave afterward? He wasn't certain how he would handle this. Doyle felt for the folding knife he kept in his pocket. The gun was a last resort due to the noise.

The knife wasn't much better. God knew what kind of mess it would make and there was no guarantee it would be quiet. If he could slash Tass's throat first, he might be able to keep the chaos in check. But he'd still leave traceable evidence. Possibly get injured himself.

Doyle started to squirm out from his hiding place. The room was dark, and the couple was still on the couch. He silently stepped toward the doorway of the kitchen. The knife was now open and in his hand, ready for action.

The woman let out a yelp. She sprang upright on the couch. She directed a string of curses at Tass in both English and Spanish. The old drug dealer started to laugh, then cackled at her.

Doyle stepped forward for a better look. He blended into the shadows of the dark room. Now he saw Tass's pudgy figure next to the woman on the couch. He tried to caress her face, but the woman knocked his hand away. She was angry. This might work out.

Tass spoke in soothing tones. His Spanish had an accent that took Doyle a moment to recognize as actually from Spain. It might be considered a classy accent, but whatever he said didn't soothe the pissed-off woman. She stood up, straightened her clothes, and marched out of the apartment with as much dignity as she could muster.

At the front door, the woman spat a few more insults at Tass before turning, slamming the flimsy door as she left.

Tass groaned from the couch.

Doyle now stood in the doorway to the kitchen—in full view if Tass looked up and there was a little more light. Doyle flipped on the switch in the kitchen, and the entire apartment lit up.

Oscar Tass's head snapped up, but he didn't say anything or reach for a weapon.

Doyle leaned against the doorframe with his arms folded. He didn't know why he'd turned on the light and given himself away.

Tass settled back on the couch. He finally said, "So you're the bastard who's been picking off my associates one by one."

"I tried to be efficient and get you and Rios at the same time."

"Instead, you shot his little groupie. All she wanted to do was live the high life and work for us."

"She had a gun. That makes her fair game."

"No, you're right, white boy. She was tough and passed our first initiation by killing a runner for another organization. Shot him right through the eye." Tass shook his head. "Pretty little thing. Until you put a bullet through her face." He moved on the couch. "What you got for me? A bullet?"

"Since we're chatting, I'll give you the option."

"Okay. Leave and we'll forget the whole thing."

Doyle let out a snort of laughter. "You know that can't happen."

"Then tell me who sent you and why."

"I can't do that."

Tass stood up from the couch and faced Doyle across the room. He started to reach behind his back.

Doyle lifted his shirt to show the butt of his Beretta.

Tass slowly removed his hand from his back to show Doyle he

was holding a knife. A long, curved knife. Too fancy for most uses. "You're going to have to shoot me and alert the whole building. And I got a lot of friends in this building." He waved the knife to intimidate Doyle.

Doyle smiled. "You're hoping to scare me into leaving quietly. Nice try." He brought his hand up to reveal his own knife, which he'd been gripping by his thigh. He showed Tass the four-inch practical blade. This was at least more interesting than most of his hits. He stepped all the way into the living room, a few feet from Tass.

Tass charged him like a rhino. He was about as unwieldy as a rhino too. Doyle easily stepped to the side and arced his blade up, slicing the bigger man's throat and severing part of his ear.

Then he wasted no time before turning and stabbing Tass in the lower back, away from any ribs. His arm moved like a piston. Two, three, four times, finally finishing after a dozen jabs. The blade disappeared to the hilt with each strike.

Tass collapsed without a sound. The thin, cheap carpet turned dark as blood flowed from all the wounds. His eyes and mouth were wide-open.

Doyle wiped his blade on Tass's ruined plaid shirt. Then he took a moment to look around the room to make sure he hadn't left anything that could be used to identify him. No bloody footprints. Nothing. He took a paper towel from the kitchen and wiped down anywhere he had touched.

He lingered at the front door, surveying the apartment. Nothing out of place except a giant lump of a useless human on the floor. Tass's face had drained of blood, giving him a ghostly look.

That seemed fitting.

CHAPTER 67

MY MORNING STARTED when a bad dream jolted me awake. I guessed it was Mary Catherine's concern about the baby. I dreamed we were in a doctor's office and they were giving us bad news. But like a lot of dreams, it wasn't clear to me what the bad news concerned. It left me unsettled, and I lay there quietly, staring up at the ceiling.

I didn't hear any kids, so I guessed it was early, maybe sometime around 6 a.m. It had been the longest night's rest I'd gotten in a week. The family dinner with Trilling and his new paramedic friend had been a great success. It had made me happy to see everyone getting along. Even though my grandfather had overindulged in the pinot noir a little, I couldn't help but smile, thinking how his long-winded stories entertained the kids.

I slipped out of bed without waking Mary Catherine and padded through the apartment, hearing the first stirrings of the morning. I headed into the kitchen and started breakfast, which always required at least a dozen eggs as well as ham, turkey bacon, an assortment of cereals and fruits, and three different kinds of milk: whole, skim, and almond. The entire process took some time to accommodate the kids waking and coming out at different times.

While I concentrated on flipping the eggs perfectly, so they were actually "over easy," Juliana walked into the kitchen fully dressed.

"Where are you going so early?"

"Got a lot of work to do today and I want to meet with some people at school this morning to go over some class requirements. It may not be Ivy League, but City College is still a college. Don't worry. Brian said he'd take the kids to school."

"I can do it. Brian's got a job. You guys have covered for me enough. And for the record, I think City College is a good school. A really good school. I'm proud that you go there."

That earned me a weak smile from my oldest child. Without any more conversation, Juliana just said, "Bye." And walked out the door. It all felt a little awkward. Then I tried to put it in context with her reaction to Trilling the previous night. I still didn't get it completely, but I knew it had to do with him.

Just then the other kids started filing out of their bedrooms and moving like zombies toward the kitchen. I handed out plates with food randomly piled on. The twins both took plates out of my hand without acknowledging me in any way.

While everyone was eating, I slipped back into the bedroom and got dressed for work. Mary Catherine turned in bed and said, "Come lie down with me for a bit."

"That's the best offer I've heard in a long time. But I need to get the kids to school in a little while."

"If that's all I can get, I'll take a little while."

I sat, then stretched out on the bed next to my beautiful wife. Her tangle of golden hair shot through with glints of red made it look like she was a feral child. Of course I didn't say that.

Mary Catherine said, "Any crises this morning?"

"Nothing really. Juliana shot out of here like a missile without eating or talking to anyone. I think it might have something to do with Rob and his date last night."

Mary Catherine propped herself up on her elbow. "Really, Dr. Phil, that's your analysis?"

"Why? Am I wrong?"

"No. You actually got it exactly right. Juliana has had a crush on Rob Trilling since the first day you brought him home."

"Rob does attract pretty girls. Why do you think that is?"

"You think it might be because he's good-looking, polite, smart, loves his family, and has a good job? Gee, that's a tough one to figure out."

I had to laugh at Mary Catherine's sarcasm. She knew me better than anyone. And this was one of my blind spots. Especially when it related to my own children. Criminals and murderers were more in my comfort zone than relationships.

We chatted for a few moments. She kissed me lightly on the lips. That turned into a little more serious kiss. Before I knew it, I lost track of time until Eddie knocked on the bedroom door and said in a low voice, "Hey, Dad, we only have fifteen minutes to make it to school. Sister Sheilah will never let you forget it if we're late again."

I looked at Mary Catherine and said, "Duty calls." I got the kids to Holy Name with almost a full thirty seconds to spare.

CHAPTER 68

I WAS SURPRISED to see Terri Hernandez huddled with Rob Trilling and Walter Jackson when I stepped through the office door. They sat at a table surrounded by desks that were rarely used. We called it the temporary duty area. That's where detectives who were helping us could do their work. As I came closer to the trio, I realized this was not a social get-together. Instead of greeting them, I simply said, "What's wrong?"

It was Terri Hernandez who turned to me and said, "Another drug dealer was killed."

"Trilling said you thought it was a domestic. Did you learn something new?"

"That was Saturday night. *Last* night, a guy named Oscar Tass was murdered in his apartment. We even have the time of death narrowed down to a tiny window. He had his on-again, off-again girlfriend in the apartment. They had some kind of argument and she left. When she came back less than twenty minutes later, Tass was on the floor with his neck slashed and almost a dozen stab wounds in his lower back. Someone who knew what they were doing didn't want to take any risks with him surviving. Forensics hasn't come up with any decent leads. It looks to me like it was a professional."

Trilling added, "And Sunday night's victim was friends with Saturday night's victims."

I eased into the chair at the next desk. "That also makes Saturday night's shooting look more like a hit than a domestic."

Terri said, "Exactly."

I took a few minutes to fill Terri in on the investigations I had been working quietly for Celeste Cantor, with Trilling's and Walter's help.

Terri said, "I've also been trying to find another drug dealer — or, supposedly, former dealer — Trilling and I talked to last week. His name is Silbas. He's not answering his calls and he wasn't at home when I knocked on his apartment door. I think we should make an effort to find him. Or maybe he's already been crossed off someone's list."

I looked over at Walter Jackson. "You were the first one to bring up the link between former arrests by the Land Sharks and drug dealers being murdered. We combine that with the retired cops, it's a pretty serious body count. The situation seems to be spiraling into something big. Really big. And a little unsettling. And the one thing they all had in common was some connection to Richard Deason. The closest connection we have to him is his son, Antonio. We don't have any idea what their relationship was like. We also have almost no idea what Antonio has been up to, beyond the makings of a drug deal with your gang in the Bronx."

Terri looked at Trilling. "We know what Antonio's been up to. Following in his father's footsteps."

I said, "Walter found some family connections from the mother's side. One of the uncles looks like he's a mercenary type. Maybe he's doing the killings on behalf of his nephew. Or, more likely, hired someone to do them."

Walter Jackson said, "That's a lot of territory to cover. Where do we start?"

We hadn't heard anything from Rob Trilling yet. I turned to him and said, "What do you think?"

As always, he took a moment to answer. He wasn't being sly or coy. He was being thoughtful. "Looks like the most obvious course would be for us to go back to SoHo, keep trying to follow Antonio Deason and see exactly what he gets up to during the day."

I looked at Terri and Walter and said, "He's really starting to get the hang of this whole investigation thing."

Walter said, "He's learning so fast, he's in a class by himself."

Everyone groaned at that pun. It was the first time I'd ever seen Walter look defensive. He raised his hands and said, "C'mon, I came up with that one on the fly. I deserve a little credit."

The three of us were already thinking of our surveillance plan.

CHAPTER 69

HOMICIDE DETECTIVES DON'T typically conduct surveillances of suspected drug dealers. Following those suspects is work more often done by the narcotics squad. I did a couple of surveillances when I was on a robbery unit years ago. We developed a suspect for a series of robberies, then tried to follow him. I wouldn't say it was a waste of time, but it did not resolve the case. Only once did we actually observe a suspect as he attempted to commit a robbery. And even in that case, we were working on a tip from an informant.

One time I *did* follow a homicide suspect all the way from Manhattan to Buffalo. Most of it was on the highway, and it was pretty easy for two cars to keep up with the suspect. The New York State Police helped quite a bit. An inspector with the State Police named Bud Wilson arranged for us to be relieved at night and get a few hours' sleep.

The next day, we followed the suspect all the way back to Manhattan. We never saw him meet with anyone or do anything suspicious. He stayed at a cheap hotel. We couldn't tell if any of the people who came and went were there to visit him. The craziest part was that as soon as he got out of his car back in Manhattan, his estranged wife walked out of the building and shot him in the head.

At least we made one arrest for homicide. Turns out he had been visiting a girlfriend in Buffalo at the low-rent hotel, but no one had noticed the woman going to his room. I hoped today's surveillance would go better.

It was a nice change of pace. The skies were clear and there were no visibility issues. It got me out of the office and made me think, at least for a while, that I was in control of the investigation. But surveillance still isn't my thing. Hernandez sat at one end of Antonio Deason's block in her SUV. Trilling and I were in my Impala at the opposite end of the block.

We caught a break a few minutes after we'd set up our surveillance of Antonio's apartment in SoHo. The electric Porsche that I'd heard so much about came down the street and stopped directly in front of his building. I expected Deason to hop out of the car so was surprised when instead a dark-haired woman in her thirties stepped out. Deason came from the building immediately, spoke to the woman, then got into the Porsche by himself and pulled away from the curb.

It was at that moment I realized we should've had more officers working this surveillance. If we'd had more people, someone could've stayed to see where the woman who got out of the Porsche Taycan went. Was she his assistant? His girlfriend? Did she work at a mechanic's shop and was returning the vehicle? All questions I knew would have to be answered as we watched Antonio Deason drive away.

Terri Hernandez fell in behind us. If we didn't switch up leads, anyone we were surveilling might notice the same car tailing them after a while. Cops have been doing it the same way for decades.

Not long into our following Antonio Deason, less than five minutes, a blue Chevy Tahoe came off a side street as we were pulling up to a stoplight and stopped between us and the Porsche. When the light turned green, the Tahoe didn't move.

I honked, but in Manhattan that's about as effective as blaming other people for your problems. I stuck my head out of the Impala's driver-side window hoping to spot which direction Deason had taken. All I saw was his left hand extended out of the window, shooting us the bird.

The Tahoe finally started to move slowly through the intersection, but there was no way I could get around it. Hernandez had raced ahead on a parallel street. After a few minutes we realized we'd lost our target.

Trilling turned to me and said, "What do we do now?"

"That is a really good question."

CHAPTER 70

KEVIN DOYLE SAT in the comfortable Kia he'd rented under the name Dave Allmand. He rarely rented. It was tough to explain to Avis how a bumper got damaged. He preferred to use a stolen car when committing a crime. He had a discreet little electronic device that got him into almost any somewhat newer model, and he went old-school with older models. But some days, like today, he just needed a nondescript vehicle he could use to check out a number of places around the five boroughs.

He was parked in a loading zone. The sign didn't matter because he didn't intend to leave the car. Doyle just sat there, staring at the message on his burner phone. His employer wanted him to keep an eye on an NYPD detective named Bennett. They told him to make a contingency plan in case the detective got too close. There were two attachments to the text, intel sheets just like the ones that had been provided for his other assignments here in New York. One was on Bennett, and the other was on another NYPD detective named Robert Trilling, an Army vet. *Shit*. This assignment kept getting worse. Just when he thought he'd almost finished, they threw this at him.

Doyle looked up from his phone. There were very few people on the street, for some reason. Usually this part of Brooklyn had more foot traffic. It did give him a clear line of sight to the building he'd been watching for the last hour: the diner where Tammy worked. He was stuck on her. There was no way around it.

This particular position gave him a view of both the front and the rear of the diner. The wide windows on the side of the building let him look all the way inside. There were two people at the counter and two occupied booths. He had caught a couple of glimpses of Tammy running food out to the booths or chatting with the men sitting at the counter.

Then he saw the back door open. An older man shuffled out and tossed something into the dumpster at the rear of the building. He was big. Maybe six foot four and a little overweight. This had to be Tammy's tyrannical uncle. He wore a white T-shirt and blue work pants with an apron. It had to be him.

He lingered by the dumpster, just a few feet from the road. Then the man took a pack of cigarettes from his chest pocket and lit one.

It felt like God was testing Doyle. It would be so easy to drive by and pop a couple rounds into the man. Or maybe wait and let him get close enough to the street that Doyle could hit him with the car. But not this car. This was a rental that would get examined upon return. Even though he'd used a fake name, Doyle never would let someone come that close to his real identity. No, he needed to think this through. He had enough to do for the time being without worrying about someone else's problems. It didn't matter how pretty she was.

He glanced in the diner and saw Tammy leaning close to one of the men at the counter. Doyle picked up the monocular he'd bought from his Israeli contact and zeroed in through the window. Everything was crystal clear. He hadn't been steered wrong about this monocular. Unfortunately, what he saw was Tammy fawning over a big biker-looking dude with a sleeve of tattoos on his right arm. Then Doyle noticed the Harley parked on the street a little farther down from the diner.

It didn't take a genius to figure out why Tammy was all over this guy. It made him a little angry. Maybe jealous. That was not something he was used to.

Doyle took a moment to look at the rear of the building just as Tammy's uncle was walking back inside.

He threw the Kia into gear and cruised past the diner slowly. His face burned as he saw Tammy flirting with the biker.

CHAPTER 71

A FEW HOURS after losing Antonio Deason in traffic, Rob Trilling and I were back in SoHo, watching his apartment again. Our new plan wasn't much better than our last one. Trilling had a cheap tracker he intended to slip onto the inside of the car's bumper. He wasn't super familiar with this model of car, but he was convinced he'd find a place where the magnetic back of the tracker would stick.

This tracker was not an official NYPD piece of equipment. We didn't want to risk explaining a potential loss of a tracker on an unofficial case. Instead, I'd sprung for a tracker that worked off a smartphone app. It wouldn't be nearly as effective as one of the NYPD trackers, but maybe it would give us an edge in our next surveillance.

Terri Hernandez was gathering more information on the weekend's murders. With everything she had learned, she now strongly suspected they had been committed by the same killer who'd orchestrated the faux suicides and accidents among the retired NYPD cops.

I knew how territorial the precinct detectives could be about homicides. I'd experienced it myself. I also knew there weren't many who could stand up to Terri Hernandez when she started to insist on things. It was one of the reasons I enjoyed working with her so much.

I turned to Trilling. "You sure you know how to work that thing?"

"Piece of cake. The app's installed on my phone. Should go like clockwork. I only need forty-five seconds to plant it securely."

"I hope we get it. I don't know if that was some kind of car service that dropped the Porsche off earlier or what. Either way, I think the car will eventually end up back here in front of his apartment. Even if only for a few minutes."

Trilling said, "Obviously, because he shot us the bird as he drove away, Deason knows we're looking at him."

"Yeah, I have a feeling our clumsy attempt at interviewing him might've tipped him off."

Just then, the Porsche rolled down the street past us and parked in front of the building. Antonio Deason hopped out and headed into the building without looking back.

As Deason disappeared into the building, Trilling got out of my car and hustled up the street, then paused for just a few seconds by the Porsche. He bent down like he was looking at something on the ground, then slapped the tracker under the car near the rear bumper.

Trilling casually stood up, walked past the car, lingered in front of a store, then came back to my Impala. He held his phone out to show me the app.

Trilling said, "Looks like it's working perfectly. Next time he leaves, as long as we're within a quarter mile, we'll know exactly where he's at."

"I don't think he's going to be inside long. The way he parked and hustled into the building makes me think he's leaving again soon. Let's sit tight and see what happens."

About ten minutes later, Antonio Deason walked out of his building's front door, dressed in a nice sport coat. He was talking on his cell phone. He walked directly to the car and got down on his knees. He spoke on the phone again, then stood up and moved to the rear of the Porsche. He reached under and pulled the tracker off.

Deason looked up and down the street. Then he dropped the tracker on the ground and mashed it with the heel of his shoe.

Trilling said, "I guess we go to plan B."

"This whole case is a plan B. Not typically the best way to go about police work. But in this instance, we'll go with your other idea and we really will hope for the best."

CHAPTER 72

ROB TRILLING WAS trying to forget about the failures of his day at work. He had no idea how this guy Antonio Deason had figured out so quickly that he was being watched. Terri Hernandez said it had to be counter-surveillance. Whoever was conducting it was really good. None of them had seen anyone watching.

Now, in his apartment, Rob had collapsed on the couch, watching a rerun of *Friends* with his five roommates. They liked it, and it was apparently a highly recommended show for English-language learners. He just needed a distraction. The women were pretty good company. They didn't say much but appreciated his presence.

The youngest of the women had recently adopted the name Katie. The woman whose English had improved the most, and who had revealed herself to have one hell of a sense of humor, was now calling herself Sylvia. Sabiha, Ayesha, and Fareeha had said they preferred their traditional, Urdu names.

Rob watched the TV as the characters sat down to a meal together. Then came a firm knock on his apartment door. Everyone froze.

Even though the women were living in New York legally, and Rob had agreed to sponsor and house them during the lengthy legal proceedings, it didn't change the fact that surprise visits to the apartment still alarmed the women. Part of it was their upbringing and part of it was fear of their vague immigration status in the US. They also were worried that the building's superintendent, George Kazanjian, might evict them. George liked Rob, and the women were careful to always leave one at a time to maintain the idea that Rob lived with just one woman. But there was no telling what he might do if he found out six people were crammed into Rob's small apartment.

Luckily, George didn't seem to be particularly observant.

Rob bounded off the couch and slid to a stop next to the door. He stayed motionless and silent for a moment. Then the knock came again.

He looked over his shoulder, relieved to see that his roommates had all scurried into the bedroom and shut the door behind them. It was a drill they'd worked on several times—twice when George had knocked on the door about something and several other times when a neighbor had come to the door for one reason or another. Each time the women had been able to race into the bedroom unseen.

Rob steadied his voice and said through the door, "Who is it?"

"Juliana." It wasn't a shout, but it didn't sound that friendly either.

Rob took one more glance over his shoulder. The women had even picked up the glasses they had been drinking from. Except for one. That, along with Rob's glass, could be trouble. He didn't have time to fix it. He opened the door.

As usual, Rob was amazed at how beautiful Michael Bennett's oldest daughter was. Dressed in jeans with an all-weather jacket, Juliana looked like she could be a model for a fashionable outdoor company. She also wasn't speaking. She just stood there, staring at him, her expression unreadable.

Finally, she said, "Are you going to invite me inside?"

He almost jumped in response. "Of course, come on in." He stepped wide and waved his hand like he was introducing her onstage.

Juliana stared at the two glasses of water sitting on his scarred coffee table in front of the couch. She scanned the room and her eyes fell on the closed bedroom door. She took a step in that direction.

Rob said, "I'm not sure what's going on, Juliana. Why are you here?" That kept her from walking any closer to the bedroom.

Then she turned to Rob and said, "Can we talk?"

CHAPTER 73

KEVIN DOYLE HAD left the rented Kia parked a couple of blocks away. He was in Queens, following up on the instructions he'd received. He'd already watched the lead detective, Michael Bennett, and seen his fancy apartment building on the Upper West Side. He was curious how an NYPD detective could afford to live in such a nice building. More importantly, the building had excellent security and a doorman.

He also knew that Bennett had ten kids. That was old-school Catholic as far as Doyle was concerned. He knew several Catholic families from his parents' generation who had eight or more children. But you didn't see it much nowadays. Bennett's children were another roadblock. There was no way Doyle was gonna risk harming a child for his job. Hell, he didn't even want to do anything to Bennett. But if people were getting nervous that Bennett was too close to the truth, Doyle wouldn't have a choice. He liked to think that he was in control, but there was always someone else pulling the strings. He had decided a long time ago that if someone was going to be in charge, at least he was going to make some money at it. He didn't mind the government work he'd contracted over the years. But compared to some of the private jobs he had done, it was like working for a charity.

He looked again at the information sheet he'd been given. He'd been watching the apartment building where Bennett's partner, Rob Trilling, lived. During the afternoon, he hadn't noticed anything unusual, except that there were several young women who all looked alike coming and going from the building. All of them were about the same size and age, and they all dressed similarly and had dark hair, brushed straight down their backs to just over their shoulders. Curious. But probably not even related to his target.

Doyle had been lucky to see Trilling walk into the building. He seemed almost too young to be both an Army veteran and a detective. He was about six feet tall and very lean. Doyle had stayed at his position on the corner, sitting on a bench in a small park that bordered the street, and glancing over his right shoulder occasionally to look at the apartment. A young mother was watching two small boys kick a ball over the little patch of grass. It made him nostalgic for his own childhood in Brooklyn. He and his siblings spending a whole afternoon with nothing but a ball. They'd make up games and be so tired by the end of the day that they'd fall into bed with their clothes on.

About forty minutes after Trilling had arrived home, Doyle was surprised to see a young woman get out of a sedan with an Uber sign in the front window. She was stunning, with long, flowing dark hair. Doyle thought she seemed familiar. When he looked back at Bennett's information sheet with pictures of his children embedded in the document, Doyle recognized the visitor as Bennett's oldest daughter, Juliana.

She had to be going to Trilling's apartment. It was too much of a coincidence that she would show up here otherwise. Doyle took a moment to wonder whether the senior detective knew that his daughter and his young partner had a thing going on.

As Doyle looked over his shoulder, watching Juliana Bennett walk into the building, he felt something on his leg and jumped. Too many years in the military and combat zones had eliminated any chance he had to seem calm when something like that happened.

As soon as he turned, he realized one of the boys had kicked the ball across the small park, hitting his leg. Doyle reached down and held the ball out to the little blond boy. The boy only approached when his mother and brother came with him.

Doyle said, "That was a good kick."

The little boy smiled and looked back at his mother.

She had an Eastern European accent. "I'm sorry we disturbed you."

"You're not bothering me at all. I like to see kids outside playing."

The young woman thanked him, and the boys ran off with the ball.

As Doyle watched them leave, he thought, *I bet she wouldn't ask me to kill one of her relatives.*

Then he focused his attention back on his potential target's building.

CHAPTER 74

ROB TRILLING WAS trying not to fidget as he and Juliana sat on his living room couch. George Kazanjian had found the couch for him in an empty apartment. It had served him well and was comfortable. But now, with Juliana sitting only a few inches from him, he was aware of the old couch's many flaws. The brown cloth was threadbare on the armrests. There were more than a few holes, exposing the batting. And if Juliana scooted back to the far end of the couch, she'd realize there was a spring missing.

He tried to focus on his guest. "What would you like to talk about?"

Juliana took a moment. She didn't seem upset and wasn't crying. Finally, she said, "I can't believe you brought a date to our house for dinner."

"Your father said I could bring someone."

"My father still thinks Jane and I dream about teen pop stars. I'll always be his little girl. He doesn't have a clue about modern relationships."

Rob wasn't really sure he had much of a clue himself, especially when Juliana continued.

"You bringing a date over to my family's apartment really hurt my feelings. And the fact that she's so pretty and seems so nice, and you seem to be so into her, only made it worse. How long have you been seeing her? Is it serious?"

Rob didn't know how to respond. "Mariah and I have only gone out a few times."

Juliana leaned back, then looked down at the coffee table. "Please don't lie to me. I'm not an idiot. There are two glasses on your coffee table. There's still ice in both of them." She looked over her shoulder at the closed bedroom door.

Rob took in a lungful of air, then let out a long sigh. "I swear it's not what it looks like."

"It looks like you're a normal guy dating a pretty girl. I get it. I didn't mean to surprise you while she was here. I don't want to make a scene. I'm not here to fight your girlfriend. I just wanted to tell you how I felt. You hurt my feelings."

He wanted to say there was nobody here. But that wouldn't be true. Rob already felt terrible to hear he'd hurt Juliana's feelings. He never wanted to do something like that. She was a great girl.

He made up his mind. He stood up from the couch and padded across the tiny living room to his bedroom door. He waited until Juliana had turned to look at him. He reached over and grasped the door handle but didn't turn it.

Juliana said, "You don't have to do this, Rob. I'm not looking for a confrontation."

Rob turned the knob quickly and opened the door. Three of his Pakistani roommates almost tumbled out onto the living room floor. They had obviously been listening at the door. They all straightened and tried to look nonchalant.

Rob shook his head as he said, "Juliana, these are my roommates." He stood silently as all five of them shuffled into the living room.

Juliana was stunned silent. Her mouth fell open as she stared, then she finally mumbled, "I don't understand."

Sylvia said, "We are maid service?"

Rob had to let out a quick laugh. He wondered if Sylvia could make it as a stand-up comedian. Juliana just turned and continued to stare at Rob, waiting for an explanation.

The women walked over and assumed their usual seats, either around the couch, on the floor, or in the single recliner. Rob cleared his throat, then tried to briefly explain how the five women had all ended up living here with him. He let each of his roommates introduce herself and verify his crazy-sounding story.

"And my dad knows about this?"

"Yes, he does. He and your great-grandfather helped me get some assistance to buy food and get them medical care and legal help."

"How does Mariah feel about this situation?"

"She has no idea."

"And this is why you never invited me to your apartment?"

Rob paused. "To be completely honest, I'm not sure I would've invited you even if I lived alone. I told you about my concerns. I'd never want to do anything to screw up my relationship with your father. And I'm pretty sure you could do a lot better than me."

Juliana looked around the room at the five women. She

seemed to make up her mind. Then she stood up and said, "I doubt I could." She reached over and gave him a quick kiss on the lips. "I have to get back to the playhouse. I'm really glad I came by to see you."

Rob still had a goofy grin on his face for a full minute after Juliana had left the apartment.

Sylvia said, "She nice girl. You should date her."

"If only it were that simple."

CHAPTER 75

I GOT INTO the office pretty early. Juliana seemed to be back to her old chipper self. She was a godsend in the mornings. She stayed on the younger kids to make sure they had packed everything they needed for school, helped me make breakfast, let me leave for the office early, then took everyone to Holy Name.

Juliana said Sister Sheilah told her this was the longest streak of everyone being on time she could ever remember. That was an absolute jab at me. I did have a tendency to run a little late, at least when it came to getting things done in the morning. I didn't think Sister Sheilah always noticed, but now I knew she really did keep some kind of ledger. I had suspected it when I was a student at Holy Name and she was a brand-new teacher. To Sister Sheilah's credit, she never held my morning tendencies against any of my children. In fact, she was one of the best supporters and advocates for kids I had ever known. Not that I would ever admit that to her.

By the time I sat down at my desk, Walter Jackson was already working quietly in his office. I knew if he didn't come out with a pun or joke, he was probably working on something pretty important. I took advantage of the quiet time.

I laid out everything we'd discovered about Antonio Deason. Which wasn't all that much. Not that it necessarily mattered, but he had had pretty good grades when he was at the University of Miami. That was just one of many pieces of the puzzle. I was trying to figure out how a good college student would turn into a drug kingpin. He'd barely known his father, who'd spent his last years in prison.

Frankly, if Antonio had talked to us the first time Trilling and I went to his apartment and had some reasonable alibis, he might not still be on our radar. But it was the way he had so easily detected our surveillance attempts that made me consider him a potentially serious player on the drug scene. Not many organizations can afford to have people conducting counter-surveillance. Counter-surveillance requires trained people. Not just someone recruited off the street. Someone with some smarts who understands what cops or other drug dealers do when they try to follow someone.

It was a mystery that I intended to solve.

Trilling wandered into the office about an hour after me. He was still early according to his schedule, but late compared to his usual arrival time. I glanced up from my desk and he nodded. We exchanged quick greetings and he sat down at his desk.

Something was off. My young partner was fidgety as opposed to his usual dead calm.

I said casually, "What'd you get up to last night?"

Trilling was quick to answer. "Um…ah…nothing really. Why?"

"Just curious. Why are you so antsy? Your new girlfriend giving you problems?"

Trilling flinched. "Mariah's not my girlfriend."

"No? Then why'd you bring her over for dinner?"

"Let's call it an error in judgment. I'm not used to women paying attention to me."

"Sounds like you guys might have had a fight."

"No, in fact I'm supposed to see her later. I don't know what I'm going to do."

I wasn't sure why he was so worked up. I didn't want him to think I was prying. But I was interested in his life, and I'd been happy to see him with a date.

"Everything okay?"

Trilling surprised me by sort of blurting out, "Look, Juliana came to my apartment last night. I swear nothing happened. I introduced her to my roommates."

I focused on the last part of his statement. "All five of them?"

"She was fine with it. She appreciates what I'm doing."

I chose my words carefully. "The world didn't end. Juliana's a smart girl and she understands people. She's got very good insights."

But Trilling was still upset. "I was trying to find a way to let Juliana know I wasn't right for her. She told me I hurt her feelings by bringing a girl to dinner. I screwed up and I know it. I should have at least given her a heads-up before bringing Mariah over to your house. I don't have that much experience with women. They're confusing."

I said, "Tell me about it."

CHAPTER 76

WE FINALLY CAUGHT a break, as far as resources. Terri Hernandez knew of a few NYPD helicopter pilots who were testing a new helicopter with no markings on it later in the day. She had enough leverage on the pilot to get him to take her up. She told him what we were doing as far as surveillance and how we'd been burned a couple of times. The pilot's biggest concern was flight paths over the city, but he thought he could work it out.

Now I was driving a seized Cadillac that the narcotics team let me borrow. Trilling was in an unmarked Ford Explorer he'd borrowed from the Harbor Unit. Like Hernandez, he knew one of the young officers on the unit and had somehow talked him into letting us use the Explorer for a few hours.

We knew better than to set up right at Antonio Deason's building again. That approach hadn't worked out well for us before. We had the perfect answer to our problem: Walter

Jackson. Although it was a simple, safe assignment, I could never tell Harry Grissom that I used a criminal intelligence analyst in this way—there were strict rules about not putting them out on the street.

In any case, all I asked Walter to do was go window-shopping down one side of the street and up the other. He had his cell phone with him and was to call me once he identified the Porsche Taycan on the street. Then he could continue taking his time strolling along until he saw Deason come out of his building and hop into the car.

As soon as I got the call from Walter, I used the radio to contact Terri Hernandez. Within about thirty seconds, I spotted a helicopter overhead, at a very high altitude. Given the number of helicopters that flew across the city on a daily basis, you would've had to really be paying attention—like I was—to notice this one.

Almost immediately, Hernandez came on the radio and said, "The target is moving north on Greene Street."

I didn't even have to coordinate with Trilling. We were on parallel streets with our eyes open for counter-surveillance.

Then Hernandez again came on the radio. "The target just turned east on Houston Street."

So far, even in the heavy traffic, this was a much easier surveillance. We didn't have use of a helicopter often. At least not for surveillance. I wasn't sure how long we could use this one. I told Hernandez once we had him at a location we could cut the flight crew loose. Trilling and I would see what we could find out from there.

Hernandez guided us north on First Avenue, then notified us that Deason had parked the Porsche near Bellevue Hospital and was on foot walking west on 26th Street. One minute later,

Trilling came on the radio. "He just walked into an Italian restaurant on Second Avenue. It's called Rocco's Hideaway. He didn't meet anyone out front."

Hernandez told us to stand by. She was getting dropped at the Bellevue helicopter pad and would be there in a few minutes.

Trilling and I set up to observe the restaurant from different points on Second Avenue. I could see it was upscale and fairly small. Deason sat at a table near the back, talking with a tall, well-dressed Black man I couldn't see clearly. I tried to get a better view from a couple of angles. Because of the late-afternoon hour, they looked like the only customers. That also made it tougher to do any kind of surveillance, especially since Deason had seen me and Trilling when we tried to interview him, so neither of us could just walk in and expect not to be recognized.

Then Hernandez showed up. She handed me a little backpack. "What's this?" I said as I took it.

"It's my NYPD raid jacket that I was wearing in the helicopter, along with a hairbrush and a few other items I used to freshen up after my wild ride over the city." She shook her hair out, then looked at me. "I'm assuming you want me to go into the restaurant. Since I was the only one smart enough not to identify myself to him."

All I could do was smile.

Hernandez walked in and sat at the table closest to the front window. After a few minutes, I got a text from her saying that Deason and his dining partner were chatting too quietly in the corner for her to overhear what they were saying.

After almost an hour and a half, Deason and his companion came out of the restaurant. Hernandez stayed at her table near the front door. I decided to take another risk. After we let Deason walk away, I rushed inside. Hernandez didn't acknowledge me or give away her identity.

I wasn't sure what I was hoping to find. Maybe the name of Deason's dining partner on a credit card slip. I introduced myself and showed my ID to the waiter. He clearly didn't want to be involved with the police. He led me down a narrow corridor to an office in the back.

The manager was a petite Italian woman named Mari. Unlike the waiter, her immediate smile when she heard I was with the NYPD told me this might work out.

Mari said, "My brother's a cop on Staten Island. He's only been with the NYPD two years."

We chatted about her brother and how the two of them grew up in Brooklyn, then I asked her if I could see the credit card receipts for a customer who'd just left the restaurant.

The manager led me back out into the dining area. As we were talking, Hernandez cleared her throat and then coughed loudly. It made me look up.

That's when I saw Antonio Deason stick his head in the front door.

He looked at me, smiled, and said, "You're gonna have to do better than that."

I had no idea how this asshole was a step ahead of us on everything we did. But this was going to change starting right now.

CHAPTER 77

KEVIN DOYLE HAD been keeping tabs on both Michael Bennett and Rob Trilling. This was not an assignment he would appreciate if he was told to move forward. But he had to be prepared. Clearly, Bennett had years of experience on the streets of New York. Trilling was young and in shape. Either would be a challenge. Plus, he'd have to get out of New York immediately. Although the general public tended to accept active-duty police fatalities with just a shrug, the cops would be relentless looking for him. It was the same in every country.

Doyle was once contracted to kill a police captain in Beirut. The captain had been on the take and was allowing shipments of supplies for refugees to be pillaged before being sent on to Syria and elsewhere—places that desperately needed them in order to see another sunrise. To Doyle, this was the worst kind of criminal—a corrupt cop taking food and supplies from people who need them.

It had been a fairly simple job. Doyle made certain not to do anything that this jerk's family might see. His kids didn't need to be traumatized. He simply took a long shot with a scoped rifle and hit the police captain as he came out of his office.

Doyle had wasted no time employing his escape plan. Even with his resources and experience it was a tighter escape than he would've liked. The cops contacted the military and were able to close off Beirut in less than twenty minutes.

Luckily for Doyle, who was traveling with an Irish passport, the cops were certain the assassination was the work of a local terrorist group loosely affiliated with some of the larger, better-known groups. Doyle was allowed to pass through their perimeter, and he was out of the country a few hours later.

Doyle later heard from some of his associates that the cops hadn't let up the pressure for nearly three weeks after the police captain's assassination.

Now, on the streets of Manhattan, he watched as Bennett and Trilling both pulled up to their office building in unfamiliar cars. Bennett was in a Cadillac and Trilling drove a blue Ford Explorer. Doyle figured they'd been out on surveillance again. They were definitely poking around the same people as Doyle.

He still held out hope that he wouldn't get the order to do anything to either of the cops. But Doyle had found he rarely got what he hoped for.

CHAPTER 78

ROB TRILLING AND I stepped into Walter Jackson's office. Walter sensed how dejected we were from the failed surveillance. He didn't even try one of his puns on us. I guess every screwup has a bright side.

I knew the team looked to me for ideas. But clearly Antonio Deason had a strong network behind him. I didn't see any way to move forward without bringing in a narcotics team used to complex surveillances. And I was pretty sure that wouldn't go over well with Celeste Cantor. Terri and Walter weren't even supposed to know about any of this investigation.

Walter had a map of the city on his wall, with red pins marking the sites where drug dealers had been killed in the last two months and a blue pin marking where retired cop Roger Dzoriack had died. He also had two blue pins north of the city, representing Tabitha Arnold's death from carbon monoxide poisoning and Lou Sanvos's car accident, plus two more blue pins to the south, representing Ralph Stein's and Gary Halverson's deaths in Florida.

Trilling said, "Hernandez and I talked to a guy named Silbas. We were asking about the death of his godson in a shooting. I know Hernandez has been trying to find Silbas the last couple of days with no luck. It's like the guy just vanished. I wonder if we need to add him to your map, Walter."

The big man said, "I got plenty of red pins."

I was barely following along with their conversation. I said out loud, "What about the informant you and Terri have been using in the group? Is he worthwhile?"

Trilling shrugged. "He's worn a transmitter for us a couple of times. He's trying to work off an assault charge. He's not super helpful, but he's done what we've asked. I don't know if we can get any more help out of him. He's always reluctant. If he wasn't looking at so much time, I think he would have told us to get lost a long time ago."

"So you don't think he'd be willing to do a little extra and clue us in to when Antonio Deason is coming to their clubhouse?"

"I doubt it. He's stubborn and cocky."

"That's a terrible combination for an informant."

"I don't have a lot of experience, but Jaime Nantes *does* seem like a bad informant. Hernandez doesn't like to deal with him at all. He looks at her like she is some kind of meat on display."

I considered this, then said, "We need to find a way to motivate him." I turned toward Walter, knowing he had already figured out some angles.

Walter typed away on his computer and said, "I pulled Jaime Nantes's file up. He's got a long record. Lots of assaults and possessions with intent to sell. Surprisingly, he's never really done any time. Maybe that's why he agreed to cooperate."

Walter got that look on his face he gets when he finds something interesting, and he started clicking through links. His mouth dropped open a little bit as he concentrated. I knew the look well. My anticipation grew as he followed more and more links. Finally, I had to ask him outright, "Walter, what've you found?"

It was like startling him out of a nap. His eyes cut up to me, then flicked over to Trilling. "I found an old warrant that was rescinded. It's six years old."

I said, "Why would a six-year-old warrant that was rescinded be of interest?"

"It's for child pornography. It looks like the FBI did the investigation."

I sat back and considered this for a few moments.

Trilling said, "You guys are going to have to fill me in. I don't understand why an old child pornography warrant could be important if it was already rescinded."

"It's not so much that it was rescinded. It has to do with the charge. No drug dealer wants anyone to know he was involved in child pornography."

"But it was rescinded."

"Those sorts of legal distinctions don't mean anything on the street. His buddies would flip out if they heard about this."

Trilling said, "How does it help us?"

"It might motivate him. We have to indulge in a little blackmail, but it could get us a decent contact for when Antonio Deason is moving and what he's doing."

Trilling said, "I'm not sure I like the idea of blackmail."

I smiled and said, "Don't knock it until you've tried it."

CHAPTER 79

I WAS MENTALLY drained by the time I got home. But the twins greeting me with a hug and a cheerful hello turned that completely around. It's easy to make jokes about how it's exhausting having ten kids. Reality is much different. I genuinely look forward to coming home every day. Usually, it is the youngest girls who greet me with the most enthusiasm. Teen girls usually don't show much interest in their parents coming home from work. I just happened to catch Fiona and Bridget as soon as I walked in the door.

My grandfather was sitting at the kitchen counter with a glass of pinot noir. He was chatting with Ricky, who was taking something out of the oven.

As I approached, I asked, "Everything okay?"

Seamus lifted his glass. "Right as rain, my boy. Right as rain."

I looked at Ricky. "Whatever you're making smells fantastic."

Ricky glanced over his shoulder from the oven and smiled.

"It's Chicken Marsala. I hope this is what I'm gonna make for my audition for *Rising Chefs*."

My grandfather said, "If it tastes as good as it smells, they won't even hold a competition. They'll just name you the winner right away."

My grandfather always knew exactly what to say to the kids. That's why they all gravitated toward him. When I thought about it, I'd felt the same way about him when I was a child. He'd worked hard, long hours at his bar. But he'd never neglected me. When I came home from school, he knew exactly what to say to keep me engaged in my schoolwork and activities.

I checked in on Mary Catherine, who looked better every day after a week on bed rest.

She said, "I *will* be sitting at the table for Ricky's big dinner tonight. And I'm not interested in an argument. Is that understood?"

I had to smile. "Yes, ma'am."

Ten minutes later, with assistance from Jane and Juliana, we had Mary Catherine seated at the end of the dinner table. She almost looked like a royal sitting on a throne. The kids fell over themselves making sure she had everything she needed. I saw a future for Trent as a concierge. He was attentive and polite, and had a sense of when to back away.

Ricky called for help serving in the kitchen. An assembly line of kids managed to get all the filled plates onto the table while they were still piping hot.

He also did his little show before we started eating, taking the lid off the remaining Chicken Marsala. "As you can see, we're using chicken instead of veal." He shot a dirty look at Jane.

Jane said, "The twins and I won't eat veal. We barely want to eat chicken."

Ricky sort of shook his head and continued. "The sauce has a traditional base of Marsala wine but is from my own secret recipe. Plus a generous helping of yellow onions and portobello mushrooms. The vegetable side today is glazed brussels sprouts. I would've paired them with the wine, but Gramps drank most of it."

The dinner was exactly what I needed—listening to the kids talk about their day, the easy chatter between siblings, and an occasional story from my grandfather. Best of all, Mary Catherine was sitting right next to me. Although she wasn't as talkative as normal, she had a decent appetite.

Seamus said, "Ricky, my boy, if this doesn't win you that competition, it's rigged. I hope they don't take points away from you because you don't have an Italian last name."

Ricky had a big grin on his face. He had made a giant dinner and there was almost nothing left. Even Bridget, who tended to be a little mean to her brothers, said, "I agree with Gramps— this is the best dinner I've ever had."

I just soaked in the banter and compliments. It was nice to see Ricky getting the credit he deserved for his talents in the kitchen.

Then Mary Catherine grasped my hand on top of the table. At first I thought it was a romantic gesture. And I felt the pressure in her grip. I turned to her and said in a low voice, "You all right?"

She shook her head and mumbled, "No. We need to go to the hospital. Right now."

I felt panic race through my whole body. It was all I could do to stay calm and not alarm the children. It was Mary Catherine who took charge.

She looked over at my grandfather. "Seamus, I'm not feeling well. Michael is going to take me to the hospital. You're going to make sure these children focus on their homework and not worry about me." Then she turned to each of the kids and gave a little message. To Ricky, she said, "Dinner was fantastic." She turned to Juliana and said, "Thank you for taking charge of so much." She worked down the line while I gathered my keys, wallet, and phone.

A few minutes later we were racing to Mount Sinai.

CHAPTER 80

KEVIN DOYLE HAD been texting back and forth with his employer. The little burner phone he'd bought from a kiosk in a shopping center on Long Island didn't have the best on-screen keyboard.

He was sitting in his rental car a block down from the diner where Tammy worked for her uncle. He couldn't get the pretty triathlete out of his head. He noticed that the big tattooed guy was back in the diner tonight. She did work fast.

Doyle had been using the quiet time to communicate with his employer. A call might've been easier, but he felt like this was safer.

Then the text came through that he didn't want to see. It might be time to take action. Stand by. It'll take a little while to work it out.

He knew that probably meant Bennett. He really hadn't wanted to do anything like this. Killing the retired cops was bad enough. This felt like a sin. An even worse sin than the ones he had already committed.

Doyle texted, Bennett's tough.

I'll send you some help.

Can they be trusted?

No names. Just backup.

So he wouldn't be able to tell anyone anything even if he got caught.

Doyle considered it. He rarely worked with partners. When he first got into the business, after his stint in the military, some of his government employers would send a second along. They were rarely much help. He always felt like they were there to snitch more than anything else.

Doyle tried to look on the other side of the coin. If he lined everything up properly, maybe he could have his partner take the shot. That wouldn't feel as bad as Doyle pulling the trigger himself. Finally, he texted his employer and said, Okay. I'll take the help.

The next text was right to the point. Nothing fancy. No collateral damage. Just eliminate him. I'll text you where and when to meet your partner. Might be a couple of days. Keep on other jobs until you hear from me. It was followed by a smiley face emoji.

It didn't lighten his mood.

Doyle was apprehensive about using someone else on this job. But he saw all the potential positives. This job and visit to New York had not turned out the way he thought it would. He had too many professional and personal ties here. But it had convinced Doyle he needed to step away from this business. He made up his mind. This was his last job.

He looked through his windshield one last time. Although the diner was busier than usual, Tammy was lingering at the end of the counter, chatting with the biker-looking dude. She even reached up and touched his scraggly beard. It made Doyle's stomach turn.

He thought about what would happen if he took Tammy up on her offer. Now he realized he'd have to deal with the biker if he wanted to talk to Tammy again.

Maybe Bennett would be his second-to-last job.

CHAPTER 81

FOR ALL OF its notoriety, Mount Sinai Hospital in Manhattan made great efforts to put us at ease once we arrived at the emergency room. They weren't fooling around with a pregnant woman who was experiencing extreme pain in her lower abdomen and a shortness of breath. The stress of the situation was starting to give me similar symptoms.

A young nurse held Mary Catherine's hand for a moment and said, "We're waiting to take you down for an ultrasound. I know it sounds crazy but try to relax. I think your shortness of breath is just anxiety." He sounded pretty confident in his diagnosis.

Mary Catherine squeezed the young man's hand. The nurse flinched. To his credit, he didn't try to snatch his hand away from her. This was not his first rodeo.

We sat alone in the pleasant examination room. This didn't seem like the kind of room where they brought gunshot victims.

A padded chair sat in the corner. Instead of a hard examination table, there was a bed with a real mattress. Mary Catherine looked comfortable enough on the bed, which took up almost all the space in the room.

I tried to make small talk in an effort to keep Mary Catherine's mind off things. Eventually, the conversation did come back to kids and family.

Mary Catherine said, "We're going to be older parents, aren't we?"

I laughed and said, "This is one of the few times the word 'we' doesn't really apply. You're quite a bit younger than me. I'm surprised no one has asked you if I'm your father." That had the intended effect as Mary Catherine started to laugh.

I said, "I'm going to be one of the oldest fathers on the soccer field."

"Oh, stop it. You know that's not true." She paused for a moment. "Mr. Dunkel down on the first floor is fifty with twin two-year-olds running around the house."

"Okay, you got me. I just feel like I'm the oldest father."

"You're the best dad I've ever seen. I can't wait to see you interact with our baby."

"I can't wait either."

Then Mary Catherine burped. Not a dainty Irish-lass burp. More of a professional-wrestler-after-eating-a-steak-dinner burp. It was impressive. I tried not to smile, but the embarrassed look on Mary Catherine's face was priceless.

Then she did it again. Before she could say anything, she broke wind. Twice.

I worked hard to stay next to her. It wasn't the easiest thing I'd ever done.

Then she looked at me and said, "Oh, my God!"

"What? What is it?" Panic bubbled in my stomach.

Mary Catherine said, "I feel so much better." She burped again. She looked at me with a serious expression. "You think all I was feeling was gas?"

"You have been eating a pretty bland diet and intentionally not moving much. Ricky's dinner was superrich."

We waited to have an ultrasound just in case, but everyone agreed, this was a case of acute Chicken Marsala gas. Everyone except Mary Catherine got a pretty good laugh out of it.

When we were back in the car, headed home, Mary Catherine said, "I need you to promise me not to tell anyone about this."

I smiled. "That's a promise I'd hate to keep."

"I'll tell the kids it was gas. But I'm not going to explain how we figured it out."

"That's the best part of the story!"

"And the last thing you will ever reveal. That is, if you want to live long enough to see our baby."

That sounded like an offer I couldn't refuse.

CHAPTER 82

THE STRESS OF the last week, coupled with the pain she'd felt earlier in the evening, caught up with Mary Catherine. Just the short drive from Mount Sinai back to our apartment was enough for her to doze off.

I wanted her to sleep so badly that I just sat in the car with her for twenty-five minutes after I'd parked. Then she opened her eyes and said, "That was a quick ride from the hospital." I chuckled as I hustled around to the other side of the car to open the door and help her out.

As we slowly made our way through the lobby and into an elevator, Mary Catherine said, "I want to think of a way to explain this without making it seem like it was Ricky's fault that the dinner gave me the pain."

"You mean you want to avoid saying you had a massive gas attack."

"No, smart guy, I don't want to shake Ricky's confidence."

I knew that was her true concern. It was just fun teasing her. I thought about it for a moment and said, "We don't have to tell them anything about it. We'll just tell them everything's fine, and the doctor told us not to worry." Mary Catherine seemed satisfied with that plan of action.

We were both shocked to see everyone awake and still sitting around the dining room table as we walked through the front door. Before Mary Catherine could start scolding anyone, the whole group, including my grandfather, sprang from the table and rushed to give her a hug. She couldn't say one word about the kids being up past their bedtimes.

We assured them everything was all right. Just as I was about to follow our plan and tell them the doctors said not to worry, Eddie gave Mary Catherine another big hug.

And she broke wind. Loudly.

No one dared snicker. But everyone seemed to be staring at Mary Catherine.

Then my wife burst out into laughter. She admitted everything and told the kids exactly what had happened. She turned to Ricky and said, "Your dinner was *so* good, I couldn't stop eating it. As long as the guy who hosts that show isn't pregnant, you shouldn't have any problems."

We were about to force everyone to their bedrooms when I glanced out into the living room. Something didn't look right. I couldn't quite put my finger on it. I was still looking out into the living room trying to figure it out when Shawna spoke up.

"I did it. It's my fault, Dad."

I looked down at my second youngest. "What are you talking about, sweetheart?"

"I spilled red Gatorade on the carpet. I cleaned it up the best I could, but it didn't all come out."

Brian spoke up. "It's really my fault, Dad. I moved the sofa to cover the spot until I could get it shampooed tomorrow. We just didn't want you guys to worry about something like this when you came home."

I turned and looked at my grandfather.

Seamus just shrugged and said, "I'm sorry. I dozed off. But I did approve the plan after the fact."

That was the straw that broke Mary Catherine's resolve. She started to laugh. Then I started to laugh.

Mary Catherine looked at me and said, "We'll be fine older parents. Look at this bunch. Not a liar in the whole crowd. That's good parenting."

CHAPTER 83

BY MIDMORNING THE next day, I found myself on surveillance with Rob Trilling again sitting in the passenger seat. I was on the phone with Terri Hernandez, who was in court in lower Manhattan. We were talking over one of the most sensitive subjects: informants.

I said, "Are you sure you're okay with Trilling and me talking to your informant?"

"I'm going to be stuck in this trial all day. I know we can't wait on this case. Just be careful with Jaime Nantes. He may have worn a wire for us, but I don't trust him."

"You don't trust anyone."

"Mike, I'm serious. This guy could turn on you. And I'm not sure your plan of bringing up some old warrant for child pornography is the best idea. He may just decide to run. Leave New York altogether. That's the easy solution."

I said, "I hear you. We'll be careful. I just don't see any other choice going forward."

Terri said, "Tell Super Jock I'll give him the benefit of my experience when I get done with this trial appearance. Until then, you need to keep an eye on him."

"Sounds like you're finally warming up to him."

"I just know how little a rookie really knows. I don't want him doing anything stupid."

Right after I hung up with Terri, Trilling pointed down the street toward the warehouse. "That's our man, Nantes."

Jaime Nantes didn't look much like his last booking photo. He was a little sloppy, with a gut he tried to cover by leaving his shirt untucked. Or maybe he left his shirt untucked to hide a gun. Either way, it wasn't a very good look. His unkempt beard and curly hair were both streaked with gray and looked like they could use a good washing. He took a long drag from a cigarette, then flicked it onto the sidewalk. He then crossed the street and headed toward his typical destination, a tiny restaurant called Island Delight connected to a bodega near the drug gang's clubhouse. The sign in the window was handwritten and someone had run out of room so there was no *t* on the end of "Delight."

I sensed Trilling tense up when Nantes passed a teenage girl. The look he gave her set me on edge as well.

As if he were reading my mind, Trilling said, "Now that I know about the child pornography allegation, seeing him anywhere near a young woman pisses me off."

"What's this guy like to deal with face-to-face?"

"I never really had to talk to him. I usually sat in the back. But I noticed Hernandez was really short with him whenever we collected the transmitter after a meeting. It's clear she didn't think much of him."

"Really? Our Terri doesn't think much of a guy with a long criminal history trying to work off an assault charge? It doesn't sound like her."

That made Trilling laugh.

I reminded him, "No matter what this guy says or does, don't lose your cool. Once he finds out we know about the child pornography warrant, he may get hinky."

"He may get what?"

"Hinky. You know, squirrelly." I looked at Trilling. "You're just busting my balls. You know exactly what I'm talking about."

Trilling kept that goofy grin on his face. And that's what made me laugh.

We didn't waste any time. We wanted to be inside by the time Nantes stepped through the door.

We got out of my car and casually walked toward the restaurant.

CHAPTER 84

KEVIN DOYLE PUT off doing anything about the cop, Bennett. He still had plenty of jobs to complete. He'd deal with Bennett when the time was right and he had his ducks in a row.

Doyle examined the interior of his current car, a stolen Ford Taurus. He'd taken it from a construction site in Brooklyn. Now he realized the owner was some sort of building inspector. He wouldn't keep this one too long. He was only using it for one job. And right now, he was watching as his target walked from the gang's warehouse in the Bronx to a restaurant where he ate almost every single day.

The target's name was Jaime Nantes. He was every bit as bad as or worse than all the drug dealers Doyle had taken out so far. At the moment, he was under indictment for assault with a firearm. Apparently, a stockbroker in lower Manhattan had decided Nantes's price for cocaine was too high. He refused to pay, so Nantes took the business dispute into the restroom of the club where they met. Following a short discussion, Nantes pulled out a Colt .45. After smacking the stockbroker in the face with it several times, Nantes stuck the pistol in his customer's mouth. All this was generally accepted business tactics in the world of narcotics. Nantes's problem occurred when the bouncer had to use the bathroom and walked in on the disagreement.

The bouncer was a former Marine and quick on his feet. He barreled into Nantes and his customer, knocking the pistol to the ground. Nantes was in custody a few minutes later.

Doyle liked to keep little tidbits of information like that in his head before he took out a target. It was his way of rationalizing what he did for a living. Like most people, Doyle wanted to do the right thing. He wanted to make the world a better place. No one could argue that running down a guy like Nantes would help society a little bit.

The problem with today's assignment was a restaurant down the street from his target. It was a chicken place. A busy chicken place. Cars were lined up into the street to go through the take-out lane. Occasionally, cars blocked his view of the street. It was frustrating, but it also gave him a little more cover.

Doyle knew Nantes's schedule pretty well. Now he could see Nantes walking down the sidewalk toward Island Delight. He knew that his target always spent about thirty minutes in the little restaurant, then walked the exact same path back to his drug gang's headquarters. That's what Doyle was counting on. He'd be able to catch Nantes when he crossed the street, then keep on driving until he saw a good place to dump the car. Though first, Doyle thought he might try the chicken.

He could be back at his hotel in Brooklyn by midafternoon.

He wanted to be done with this assignment. He also was hoping that if he left town quickly, he'd be able to avoid trying to take on Bennett and his partner.

Doyle was tempted to act rashly. He wanted to pull out of his parking spot, dodge a few chicken customers, and run this son of a bitch down right now. But that wasn't in his nature. He was an excellent planner and that wouldn't follow his plan.

Instead, he let Nantes walk through the door to the bodega and Island Delight intact and healthy.

At least for now.

CHAPTER 85

ROB TRILLING AND I sat at Nantes's usual table in Island Delight, the little restaurant connected to the bodega. We ordered a couple of Cuban sandwiches. Trilling went with a regular Coke while I tried something new: an orange soda made with real cane sugar. Holy cow was it sweet.

This place was only a few blocks from where the Salazars' bodega was located. I was sure they knew the owners here too. There was just enough distance from the clubhouse that the Salazars' bodega wasn't one of the gang's hangouts. I was happy the Salazars didn't have to deal with this group directly.

I knew Jaime Nantes would recognize Trilling sitting at his usual table as soon as he walked in. I intended to use that short period of disorientation to pounce on the scumbag and get him to help us.

Nantes walked in the door and greeted the woman behind the

counter. He turned toward the restaurant and the four tables set up in the cramped space. As soon as he noticed Trilling, he froze. Then he glanced around to make sure no one else he knew was inside the bodega.

I slid out the chair next to me.

Nantes took the hint and cautiously sat down. The first words out of his mouth were "Where's Hernandez? That's who I deal with."

Trilling said, "She's busy."

"Then come back when she's not busy."

That's when I decided to step in. I didn't want this guy trying to tie Trilling up in verbal knots. Besides, it's tough for any father to sit across from a creep like this and not do something. I don't know if it was anger or disgust, but I had to speak up.

I said, "Settle down. We just want to talk to you for a minute. Detective Hernandez has more important things to deal with."

Nantes said in a low voice, "I don't know what you guys want. I already wore a wire for her and this redneck. I'm doing everything I'm supposed to do." Nantes looked at me and said, "Who the hell are you anyway?"

"Michael Bennett, homicide."

"So this is still about them murders, huh?"

I just said, "Yep."

Nantes looked at the floor and shook his head. Then he said, "I done all I'm gonna do."

I didn't wait to drop our ace in the hole. "We found some old paper on you."

"I ain't got no warrants. They'd have come up while I was working with Hernandez and this guy." He cut his eyes to Trilling like he had been cheated. Then he looked back at me and said, "What old paper?"

"A child pornography charge."

Nantes flinched. "I worked that off with the FBI a couple of years ago. Just a bunch of bullshit."

"It may be bullshit. But you still don't want people talking about you molesting children. It's bad for business."

"That's not cool, man. I wasn't convicted of nothing."

"But you had to work it off. That tells me you *did* something. Doesn't matter if you were convicted or not. Your guys might consider the fact that you worked off a charge as bad as the child porn itself." I just sat there and stared in silence. That had to be tough for Nantes to deny.

Finally, he said, "You want something from me or you wouldn't have come here. What do I need to do to get out of this?"

I said, "We need you to get enough info on someone for us to charge him. We want to hear and see everything he does."

Nantes looked between Trilling and me. Then he said, "Who are you talking about?"

"Antonio Deason."

CHAPTER 86

JAIME NANTES LOOKED at me like I was crazy. I could have slapped him and gotten the same response. Finally, when neither Trilling nor I filled the silence, Nantes said, "I don't know about that. That's a lot of risk for a charge I've already taken care of. I knew Deason's dad. If Antonio's anything like his old man, I don't want to get on the wrong side of him."

I said, "We're just looking for a little help. Tip us off when he's leaving with some product. Something like that. You don't have to do anything dangerous. Just be our eyes and ears."

Nantes had to think about that one. I didn't push too hard. We were already out on a limb. This was much closer to blackmail than it was to law enforcement. But I was getting desperate.

"How well do you know Antonio?" I asked.

"I've recorded a couple of conversations for Hernandez when the guy was over at our warehouse."

Trilling cut in. "Technically you just transmitted the conversations. Detective Hernandez made that clear."

Nantes shrugged. "Whatever. You guys already know he's been coming by our warehouse or you wouldn't be talking to me now."

"Have you had any dealings with him outside of the ones Detective Hernandez heard?"

Nantes shook his head. "I'm trying to *stay out* of trouble, not get into more of it." He took another pause and then added, "This doesn't sound like something I want to do."

I immediately stood up from the table. Trilling followed my lead. I said, "Okay, do what you need to do. It's your choice." I started to turn and I mumbled, "Good luck."

That took all the defiance out of Nantes. He barked, "Wait, wait. I have another idea."

I hesitated, then partially turned to hear him out.

Nantes said, "I can show you some documents back at the warehouse. Stuff that would bury Deason. His name is all over them."

Trilling asked the important question. "How do we do it without the other guys at the warehouse seeing?"

"There's no one there right now. We got at least an hour." Then he looked at me and said, "Your choice." He stared me down as he stood up and casually walked to the front door, then turned around to hear my answer. His right hand rested on the door.

Maybe this guy wasn't the dumbass I thought he was. It was worth the risk. I said, "Let's go."

CHAPTER 87

KEVIN DOYLE CURSED the timing of the car that stopped directly in front of him. It almost completely blocked his view of Island Delight and the bodega. He'd seen Nantes standing on the inside of the glass door. It looked like he was talking to someone inside the bodega. But an older Chrysler minivan with a couple of kids in the back blocked him. They were in line to get take-out chicken.

Doyle didn't want to call attention to himself by doing something crazy, like backing over the curb and going across the sidewalk. There were too many potential witnesses who could then identify him later. He didn't want to risk it on what was possibly one of his last days in New York.

Doyle patted the pistol he'd shoved into his belt holster. The gun was a distant backup plan. He had time. If he didn't see the opportunity today, he could come back tomorrow. That may not have been his preference, but it was an option. He took a deep breath and concentrated on the word "patience." Patience was the motto of every successful contract killer in the world. If you rushed a job, you'd be caught. It was that simple.

Then he thought about Tammy at the diner. Maybe she was influencing his haste to get out of the city. Romantic entanglements always caused complications. Even ones he wasn't pursuing anymore.

Perspiration formed on his forehead. Just because he knew he had to be patient didn't mean he liked it. He'd almost rather be under fire than have to wait like this. Even the cute face of the little girl in the car seat in the van didn't calm him down. She turned, stared out the window, and smiled at him.

Doyle mumbled, "Tell your mom to move forward." And just like that, the minivan moved forward one space. It was like magic. Doyle didn't wait for the next car in line to fill the gap. He pulled out onto the street. This wasn't ideal, but it was better than being trapped in the parking spot.

He could still see Nantes standing just inside the door, talking to someone. Doyle took a breath and let Nantes continue his conversation. It was probably the last one he was ever going to have.

CHAPTER 88

I KEPT MY cool and didn't yell at Jaime Nantes to get moving. The scruffy informant was stopped at the front door, one hand resting on the rail to push it open. He turned to look at me and Rob Trilling following directly behind him.

Nantes said, "C'mon, guys, don't crowd me on the way back. I can't be seen walking with you two. In this neighborhood you'll be made for cops before we take three steps out of this bodega."

Trilling and I exchanged glances.

Nantes added, "I promise I won't go inside the warehouse without you. I won't be out of your sight." He looked past me to make sure no one inside the bodega or restaurant was paying attention to us. Then he added, "We need some level of trust or this ain't gonna work at all."

Reluctantly, I nodded. But he kept standing at the door. I realized Nantes was waiting for Trilling to approve the plan as well. I guessed it was because he'd been working with Trilling, and this was the first time he'd met me.

My partner said, "None of us will walk together. I'll be behind you and Detective Bennett can be a few dozen feet behind me. Just three individuals walking down the sidewalk."

Nantes said, "You'd be surprised what some people notice. The older women sit in their apartments and watch the sidewalk like they used to watch soap operas. But I can live with the three of us spread out."

I nodded again. Nantes turned and pushed the door open. He stepped out onto the sidewalk and paused. I noticed him look both ways. He still hadn't moved from the doorway. The street wasn't busy. I wasn't sure what he was looking for. Then I had the uneasy feeling he might try to double-cross us. Even if he ran right now, I had no probable cause to chase him. We were essentially threatening him into helping us.

Then he walked straight into the street, crossing it quickly. He slowed once he reached the sidewalk on the other side.

Trilling and I took a slightly different route.

Trilling said, "You cross the street and I'll hustle up this sidewalk. That way we might be able to corral him toward the warehouse, or clubhouse, or whatever the hell they call it."

I stepped out of Island Delight. Nantes was already heading up the street on the other side. While I stood there, checking for traffic, Trilling slipped out of the bodega and started striding quickly on a parallel course.

My sixth sense told me this was not going to go the way I hoped it would.

CHAPTER 89

KEVIN DOYLE HAD managed to pull his stolen Ford Taurus onto the street without drawing too much attention. He was essentially parked in the middle of the street as if he was waiting to turn left. At least he had a clear view.

Jaime Nantes stepped out of the bodega. He was alone. Whoever he'd been talking to inside didn't exit with him. Nantes paused and looked up and down the street. For a moment, Doyle was worried he'd been spotted. Why was the drug dealer so nervous today? Doyle had watched the man on the same street three different times and he'd never seemed jumpy before.

Then Nantes really surprised him. Instead of walking down the sidewalk and crossing the street at the next block, like he always did, Nantes crossed directly in front of the bodega. This was not part of his usual pattern.

Doyle muttered, "Shit." But there was nothing he could do.

He considered the route to the gang's warehouse. Nantes still had to cross another street. It would just be a little trickier to hit him with the Ford there.

Doyle went around the block so no one would notice the Taurus. He hit the gas a little hard. The wheels squealed as he took the next corner. If his calculations were correct, he had plenty of time to get into position and catch Nantes as he crossed the next street. In fact, this might have worked out for the best. There was less traffic and no crowded restaurants were nearby.

He quickly glanced up and down the streets. There were a couple of people around but no one particularly close to where Nantes was walking. That's who he was focusing all of his attention on. The casual gait, the sloppy shirt, the unkempt salt-and-pepper beard and messy hair. He was fairly easy to pick out.

Doyle drove slowly, inching along at a couple of miles an hour. As Nantes approached the intersection that he needed to cross, Doyle eased on the gas and picked up speed. Given what he knew about Nantes, this wasn't going to bother Doyle much at all.

Now he had the Ford Taurus rumbling a good thirty-five miles an hour. Nantes was stepping off the curb. Doyle's peripheral vision picked up on someone else crossing the other street in the intersection, but it was like he had tunnel vision as he focused on the drug dealer. There were no other cars nearby. This was perfect.

Just as Doyle entered the intersection, Nantes looked up and noticed the Taurus.

As Doyle prepared for the impact, something remarkable happened. The man who'd been crossing the other street darted through the intersection, grabbed Nantes's arm, and jerked him out of the way of the speeding car. The man moved so fast, Doyle didn't even get a decent look at him. All he knew was that the guy had dark hair and the reflexes of a cat.

The Ford's bumper had missed Nantes by a matter of inches. After passing through the intersection, Doyle just kept driving. He was confident no one had seen his face and it would simply be assumed that he was a poor driver. No one would even call the police. There was no accident. No injury. And Nantes was too stupid to think it was any kind of planned attack. Doyle was sure the drug dealer wouldn't change his usual routine.

Doyle turned onto Crotona Avenue and drove until he was a couple of blocks from the Bronx Zoo. It took only a minute to wipe down the interior of the Taurus. He used a screwdriver to crack the steering column and start the car. Just to be on the safe side, he left the car idling with the windows rolled down. With any luck, someone might see it and take it for a ride themselves. If not, it might be a while before anyone found the Taurus by the zoo.

Doyle walked as casually as he could a few blocks north and west. He went into the nearest subway station and jumped on a 2 train.

He thought back to his mantra: patience.

Tomorrow was another day. Tomorrow Doyle would find a different car and do the whole thing over again. But that meant he had another day or two in New York. More time to think about Tammy. And more time for his employer to decide what they were going to do about Bennett.

This had not been his best day.

CHAPTER 90

I CAUGHT UP to Rob Trilling and Jaime Nantes on the sidewalk near the warehouse. I'd seen the whole incident from half a block away. I couldn't help saying to Nantes, "I guess you didn't mind Trilling being a little close to you during your walk."

"I never seen no one run like that. That cat is fast. I probably could've jumped out of the way, but I appreciate him looking out for me."

I looked at Trilling. "That really was some spectacular shit. I know the Army didn't teach you to move that fast. That's natural talent." As usual, my partner barely acknowledged the compliment. He just smiled and looked up the street toward the warehouse.

I guessed Nantes was so happy with Trilling that he didn't mind us walking with him the last half block to the building. He slid a key into a sophisticated lock in the warehouse door. I expected to see a hot, dusty space with wide-open bays as soon as we stepped inside. Instead, there was a series of rooms with one big common area. The air wasn't stale, which meant they had a good ventilation system. They probably could even keep this giant place cool in the summer.

Then Nantes called out to someone loudly, in Spanish. His voice carried and echoed through the empty rooms. He spoke too quickly for me to follow a word of it.

I grabbed him by the shoulder, while my other hand, by habit, touched the Glock in its holster at my hip. "Who else is here?"

Trilling was already on alert, his hand pulling out his own gun and his head moving in every direction. There were too many hallways in this place to get a good eyeline.

Terri had warned me about Jaime Nantes. I hadn't listened.

I kept a grip on Nantes's shoulder and shook him. "Who the hell did you call out to?"

A voice behind us said, "He was calling out to us."

When I turned, Trilling was already raising his hands, his Glock 19 dangling by two fingers. I moved my own hands, palms up, away from my body, away from my still-holstered firearm. There were three men holding submachine guns on us. Two on one side of the hallway, one on the other. They weren't going to get caught in a crossfire.

Nantes jerked away from me. He took a couple of steps and said to his friends, "Call Deason and tell him to come here. We have a present for him."

CHAPTER 91

THE GANG SAT Trilling and me at a folding table. We were told to put our hands palms down on the table in plain sight. No one said anything else as our firearms were taken away. When I started to ask a question, a big burly guy said, "Shut up. This ain't court. You don't get to argue your case."

So we sat there in silence. I should've been scared. Maybe even terrified. Instead, I was more embarrassed than anything else that I'd let a moron like Jaime Nantes trick me into getting captured by drug dealers. I hoped this didn't get out and spread around the department. I'd never live it down.

I was impressed with Trilling. He kept his cool. I had no idea what he was thinking, but I liked how he kept looking around the room. I knew he was marking exits in his head and searching for weaknesses.

The gang was sharper than I'd expected. Two men stood at

opposite corners of the room with their MP5 submachine guns pointed at us.

A little less than an hour into our detention, I heard the door at the front of the warehouse open. Then I heard voices. Some were speaking Spanish and some English.

A group of men, including Antonio Deason, stepped into the room where we were being held. Deason was dressed like he worked on Wall Street. The red power tie against the blue shirt and jacket didn't fit in with the warehouse decor. He just stood there shaking his head.

He came closer to the table and said, "You guys don't give up. First you think I'm gonna be dumb enough to talk to you. Then you make a few amateur attempts to follow me. Why?"

The guy who seemed to be in charge put his arm around Nantes's shoulder. "Jaime here used his head. He got these two assholes to come directly to us. You said you wanted to see how tough we were. How about we kill these two cops as a present for you."

I felt Trilling tense next to me.

Deason looked annoyed. He shook his head. "I got a much better idea. Me and my boys are going to deal with these two, and no one will ever connect us to their bodies." He made a show of looking at each man in the room. "But no one can ever say a word about it after today. No one." He looked around to make sure everyone understood. "If you killed these two, the cops would never stop coming after you. And eventually me. But if I make it look like some kind of accident, or put the blame on someone else, it's a different story."

I said, "You've had some practice doing things that way."

Deason glared at me but didn't say anything. He looked at the men gathered around him and said, "When this is over, you'll owe me a favor." Then he glanced at Trilling and added, "Make that *two* favors."

Someone slapped handcuffs on me and Trilling and led us out to a blue SUV, where we were buckled into seat belts with our hands still cuffed behind us. We sat in the middle row, with Deason's people positioned in front of and behind us in the SUV. Then Deason jumped into the front passenger seat.

I said, "If you don't mind, you could just drop me at my office."

No one in the car thought it was funny.

CHAPTER 92

WE STARTED HEADING south from the Bronx. I felt a little more nervous now that we were out of the warehouse. There was a different, more professional aura about Deason's guys than the gang members back at the clubhouse. No one spoke. The driver focused on the road, and Antonio Deason kept an eye on us.

Even if I weren't strapped into the back seat with my hands cuffed behind me, the doors had safety locks on them. I hadn't gotten a good look at the person sitting in the row of seats behind us when they shoved us into the SUV. Deason made a phone call I couldn't hear very well, but he was clearly annoyed. That didn't bode well for us.

My hope that these guys might somehow give us an opportunity to escape seemed far-fetched.

I started asking my questions out loud. "Why aren't we tied up on the floor in the back? Why even bother putting seat belts on us?"

Deason turned in his seat to more directly look at me and Trilling. "Because you're both fucking morons."

I said, "That's a little harsh, isn't it?"

"I think it's an accurate assessment. We gave you guys every opportunity to back off. But you're too stupid to pick up the hints." Deason opened the glove compartment in front of him. I felt my stomach tighten as I wondered what he was retrieving.

Trilling was starting to lift his legs and draw them close to his body. I realized he intended to try to kick the back of the driver's seat. I tried to think what I could do to support him once he made his move. I moved my hands as far over as I could, wondering if I could release my seat belt, but my fingers couldn't even get close to the latch.

Deason held whatever he had grabbed from the glove compartment in his right hand. I tried not to flinch as he leaned toward me. Trilling got ready to make his desperate move.

It was a wallet. Deason held up his hand, then let the wallet fall open. The first thing I noticed was the gold badge. And the official ID.

Deason said, "I think you guys are morons because we're with the DEA and you're screwing up one of our biggest cases."

CHAPTER 93

I WASN'T SURE I fully believed Antonio Deason until he led us into an off-site DEA office in Midtown. They took the cuffs off us, but no one offered us our handguns back. We walked in silence down a hallway. The offices didn't look much different from our own at Manhattan North Homicide. There were a few people working at desks who showed little or no interest as we walked by.

I realized the counter-surveillance we'd come up against recently was actually DEA agents covering Deason during his undercover work. That's why they'd brought the Porsche Taycan to his apartment. It was probably a seized vehicle. The person who had been in the back seat of the SUV turned out to be the woman we'd seen delivering the Porsche to Deason the day we got burned so badly. I also realized the SUV we'd just ridden in was the same blue Tahoe that had blocked us on our first surveillance. Now all that seemed obvious. Maybe Deason was right. I might be a moron.

They took us into a comfortable conference room where the Black man we'd seen Deason meeting with at the Italian restaurant was seated at the end of the table. He gave us a grin as we shuffled in.

We all sat around the table. Another woman joined us. She wore a blue pantsuit and sat on the opposite side of the table. Her eyes gave us a stern appraisal. She was clearly management. But she was letting Deason handle the meeting.

I didn't intend to give them the satisfaction of asking a ton of questions. I just stayed quiet. I knew I didn't have to warn Trilling to keep his mouth shut. He did that on his own most of the time. He didn't seem too confused by the entire episode.

Antonio Deason sat directly across from Trilling and me. He looked a little more frazzled than in the past. He flashed his brown eyes at me, then over to Trilling. No one said anything.

Finally, Deason said, "You don't have any questions?"

I said, "I'm waiting to hear what you have to say."

"We know your reputation. That's why we brought you in here. We'd like to ensure that you don't tell anyone about our investigation."

"You mean don't tell my bosses."

"I mean don't tell *anyone*." Deason paused, then glanced around the table. The woman sitting on the other side of the table nodded her head. "I'm sure you know who I am, and that this group we're investigating worked for my father years ago. The NYPD conducted extensive investigations and made a lot of arrests back then. The NYPD unit, the Land Sharks, were the only ones who ever stopped him. But it also appears that someone in the NYPD took a lot of money as well."

"Hang on a minute. Are you saying you didn't notify *anyone* about your investigation because you don't trust the NYPD?"

"Yes."

The answer was like a slap in my face. "How did you end up investigating the same people your father used to work with?"

Deason said, "That's a smart question. I kinda didn't expect it."

"An insult and a compliment at the same time. Very impressive." That earned a chuckle around the table.

"I won't go into the details. But in my last year at the University of Miami, some DEA agents wanted to ask me questions about my father. Once they realized I hadn't spoken with him for years, we just started to chat. Next thing I knew, I applied, was hired, went through the academy, and found myself working in Manhattan. We all agreed we might be able to use my connection to my father to finally break some of the drug gangs that have plagued the city."

I said, "So you joined the DEA as a reaction to your father."

Deason said, "My father did a lot to destroy the Bronx even as he made a show of doing good works. He expanded quickly and had set his sights on ruining most of the city. That's why I started thinking of ways I could help communities instead of tearing them apart."

"We're working a series of homicides. We have no interest in narcotics cases."

"You're looking into the murders of all the dopers who've been killed over the last couple of months?"

I nodded. "We think some of them are connected to a larger case we're looking into. You—and your father—were our only known links between all the victims. Now we need to find a new suspect." I waited a few seconds and added, "Unless you did kill them and now you want to confess."

Deason ignored my comment. "Will you let the DEA handle this drug case without interference? And can we count on you to stay away from the warehouse in the Bronx and keep your mouth shut about our investigation?"

I nodded.

Deason looked at Trilling.

Trilling nodded as well.

Deason said, "You can speak, right?"

Trilling just nodded again.

I loved it.

CHAPTER 94

KEVIN DOYLE WAS in a foul mood. Actually "foul" didn't adequately describe what he was feeling at the moment. Doyle was pissed off because after yesterday's botched hit-and-run, the order from his employer instructing him to take out Bennett had come through. No more delays. His employer was sending help. If that wasn't enough to push Doyle over the edge, his so-called help was now sitting next to him atop a four-story building across the street from where Detective Michael Bennett's specialized homicide unit was located, stuck in a nondescript office building on Broadway.

Even though they'd been sitting together for over an hour, watching the office building, Doyle had yet to get any kind of decent read on the man. Other than he was a walking stereotype. He'd told Doyle to just call him "Joe." Doyle told Joe to just call him "Buddy." Joe was around fifty and a little heavy but still in reasonably good shape. His bulbous nose had been broken several times. He had a few streaks of gray in his dark, slicked-back hair.

Joe had the kind of old-school Brooklyn Italian accent Doyle remembered from around the neighborhoods and baseball diamonds of his childhood, so different from how he and his siblings spoke. Those Italian kids even called one another the kinds of names Doyle's mother had forbidden him to say. It had been exciting as a kid.

Joe had a fancy hunting rifle that screwed together at the receiver and shoulder stock, a Remington that looked like a real pro had modified it. Joe fiddled with the adjustments on the rifle but was careful not to bring the rifle high enough for anyone to notice it. Doyle just hoped he knew how to use it. He usually dismissed those kinds of rifles as gimmicks.

They'd gotten a quick view of Bennett as he parked in the lot across the street from the building earlier, but that only confirmed he was inside now. They didn't have time to act then, but now they were set up and waiting patiently for whenever the tall detective strolled back out of the building.

Their employer had set up a meeting between Doyle and Joe a few hours ago at a coffee shop. They drank a cup of coffee together and chatted for a few minutes.

Joe had looked at Doyle and said, "You must owe someone a favor, Buddy."

"Why do you say that?"

"It's rarely worth it to kill a cop. They're a funny bunch. Cops will hound you and anyone connected with you after one of them is killed. I've seen it a dozen times. I've even seen my own business partners take out one of their own employees who killed a cop and tell the cops where the body is. It's easier than trying to hide someone from a whole army of pissed-off cops."

Doyle said, "What about you? You owe someone a favor?"

Joe smiled. "I owe a lot of favors. I have to make up for some poor decisions my youngest son made. He worked for the same people I did. But killing this asshole cop, Bennett, will be a pleasure. I've owed him something other than a favor for a long time."

"You know him personally?"

"Let's just say our paths have crossed. He screwed up a lot of business deals for my organization. He even arrested my cousin and got him convicted of first-degree murder. We'll all be better off when he's off the boards."

"Was your cousin guilty?"

"Yeah, Sal was the triggerman, but that don't matter. The point is this guy has been a pain in my ass for too long." He'd nodded without being sure what the hell Joe meant.

Now, on the roof, Doyle looked over as his "help" lovingly handled his rifle. At least he, and not Doyle, would be the one taking the shot from up here. Thank God for small blessings. He noticed Joe pull a spent rifle casing from his pocket.

Doyle said, "What's that for?"

Joe gave him an evil smile, a bicuspid missing on the upper right side. "This is a little misdirection."

"How do you figure?"

"Same caliber, same manufacturer, but fired from an NYPD rifle at the Rodman's Neck range a while back. We'll leave it here. The cops will process it. They'll think the shot came from one of their rifles. Provided they have everything documented and tested the way they should."

"Still won't matter. They'll locate the gun and see it hasn't been fired or has been under lock and key."

Joe shook his head. "I'm telling you, it'll delay things. Maybe for a long time. Those knuckleheads will be off on a wild-goose chase, thinking one of their own turned bad. I think it's brilliant."

Doyle eyed his accomplice. "Where'd you get a spent NYPD round?"

Joe shrugged his shoulders. "I been around a long time. I know people. I may owe some favors, but there are favors owed to me too."

Doyle looked over at the building they were watching. "All this seems like a lot of work for a cop who may or may not even be onto something."

Now Joe had a little edge to his voice. "I told you already. Bennett is a prick. I wanted to do this at his house in front of his kids." He looked at Doyle and said, "We can still move this party over to his apartment on the Upper West Side."

The only thing Doyle was thinking about at that moment was *How hard would it be to shoot this shithead in the face, then get rid of the body?* He got ahold of himself long enough to say, "We're already set up here. Let's do it and get on with our lives."

Doyle bent his head and said a quick prayer, then crossed himself. When he looked up, Joe was staring at him.

Joe said, "You praying that everything is going to work out well and this job is going to go fast?"

"Something like that. I'm also asking for God to forgive my sins."

"You picked the wrong business to worry about sins."

Doyle was thinking he'd picked the wrong business no matter what.

CHAPTER 95

I FELT A pang of guilt for the way I'd snuck out of the apartment this morning without waking Mary Catherine. I'd gotten home very late last night after our run-in with the DEA, and Mary Catherine had been already asleep. I hadn't seen any of the kids except Brian, who'd been up watching ESPN when I walked in last night, and Juliana, who was already making breakfast for everyone this morning when I crept out of bed. She'd given me the okay to head out. I'd kissed her on the forehead and raced to the office.

It'd taken a little work, but I managed to get everyone into the Manhattan North Homicide office at the same time. Terri Hernandez was at her usual place when she visited, in the conference room, with her laptop set up at the end of the table. Trilling was at his desk next to mine, and Walter Jackson was finishing up some reports he would send us.

We'd just taken a sharp turn onto the off-ramp of our investigation. There was no other way to describe it. We'd been so focused on the homicides and how the drug gang might've been associated with them that we never considered a DEA operation might be underway. Apparently, a *big* operation.

Both Trilling and I were trying to shake off the effects of our near catastrophic visit to the gang's warehouse, our subsequent visit to the DEA, and how badly we had miscalculated our case. At least, by the end of it, we'd had our NYPD-issued Glocks handed back to us.

Based on the way Walter Jackson cleared his throat, both Trilling and I knew it was time to step into the conference room with Terri Hernandez. We went through everything from the last couple of days. I told them how Trilling had moved like lightning to save Jaime Nantes's life — before Nantes double-crossed us to his gang.

Terri surprised me by saying, "Super Jock did the same thing a few days ago." She seemed proud of the nickname.

I wasn't sure what she was talking about.

Terri saw the expression on my face and said, "Oh, my God. He didn't tell you about it, did he?" She looked at Trilling. "If I'd rescued an elderly woman and a little girl from a speeding van, that's all I'd talk about for a week. Super Jock is starting to impress me."

It was clear Trilling didn't want to spend any time on either incident. We had a fun few minutes forcing him to talk about it anyway. I wasn't sure if this young man would ever stop surprising me. I hoped not.

Then we got down to business. We took a little time to look over the details we had on each of the former police officer victims we'd identified. I wanted to find another angle to investigate, but I didn't see many new ways to look at the so-called accidents and overdoses and suicides. We made a half-hearted list of things to follow up on, like checking all the video feeds from stores along the street where Lou Sanvos had crashed. Another idea was to interview family members in each case to see if they had any idea who might've wanted to hurt their loved one. They were sort of lame assignments, but we needed to do something.

Walter asked, "What about the two guys down in Florida?"

"I was pretty impressed with Special Agent Carol Frederick. She's following up on several different issues herself, and also told her bosses she no longer believes it was a double suicide. The Florida Department of Law Enforcement has a great reputation, so I'm not worried about that case."

Then a thought flashed through my head. The kind of thought that I didn't take time to examine before I just blurted it out. I sat up in my chair to get everyone's attention. Then I said, "Roger Dzoriack, the retired detective on Staten Island, didn't have visitors."

Trilling added, "Just the super, the librarian, and maybe the neighbor next door. You told me you left your card on her door. I've called a few times to follow up, no answer."

I smiled, appreciating the little fact that my twenty-four-year-old partner was learning how to investigate, following up on a lead that had fallen through the cracks. I said, "This may be one of the few times lifting prints from different spots in an apartment might really give us a suspect. We can take a copy of Dzoriack's prints with us and eliminate them on the spot. Whatever we find that isn't the patrol officers' prints could be our suspect's."

Terri nodded. "You're right. It wouldn't work in most cases.

Too many people coming and going. But it sounds like it could be a pretty good idea at his place."

Walter said, "I'll talk to my fingerprint posse."

Trilling looked at the big intelligence analyst and said, "Your what?"

Walter gave him a paternal smile. "I have friends in all kinds of fingerprint-analysis jobs. You know, the FBI, the Department of Defense, some high-tech businesses. I know people. We can get things moving really fast. All I need is one good print."

Thank goodness it wasn't like the old days when we had to sort through fingerprint cards. I appreciated how fast today's electronic system could be, especially since a lot of older prints were already scanned into the system.

Like football players breaking the huddle, everyone rushed off to do their part of the job. Walter went to place some calls. Terri was called away on a different case and had to leave us. Trilling and I headed down in the elevator to the building's entrance, aiming to drive over and get a hard copy of the victim's fingerprints from the medical examiner.

Just as I was about to push open the front door of our building, something made me pause. Maybe I was getting skittish in my old age. I took a long moment to scan the cars parked under the elevated train tracks. It looked all clear.

CHAPTER 96

SITTING ATOP THE building with Joe was driving Kevin Doyle to distraction. The man was giving him a pounding headache. His efforts at small talk were maddening.

Out of the blue, Joe said, "I heard some of Bennett's kids are Black and Hispanic. He even has an Oriental."

"Asian."

"You knew what I meant."

Doyle muttered, "Dickhead."

Then Joe went in a different direction. "I like chubby girls. What about you?"

Doyle just shrugged.

Joe said, "I like the way they work harder and seem nicer. You know, like girls with a little meat on their bones?"

Doyle said, "I like girls that avoid guys like you."

"Funny. You're a funny guy, Buddy. I bet the girls love that.

For me, they like my cash. Not hookers, mind you. Regular girls. I used to go for Russians. Now I lean toward Puerto Ricans. We had some problems with the Russian mob and my boss won't let us chase after their girls no more. Bummer. Russian girls can be really pretty."

Doyle resisted some of the words that came to mind. "Asshole" was the main one. He had to remind himself that this was a single job, and he'd never have to see this talkative moron again. He took a deep breath and let it out slowly.

He caught movement at the front door of Bennett's office building. Someone tall was paused at the door. It looked like Bennett was checking out the cars parked under the elevated track across the street. Doyle eased back down behind the low rise of the wall on the roof. He wondered if the detective had noticed some detail that made him hesitant to come outside.

There was no way Doyle wanted to deal with Joe another day. One way or the other they were ending this assignment here and now.

Then the front door to the office building opened and both Bennett and his young partner stepped outside.

Doyle tried to keep his voice calm. "Joe, get ready. Bennett's outside."

He was surprised how nimbly Joe moved into place behind the two-foot wall with the rifle. He stayed closer to the corner of the building and placed the barrel right across the top of the wall.

Joe squinted through the scope on the rifle. "I see him."

Doyle, squatting next to Joe, shook his head. It wouldn't be a hard shot once Bennett started walking toward his vehicle. That didn't make it any easier to watch.

CHAPTER 97

I HADN'T GOTTEN more than three steps from the front door when Walter Jackson rushed out to meet us.

I'll admit Walter's health was starting to concern me. Hurrying to catch us had left him seriously winded. He leaned down with both hands on his knees while he caught his breath. I was worried he might fall to the ground. I even looked over my shoulder at Trilling to make sure I had help if needed. My spry partner was ready to jump in, I could tell.

Finally, Walter gulped in enough air to say, "Here are Roger Dzoriack's prints. Just trying to save you a trip to the medical examiner's. The prints were already in the system."

I took the sheet of paper and thanked Walter.

He said, "I talked to a buddy at the Department of Defense. He'll run any prints the moment I send them to him electronically. If you find a usable print, theoretically we could have a hit by this evening."

"You did all that in the time it took me to get downstairs?"

Walter gave me a big smile. "All it cost me was a decent pun."

I didn't want to ask him what the pun was, but he had been so helpful, I felt I had to.

He gave me another smile and said, "A young woman fell in love with a tennis player. But love meant nothing to him." Walter stood there staring at me like I needed to respond.

Somehow I mustered, "Well worth the cost."

Trilling laughed out loud, then told Walter, "I have one you can use to buy more favors."

I had to step in at that point. "We need to get going. You guys can exchange your puns and dad jokes later." I started to cross the street to my car. A garbage truck slowed as it came past me. I waited as a sanitation worker jumped off the back and grabbed one of the public trash cans under the elevated tracks.

Walter stepped in front of us, "This case has me a little shaken. You guys need to be on alert even if you're just going to look at an empty apartment."

The garbage truck started to move on. I said to Walter, "I promise we'll make it back here safely. What could happen between here and Staten Island?"

It didn't look like that satisfied Walter's anxiety in any way.

CHAPTER 98

KEVIN DOYLE LARGELY tuned out most of what Joe had to say. He had to, before it made his stomach sour. But now he was listening to the tubby hit man.

"A big Black guy just stopped them in front of the building. He's giant. I can't even see Bennett behind him. I can see the young partner. Didn't you say he was also a potential target?"

Doyle took a quick peek over the edge of the roof. He could see the gigantic man talking with Bennett and his partner, Rob Trilling. Doyle thought about the information sheet he'd read about the partner, a former Army Ranger. He blurted out, "No. Don't worry about the partner."

Joe said, "I can maybe put one right through the big guy and still hit Bennett. I can always take a second shot after they are both on the ground." He moved slightly and readjusted his position.

"Hang on a minute. Bennett's got to walk to his car. You'll get your chance. Just be patient."

Joe growled, "Shit."

"What is it?"

"A garbage truck just pulled into my line of sight. I can't see a thing."

Doyle risked another peek. This whole thing was starting to eat at him. It just didn't feel right. Bennett was just doing his job. It wasn't like he was crooked or had done anything terrible, despite what Joe said. Somehow Doyle's employer had found someone who harbored a grudge against Bennett. That didn't help the way Doyle felt at the moment.

Joe kept sighting in on the front of the building. "The garbage truck is moving on, but the big guy is still blocking my shot. I'm gonna put one through his neck, which should be just about Bennett's face."

Doyle felt like he was going to vomit. He bit his lower lip and glanced over the wall. He wondered whether anyone would notice him if he stood up. If Bennett reacted quickly, he could get out of the way.

Doyle had no idea who the giant man talking to Bennett was. He looked too big to be a detective. It would be too hard to get in and out of cars and chase people if he had to. More likely he was some kind of analyst. Doyle knew that a good intelligence analyst was worth a lot of cops, or soldiers, depending on where you worked.

Then Joe said, "Okay, I've got him. As soon as he crosses the street his whole body will be in view under the train tracks." Then he went silent.

That's when Doyle realized just how bad this assignment

really was. He glanced down at his temporary partner. Joe was concentrating and not paying attention to anything except what was in his scope. Probably Bennett's head.

Doyle felt anxious and jittery. Then he made a split-second decision. One he knew he'd regret later. He nudged Joe with his leg before he could take the shot.

Joe lost his balance and ended up sitting flat on his ass. "What the hell are you doing?"

"This isn't the place or time."

"This is the perfect place *and* time. Are you crazy? I've killed guys for doing less than you just did."

Doyle realized the mistake he'd made. While Joe sat there and stared at him, open-mouthed, Doyle reached into his pocket and, with a flick of his thumb and wrist, popped out the four-inch folding knife he kept honed to a ridiculous edge. With no hesitation, he jabbed the blade straight up under Joe's chin.

The steel blade passed through Joe's soft palate at the roof of his mouth and into his brain. It caught him midsentence. Doyle wasn't even sure what the hit man had been saying. He just stopped. There wasn't even a change in his eyes. He was still staring straight ahead as Doyle slowly withdrew the blade.

Joe flopped over onto the roof. There was some blood, but not that much. The attack was so swift his heart only beat a few times after the blow.

Doyle recognized he'd made an error. He just couldn't stand to see a guy like Joe shoot someone like Bennett. If anyone asked him, Doyle wouldn't be able to explain it. Especially in light of the fact that he had killed dozens on his own.

He'd make a quick call to his friend Amir. No one would ever find a trace of Joe's body. He'd tell his employer he didn't know what happened to Joe. He intended to say, "We tried to find Bennett but couldn't."

Doyle took a moment to unscrew the rifle and stick it back in its fancy case. Then he started to slide Joe toward the rooftop door. It only took a few seconds of dragging the fat hit man for Doyle to realize he should've stabbed him on the first floor, not on the roof.

CHAPTER 99

AFTER A QUICK stop at One Police Plaza so Rob Trilling could pick up a piece of fingerprinting equipment from a forensics tech friend of his, we found ourselves back on Staten Island in front of Roger Dzoriack's apartment. Crime-scene tape still hung across his doorway in a giant X.

I considered knocking on Lesa Holstine's door but didn't want to disturb the cats. I noticed my business card was still stuck in the other neighbor's door—strange that she hadn't been home since we were here the last time. But we were working against the clock. I wanted this done as soon as possible.

Once we were inside the apartment, Trilling showed me the high-tech camera he'd borrowed. Trilling said, "I can take a photo of the print with some oblique light and load it directly into the database from this camera. I told Walter to be on the lookout and

I'll send him an email so he can start working his magic if we find a usable print."

I broke out my old-school fingerprint kit with a brush. I don't know why I thought this might lead somewhere. Only about a quarter of crime scenes have usable prints connected to the crime. But everything about this apartment seemed to say we had a chance. One resident. Few visitors. Many possibilities. I had hope.

I checked the table near the bed. There were several finger-prints on the lacquered wood, but I easily eliminated them all as Roger Dzoriack's. Same in the bathroom and on the bedroom doorknob.

Trilling called to me from the kitchen. "It looks like there's a decent thumbprint on the kitchen faucet. It's flat and shiny. And it looks a little different from the others. We could have a winner."

I took my little kit into the kitchen, to the area Trilling pointed out. He was right. There seemed to be a perfect, com-plete thumbprint. Trilling used a flashlight and took a digital photo of the print. I checked it against both thumbprints of Roger Dzoriack. Neither matched. The victim had a big loop, and this print had a whorl in the same place. In the olden days, or what I call my earlier career, we would lift prints with tape. Just to be cautious, I ran the light brush of my kit over the print and cap-tured it on adhesive tape as well.

I checked a few more places without luck and decided I had to be satisfied with this print. I turned to Trilling and said, "How long before we can get that thumbprint in the system?"

"Already done. I texted Walter to forward the print to all of his 'posse.'" We both had a laugh at that.

Walter was hard at work by the time we returned to the office.

As soon as he saw us, he jumped from his desk and rushed forward with a sheet of paper in his hand.

"We need to buy the guys at the Department of Defense a big cake or something. They got this back to me unbelievably fast." He handed me the photograph of a young Army officer. Walter said, "His name is Kevin Doyle. He was a Green Beret. He's also applied to several high-tech firms over the years."

I stared at the photo of the handsome young man. "You think this could be our killer?"

"I've just started running a background on him. I don't see any connection to Roger Dzoriack in any way. It's not like he was a nephew who came to visit. I'd say this is a pretty good suspect."

CHAPTER 100

I SAT WITH Rob Trilling and Walter Jackson. The three of us tried to think of ways to find Kevin Doyle. Walter had quietly recruited analysts from other squads to start running his name to see if he was listed in any hotels or had taken any flights into or out of the city recently.

Walter said, "I know we're supposed to keep this whole investigation on the down-low, but what if we issue a bulletin to every patrol car in the city just to keep an eye out for him?"

I shook my head. "This is a print from a supposed suicide's apartment. It's not an official active case. I can just imagine all the questions that would come streaming in from One Police Plaza. We gotta figure out something ourselves. I don't even want to let Celeste Cantor in on this until we have more. She still doesn't know that you and Terri are on this too—that was my choice, not hers."

I noticed Trilling hadn't said much and kept fiddling around with notes and drawings. I asked him what he was doing.

He was slow to answer, as usual. But this was a different kind of hesitancy. He was forming his thoughts. Finally, my young partner said, "We both agree someone intentionally tried to run down Jaime Nantes yesterday."

I nodded.

"That means Nantes would still be on the hit man's list."

Again I nodded.

"Maybe he'll try again. Nantes isn't any the wiser. He walks down to eat about the same time at the same place every day."

"You want to do more surveillance on that little bodega when Nantes is eating and *hope* we see this guy Kevin Doyle?"

"You boiled my idea down to one clear sentence."

"You don't think it would be risky, showing up there again, after we were carted away in cuffs?"

"If you're asking me if it'll work, I'm skeptical. If you have a better idea or something else we need to work on, I'll do that. Absent either of those options, I say we head up to the Bronx. I wouldn't mind one of their empanadas anyway." He gave me a look that made me smile.

"Now you're starting to sound like a veteran NYPD officer. Never be cold, never get wet, and never go hungry."

Trilling said, "I prefer the slogan *We always get our man*. Either way, I think we should go to the Bronx."

Walter said, "I'll keep working on this guy's background. I'll call you if I can find anything worthwhile."

My phone vibrated with a text from Terri Hernandez. I read it, then mumbled, "Damn." When Trilling and Walter looked at me, I said, "Terri's tied up at a homicide scene in the Bronx near the zoo. She's going to be stuck there for quite a while." Then I muttered, "Shit, we could've used her help given how well that gang now knows our faces."

Trilling said, "You and I should be able to handle it."

I said, "What if Jaime Nantes or one of the other gang members sees us? They think we're dead."

"True. But we don't have to go *in* the little restaurant. Guess I'll skip the empanadas. This won't screw up the DEA's case at all. Our surveillance will be at either end of that street. Exactly where someone looking to run down Nantes would park."

Walter slowly nodded. "Rob's right. It's a bit of a long shot, but it might work."

Trilling clapped his hands together and said to me, "What do you think?"

I was already gathering what I needed to go.

CHAPTER 101

KEVIN DOYLE SAT in the driver's seat of an older Chevy Trailblazer. Even with some rust holes, the smaller SUV still had enough weight to splatter someone across the street. Doyle had found the car just a few blocks away. Now he was waiting in the same spot he had a day ago: next to the popular chicken place, looking down the street to where Jaime Nantes would be strolling by on his way to eat at Island Delight.

Doyle planned to make the hit *before* Nantes walked into the restaurant. He wasn't going to risk his last target getting away from him. Doyle had already texted his employer that they had not finished the job with Bennett. He left off anything about what might have happened to "Joe."

Considering how much he had to pay Amir to dispose of another body, he doubted anyone would ever have a clue what happened to Joe. Sure, someone would miss him. Eventually. But in his line of work, there were far too many suspects for anyone to blame Doyle for his disappearance. At least that's how Doyle chose to look at it.

He had very specific plans today. Finish this hit from his original contract. Collect his few belongings from the hotel in Brooklyn. Dump this shitty Trailblazer, and grab the first flight he could from LaGuardia. He wasn't even sure where he wanted to go. He just wanted out of the greater New York City area. And frankly, at this point, Doyle didn't care if he ever came back.

He knew there'd be questions about Bennett, but once he was gone and had destroyed his burner cell phone, he didn't expect to hear anything more about it.

Doyle kept his eyes on the street. He knew a knucklehead like Nantes would never realize someone had intentionally tried to run him down the other day. He'd assume it was just a bad driver. Guys like that never really thought ahead or looked at the details of life surrounding them. They simply kind of blew through the day without paying much attention. That's what Doyle was counting on today.

His mind drifted back to the diner where Tammy worked. He'd gone a day and a half without driving past the diner. He was slowly starting to get the manipulative waitress off his mind. It took him a while to realize she was a little like his employer. She knew what buttons to push to make him do different things. The difference was, he'd known his employer a long time. Tammy had picked up on his weaknesses almost immediately. That was another reason he'd be glad to leave town. He was afraid he'd end up doing something stupid if he saw her again.

Doyle sucked in a deep breath, then let it out slowly. He had tried meditation and yoga classes, but nothing ever seemed to keep him as calm as he wanted to be. His mind focused only on concerns, never on pleasure. He intended to change that.

With any luck, Doyle would be somewhere far away by this time tomorrow. Then he could focus on what he actually wanted to do with his life. And maybe forget about everything he'd done with it up till now.

CHAPTER 102

I DIDN'T WANT to use my usual Impala, so I borrowed an unmarked Nissan Maxima to head back up to the Bronx. I was driving slowly and chugging the last few ounces of a Diet Coke when I looked to my right and recognized our suspect, Kevin Doyle, sitting in a Chevy Trailblazer. I think some Coke shot out of my nose, I was so surprised. I mumbled, "I can't freakin' believe this." But actually I could. Things like this happen all the time in police work. Going the extra step often seems to give us the answer to an insurmountable problem.

Of course, I never expected this to be one of those times. Rob Trilling was never going to let me forget it. I wouldn't, if one of *my* crazy ideas bore fruit this quickly.

I used my cell phone to get ahold of Trilling. He answered on the first ring. I said, "You're not going to believe this."

"I saw the way you passed the Trailblazer. Is he in the car?"

"I didn't think I was that obvious, but it surprised me to see him so quickly." I risked a quick glance up the street to make sure that moron, Jaime Nantes, wasn't already walking toward the bodega. Although watching that scumbag get splattered by the SUV would make it an easy case against our suspect, Doyle.

I took a turn around the block, and as I came up the street, a Volkswagen Jetta in front of Doyle's Trailblazer pulled away from the curb. I slipped the Maxima into the spot and backed up until I was almost touching the Trailblazer's bumper. I'd noticed a Mercedes parked directly behind Doyle and knew he had no room to get out quickly. If the Mercedes moved, Trilling would get into place behind him. That way we'd have him trapped between us.

The dark tinting on the Maxima's windows kept Doyle from seeing me clearly. I hoped my car didn't look too much like what it was, an unmarked police car. I considered the pros and cons of calling for backup. I settled for getting on the radio and calling the dispatcher. "Manhattan North Homicide is going to attempt to make an arrest. Any marked units in the area can call me direct on the radio." I gave them our exact location and the suspect's SUV description.

I saw no reason why we couldn't sit quietly for a few minutes until a couple of burly patrol officers stopped to help us. As long as we took Doyle into custody, there wouldn't be many questions. It would be an interesting few minutes in the long, usually dull day of a patrol officer.

I called Trilling and let him know the plan.

CHAPTER 103

KEVIN DOYLE FELT a run of nerves up the back of his neck as the Nissan parked tight in front of him, boxing him into his parking spot. He focused his attention on his target. He had to get out of the spot quickly without drawing attention to himself.

Then he saw someone walking on the street alongside the parked cars behind him. It took him only a moment to realize it was Bennett's partner, the young Army Ranger, Robert Trilling.

"Shit," mumbled Doyle. "So much for karma."

Then he saw the long, lanky figure of Michael Bennett himself step out of the Maxima parked in front of him. Doyle did a quick scan of the area. He wanted to avoid collateral damage if at all possible. He figured that was Bennett's goal as well.

Doyle's mind raced with possibilities. He felt the Beretta 9mm in his belt holster. That wasn't the answer. Not here with families picking up chicken for lunch. He tried to think of a better option.

He had roughly two seconds to come up with something and all his choices were bad.

He threw the rickety SUV into reverse and stomped on the gas. The motor raced as Doyle felt the crunch of the Mercedes's bumper behind him. He had an idea, but he wasn't sure if it could work. Goddamn physics.

Then he felt the rear tires catch and the back of the SUV start to lift. He was going to use the Mercedes like a ramp to get his SUV out onto the road. He no longer cared about Nantes. His only goal was to get out of town fast.

As the Trailblazer started to roll backward, he saw Bennett make his move.

That guy had balls.

CHAPTER 104

I TRIED TO look casual opening the door of my unmarked car. There was no reason to believe that Kevin Doyle knew what I looked like.

I didn't know what it was, but something spooked the shit out of Doyle. I wouldn't say he panicked. But he made a bold decision. He threw the Trailblazer into reverse and hit the gas.

Initially, the sound of the roaring engine made me jump away from the SUV. Then I realized he was trying to make some room behind him. All I knew was the vehicle moved backward and started climbing up onto the hood of the Mercedes parked behind it.

I was so shocked by the maneuver, I wasn't sure what to do. I went with my initial instinct. I ran forward and jumped onto the hood of the Trailblazer. I glanced over to my right as I gripped the top edge of the hood. Trilling had darted into the middle of the street, away from the Trailblazer.

My knuckles rubbed against the windshield wipers as I held on to the hood like I was riding a bull. I hooked my feet on the front and side of the vehicle to give myself some stability. When I looked through the windshield I could see Kevin Doyle's face clearly. He looked just as astonished as I did.

I removed my right hand for just an instant, trying to reach my pistol. That was a worse idea than jumping on the hood in the first place. Now Trilling was starting to approach the vehicle from the side on foot. I saw him catch Doyle's attention.

Then I felt my world start to tilt. It took me a moment to realize what was going on. I could feel gravity tugging on my right side. I could see things like paper, pens, and a comb inside the Trailblazer start to fly.

The SUV had ridden up over the Mercedes's hood, but now the driver-side tire was sliding off the roof of the Mercedes. The SUV rocked, then flopped onto its side in the street. My first fear was that Trilling had been caught underneath the tumbling vehicle. That thought lasted only a moment as I was tossed onto the asphalt and narrowly avoided a Kia as it swerved to miss the rolling SUV.

I somehow came up onto my hands and knees and looked over at the Trailblazer as it lay on its side with the wheels still spinning uselessly in the air.

This had not turned out anything like I had hoped.

CHAPTER 105

I STAYED ON my hands and knees in the middle of the street for just a few moments. I had to shake my head just to clear my vision. Where the hell was Trilling? I leaned down low and tried to look underneath the SUV on its side. There was no sign that Trilling had been crushed in the street. That made me breathe a little easier for just a moment. Then I saw a flash of movement and heard Trilling's voice.

It was very clear and strong. Trilling shouted, "Police, don't move!"

I struggled to get to my feet but still felt a little woozy. Then I heard the unmistakable sound of a pistol clattering onto the sidewalk. I hoped it was Doyle dropping his gun. A second later I realized that was one hope that was not going to be fulfilled.

Apparently, Trilling had surprised Doyle on the sidewalk after Doyle crawled out of the SUV through the shattered sunroof. Somehow Doyle had knocked Trilling's pistol out of his hand. Now the two were engaged in a tense standoff with fists raised.

Trilling threw a right that Doyle blocked easily. Then Doyle stepped in and used his forearm to smash Trilling across the jaw, knocking him back against the ruined Mercedes.

Doyle stepped farther away and Trilling rushed him, then ducked and made Doyle throw a punch over his head. Trilling launched two hard kicks that left Doyle doubled over in pain. But he straightened up quickly and drove his head directly into Trilling's chin.

I didn't like the way Trilling swayed backward and crumpled onto the sidewalk. Now I was on wobbly feet but starting to regain my senses.

Doyle took one look at me and realized immediately I wasn't a threat. He could see I was barely upright. I couldn't get my left eye to focus. Doyle looked past me up the street, searching for his target, Jaime Nantes. He was a professional. I wasn't sure if he wanted to fulfill his contract or just get away. It didn't matter.

Doyle dashed through the spot where his SUV had been parked. He started to run. I thought he was running toward me; in fact, he was running *past* me. I couldn't let that happen. I didn't care how I felt.

I acted completely and utterly on instinct. I'd never had any training from the NYPD to do what I did next. Maybe it was my years watching the NFL. As Doyle ran past me, I stuck out my left arm and managed to clothesline him.

I was just the right height, and his chin caught perfectly under my elbow. It snapped his head back and pulled his feet from under him all at the same time. He slammed onto the asphalt with his head hitting last. It was as satisfying a sensation as I had ever felt.

As I looked down at the semiconscious suspect, my knees started to give out. I dropped to the asphalt and tried to make it look like I was doing it on purpose. I still had enough brainpower to reach over and snatch the pistol from Doyle's belt holster.

About that time, Trilling was back on his feet. He stepped around the wrecked SUV, holding his chin and shaking his head. Blood had crusted along his lower lip and seeped out of his nose.

Trilling calmly said, "You okay?"

All I could manage was a nod.

Now I noticed the crowd of onlookers watching this drama unfold in the middle of the street. It had been free entertainment.

Trilling checked Doyle's eyes to see how badly he was injured. I guessed his assessment was positive because he then immediately rolled the suspect onto his side and handcuffed him behind his back. It was a professional and nicely performed maneuver.

All three of us sat in the middle of the asphalt as two patrol cars screeched to a halt on either side of us. Trilling and I both raised our hands to make sure there was no confusion.

I recognized the sergeant who stepped out of the car to my right. She smiled at me and said, "I knew, when I heard your voice on the radio, shit was about to go down."

I looked up at her. "Hello, Audrina. Do you think you could help us clean up this mess?"

"I'll call in some help. And you probably need to see a paramedic." She paused for a moment and added, "You *all* need to see a paramedic."

It was like a weight had been lifted off my chest. I laughed and nodded in agreement.

CHAPTER 106

WE WERE TAKING no chances with Kevin Doyle. After the paramedics cleared all of us to leave the scene, we raced directly back to our office with our suspect. Because our squad is housed in an office building, we weren't supposed to bring handcuffed prisoners up the elevators. Which made things a little tricky because there was no way we were going to take the handcuffs off a guy like Doyle. Not after the way he'd knocked Trilling around.

We simply draped a windbreaker over his wrists. It looked like he was carrying a jacket behind him. He didn't seem to mind. Doyle seemed to have resigned himself to the situation, but he was smart and hadn't really said anything. He answered our basic questions with yes or no but hadn't offered anything else. We got him settled in the conference room, handcuffing his left wrist to a rolling desk chair and queuing up our recording equipment.

Trilling added an extra shackle on his ankle, connected to the heavy, wooden chair at the end of the table. We also made sure someone was sitting with him every second.

After I read him his rights and offered him some food, I figured it was time to get down to business. Walter Jackson was furiously working on Doyle's background. I had no doubt that Walter would find some detail we could use in the interview. We just needed to give him a little time. Doyle hadn't asked for an attorney yet, so we were free to keep maneuvering and asking questions.

We tried a couple of friendly questions but got nowhere. I decided it was time to start swinging a little harder. I looked directly at Doyle and said, "Looks like you've killed a lot of retired cops."

That seemed to hit home a little bit. Doyle looked down at the faux-oak conference table.

I kept up the pressure. "I would've thought someone with your background would understand service and duty. It's not like you're some crazy kid thinking you're fighting fascism by killing cops. You know what it means to sacrifice. You're a veteran, for Christ's sake."

Doyle nodded his head slowly. But still didn't say anything.

"We found your thumbprint on Roger Dzoriack's kitchen faucet. That's how we were able to identify you. Can you explain why you were in a retired NYPD detective's apartment just before he supposedly committed suicide?"

Doyle shook his head. But the revelation obviously shook him. He seemed a little more agitated. His left index finger started tapping on the chair where he was handcuffed. When he looked up, he was biting his lower lip.

I said, "You can't explain away your print in his apartment. You're a smart guy. You gotta realize you're all done. The only question is, are you prepared to spend the rest of your life in prison, or will you tell us why you killed these cops? Was it personal? Or did someone hire you?" I didn't bring up the dead drug dealers yet. I still wanted to appeal to his sense of duty.

Again, Doyle didn't say anything. But I could sense that he was obviously conflicted. I glanced over at Trilling, hoping he had something to add. He looked like he wanted to speak, so I nodded.

Trilling engaged Doyle directly. "I was in the Army too. I ended up in the Rangers. In one of the last combat deployments. What about you? I haven't had a chance to read your file completely."

I was surprised to finally hear Doyle's scratchy and tired voice. "I mustered out at Fort Bragg. I was a Green Beret."

Trilling said, "No shit. You've fallen a long way."

Doyle hung his head again and mumbled, "I know."

CHAPTER 107

I LEFT ROB TRILLING to try to soften Kevin Doyle up. When I stepped out of the conference room, they were chatting about their time in the military. Trilling was careful not to drift back into any incriminating subjects. We wanted Doyle to talk, not go silent.

It was late afternoon, an awkward time between lunch and dinner, but I realized we were all hungry so I got us some pizza from the little place around the corner. As I was bringing it back to the conference room, I noticed Walter Jackson working on two computers at once. That was always a good sign for an investigation he was involved in. I didn't even bother him. He seemed to be onto something fairly big. I was hoping we could use it to convince Doyle to talk.

Doyle, Trilling, and I wolfed down a couple of slices of cheese and pepperoni. It wasn't bad. The food revived me, and the off-brand cola gave me a little sugar boost. God knows I needed it.

Trilling turned to me and said, "This guy has been on some high-profile missions. He was in the mountains of Afghanistan for five months straight. Very impressive."

I saw what Trilling was doing. Showing Doyle we didn't view him as a mad-dog killer. We respected his service to the country. We just wanted to talk.

I had seen in his file that Doyle was originally from Brooklyn. "Let me guess. You're an Irish Catholic kid. You probably grew up with a bunch of siblings and cousins."

That made Doyle smile for the briefest moment possible. He said, "Two sisters and a brother. And some older cousins who lived right next door to us."

"You were never lonely."

"It prepared me for living in a barracks. Snoring and noise didn't bother me like it bothers a lot of guys in the service. As long as no one was peeing in the bed next to me, it was a step up from my childhood." He spoke as if he was remembering what his life was like before he turned into a contract killer.

I didn't push it. I sat there, thinking up my next angle of attack. That's when Doyle surprised me.

He said, "Would it be possible to speak with a priest?"

"You mean, like, for confession?"

"That's exactly what I mean. And Communion."

Trilling said out loud, "Where will we find a priest to come to our office on such short notice?"

I said, "I know one." I explained to Doyle my grandfather's position in the church, how Seamus had become a priest later in life, as a widower after having a wife and family and owning a local bar. "He may not be what you consider a typical Catholic priest, but I swear to God he's a good man. Down to his very soul. He believes in God as strongly as anyone I've ever met. And he will not tell me one thing you say. This will have nothing to do with our case—you have my word on it."

Doyle looked up at me and nodded. "I know your reputation. I'll accept your word as gold."

I was on the phone to Seamus before I even left the conference room.

CHAPTER 108

I WAS SURPRISED how quickly my grandfather showed up at the office, especially since he'd even taken the time to put on his full vestments and had brought a little satchel with everything he needed. He was ready to get to work immediately.

My grandfather and Walter chatted for a moment before I led Seamus to the conference room.

I took my grandfather aside. "I'm afraid this isn't normal circumstances. This guy is super dangerous. He's told me he won't try anything crazy if we leave him alone with you in the room. That said, I want you to stay on the opposite side of the conference table. We're leaving one of the blinds open so we can look in on you. Anything else you need from me?"

Seamus shook his head. "As long as you realize I'll never say anything about what he tells me in there."

"I don't need you to tell me anything. I'd like to know the

extent of the guy's victims list. I'm hoping if he thinks he's right with God, he'll try to make it right with us as well."

My grandfather gave me a sly smile. "If he sets himself right with God, he doesn't need to worry about being right with anyone else."

I patted him on the shoulder and walked him to the door. Trilling greeted him, then left the room to give Doyle privacy.

Doyle sat quietly at the end of the conference room table. I said, "Kevin, this is my grandfather, Seamus Bennett. You can quiz him about if he's going to talk. But I can already tell you he won't. I've told my grandfather not to get any closer to you than the end of the conference room table, and I'll be watching from outside. Does all that sound reasonable to you?"

"What about Communion?"

"When you take Communion after your confession, I'll have to come in and stand here while you do it."

Doyle said, "That sounds fair."

I left them in the conference room and sat at an empty desk right outside. Walter Jackson approached me almost immediately and squeezed into the chair next to mine. He looked anxious. That wasn't like him.

"What d'ya got for me, Walter?"

He shuffled a few pages around. He signaled for Rob Trilling to join us. I took a quick glance into the conference room. Doyle had his head bowed but was talking. I turned back to Walter.

Walter cleared his throat a couple of times, then said, "I found something I didn't expect in his background."

"Can't wait."

"Doyle was raised in Brooklyn."

"We knew that. It was in his DoD file and we've already talked to him about it."

"His father's oldest brother and family appear to have lived in the house next door. They had three girls and one boy. All would be cousins to our man, Doyle."

"Walter, we're on the clock here. Can you get to the point? Is there anything important about his cousins?"

Walter shifted his bulk in the chair uneasily. "The oldest of those cousins is a Celeste Doyle, who now goes by her married name: Celeste Cantor."

I couldn't speak. I just stared at Walter Jackson. I knew he hadn't made a mistake. This was the sort of thing he'd check from five different angles.

Everything immediately became clear. I knew what this was all about now. The Land Sharks had done something bad. And Celeste Cantor was eliminating everyone — former colleagues and criminals alike — who could derail her campaign.

Trilling looked just as shocked as I was. Then I said, "We have to move fast. She's going to find out pretty quick he's in lockup. If Doyle agrees to help us, we might be able to bag Cantor and make a decent case."

Trilling said, "Do you think he'll help?"

"I do. I don't think he would've asked for a priest otherwise." And I really believed that.

CHAPTER 109

SEAMUS STOOD UP and tapped on the door. That was my signal to come in so that he could administer Communion to Doyle. I waited just inside the door and watched silently as my grandfather prepared the wine and host and recited the litany. Doyle moved only his head to take the Communion wafer and drink from the chalice.

As my grandfather packed up his satchel and headed out of the conference room, he turned and said to Doyle, "Bless you, my son. The first step in any redemption is admitting your mistakes."

Seamus made a point of looking down at the floor and not making eye contact with me or Trilling as he hurried out of the office. I wasn't sure what that meant.

Doyle appeared decidedly more confident. Making his confession and receiving Holy Communion had clearly taken a weight off of him. He sat up straight in the chair, looked at me, and said, "I'll tell you one thing for sure."

"I'm all ears."

"I screwed up. I listened to the wrong people."

"Like your cousin, Celeste."

That had exactly the kind of effect I was hoping it would. Doyle seemed stunned by the comment. He tried to come up with the words to express it, but he was at a loss.

I said, "It looks like she had you murder a lot of decent people just so she could advance her own career."

Doyle still looked like he wasn't sure he wanted to talk about it.

"I might not be able to make a case against her. It might not even affect her campaign. You're our only link to her. We could use an assist."

Rob Trilling had stepped into the room with me. He sat down next to Doyle. They spoke quietly for a minute, Doyle nodding. Knowing the two of them had talked for a while privately, I was hoping Trilling had a better rapport with the former Army officer.

Then Doyle turned to me and said, "I'm not looking for anything off my sentence. I know I couldn't *get* anything off my sentence. But if I help you guys make a case, what would I have to do? How much do I have to admit to?"

I thought about it for a moment. "You've got to own up to the murders in this case. That's the most important thing."

"And you won't ask me any questions about my past?"

"I won't, but I can't guarantee someone else won't ask down the road." That seemed to satisfy him.

Doyle said, "If you bring me a pen and paper, uncuff one of

my hands, and bring me another soda, I can start making a list of everyone related to my cousin's case. To be clear, Celeste has been very careful. We've only met about this twice in person. But I'll do what I can."

I wished everyone who tried to help us was as sincere.

CHAPTER 110

I HAD TO recruit help immediately. This was way too much for Rob Trilling and me to handle by ourselves. First, I drafted a detective from our squad to sit in the conference room with Kevin Doyle. I told him to sit at the other end of the conference table. And not to engage him in conversation but to stay alert. I wasn't taking any chances with a former Green Beret who had already proven he really did know multiple ways to kill someone.

Trilling asked, "What do we do next?"

"Our problem is keeping this quiet. Celeste Cantor knows everyone at One Police Plaza. The Land Sharks were a popular unit. I'm worried about someone making an offhand comment that could blow the whole case against her."

"How do we get around that?"

I smiled. "I've already called in some help."

"I thought Hernandez was on another homicide. Who'd you call?"

"Dennis Wu in Internal Affairs."

Trilling looked unconvinced. He knew how much enthusiasm Dennis Wu had shown for pinning our recent sniper case on him. Trilling had felt like the Internal Affairs detective sergeant only wanted to make an arrest and it didn't matter who. I understood his concerns.

"Look, I'm not happy about working with Wu either. And I know he's a dick. But we need help, and I know for a fact he's salivating at the chance to make a case against an inspector."

That seemed to satisfy Trilling, though he still wasn't thrilled about it. I started to consider all the options we had to make a case. Clearly, the most effective and efficient method would be to set up a meeting between Kevin Doyle and his cousin, Celeste Cantor. We'd have a transmitter on Doyle and see if Cantor made any incriminating statements during the conversation.

A lot could go wrong with that plan. We'd have to let Doyle loose in public. Even if we had twenty people to cover wherever we held the meeting, the man was still a threat, and a flight risk. This is a calculation made for all active police investigations: safety versus success. Doyle had agreed to help, and it felt like he would honor his pledge. But once he was uncuffed and in public, a guy with his skills could raise holy hell.

The flip side of that was the target of our investigation now: Celeste Cantor. She was a veteran cop who had been involved in hundreds of undercover meetings over the years. She'd smell a rat a mile away. And there was no telling what she'd do if she realized she was cornered.

So I sat at my desk wondering what was going to cause me

more heartburn: a crooked cop or a former Green Beret who had just admitted to a boatload of murders. I wished we could use the Emergency Service Unit, but that risked the possibility of Celeste Cantor somehow hearing about it.

As I kept going through it in my mind, the front door to our office opened and in walked IA Detective Sergeant Dennis Wu. *Great.* I glanced over at Trilling sitting a desk away. The young officer rarely showed strong emotion, but I would describe the glare he gave Wu as "malevolent." That felt like a good word for the situation.

I nodded to Wu as he navigated the office. He was wearing his usual dark suit, though his perfect hair was a little out of alignment. I thought it had more to do with his excitement at taking down an inspector than anything else. Maybe that was how he'd made it to the office in record time. He gave off the vibe of a ten-year-old on his birthday.

He stopped a few feet from my desk and said, "If this is a prank, it's not funny."

I said, "Dennis, in what world would I entice you to come to our office for a laugh?"

Wu looked over at Trilling and said, "No hard feelings about the sniper case?"

Trilling didn't acknowledge Wu's existence. That was savage. I had to hide a smile.

Wu said, "I want to meet this contract killer and hear your plan before I agree to anything."

"I don't need you to agree. We need help, but if you're not the right person for it, I'll find someone else."

Wu considered it for a full ten seconds. Then he nodded his head and said, "You're the one on the hook for this if things go bad. I guess I can go along for the ride." He looked around the office, then turned back to me. "Why did you call me in? I'm just curious."

"I called you because you're an asshole. But you're an asshole with no connection to the Land Sharks and I know you're straight-up. All the time."

Wu gave me a satisfied smile. "I appreciate all of that. Thank you."

CHAPTER 111

DENNIS WU WAS rightfully skeptical about Kevin Doyle's motives for helping us. Hell, I was too.

Wu took me aside in the office. "I'm a little concerned about the scope of this thing. This sort of operation should have a lot more detectives on it."

"I'm worried about a bigger operation getting back to Inspector Cantor. Do you want to call in some more of your people from IA?"

Wu thought about it, then said, "Most of them are tied up on something else. Besides, I go by the old saying: *The fewer men, the greater the glory.*" He looked pleased with himself.

"Are you paraphrasing Shakespeare's *Henry V*? Or just looking to score some points for the next promotional exams?"

"Why can't it be both?"

I had to give him that one. I even chuckled out loud. Wu grinned.

Then he got serious. "You really think Inspector Cantor was out here having her cousin clean up her history just for a goddamn City Council job?"

"No, I don't. I think she has higher aspirations. Something like mayor."

Wu shrugged. "I guess it's not that far-fetched. She's smart, telegenic, and, apparently, ruthless."

Wu wanted to interview Kevin Doyle himself to satisfy his concerns about Doyle's credibility. I sat in the conference room while they spoke. I hated to admit it, but Wu was professional and efficient.

As they were wrapping up, Wu leaned in closer to Doyle. "This should go smoothly. But I want you to understand that I will do anything I have to if you try to escape. I'm not going to have a confessed murderer running around in public. I want to be straight with you right from the start."

Doyle looked past Wu to me. He said in a calm voice, "I've already explained to Detective Bennett why I'm doing this." Then he looked back at Wu. "You do what you think your duty dictates. I'm doing what I feel I need to do, to clear at least some of my conscience."

Wu slapped the top of the conference table. "We've got a rodeo."

That sounded like Wu approved of our plan.

CHAPTER 112

BEFORE WE GOT too excited about making a case, we needed Kevin Doyle to make a recorded phone call to his cousin, Celeste Cantor.

Dennis Wu, Rob Trilling, and I sat in the conference room with Doyle still handcuffed to his chair and shackled to the wooden chair next to him. We carefully cuffed his right hand to the chair as we released his left hand. We hooked a recorder to fit in Doyle's ear, which would allow each of us to listen to the call as well. We gave Doyle back his cheap burner phone and he dialed the number to Cantor's burner phone.

She answered after two rings, sounding concerned. "What's up?"

We had already briefed Doyle on what to say. "All done. But I want to meet with you for a few minutes."

"Why?"

"Need to clear a few things up. No big deal, but I'm leaving early in the morning. Can we just grab coffee or a bite somewhere?"

Cantor gave him the name of a family-owned Italian place in Williamsburg over in Brooklyn, Mama Rosa's. We had an hour and half to scout it and set up. I hated doing things on such a constricted timeline, but there were really no other choices. I felt my lieutenant's absence acutely. Normally, Harry Grissom would run interference with the brass, recruit others to help, and generally be a calming and insightful voice on an operation like this. I guess you don't really appreciate people until they're not around. When Harry got back from vacation, I intended to let him know how much I had missed him. For now, everyone was looking to me for guidance.

I rummaged around the storage closet where we kept extra equipment, recorders, transmitters, and anything else we didn't use on a daily basis. After a moment, I found an off-white heavy T-shirt our tech unit had created for us. It had a concealed Kevlar patch covering the chest and most of the stomach. I also had one of our tech guys sew a tracker into the hem of it, something we used with informants. I'd be able to follow Doyle from a program on my phone if things went bad.

When Trilling and Wu stepped out of the conference room with Doyle, I explained about the shirt. I said, "It's designed for protection against small- and medium-caliber pistols. It wouldn't do much against a rifle. But I'm going to need you to wear it under your shirt just in case."

"You think my own cousin might shoot me?"

"Until today I thought your cousin was one of the most stand-up cops I'd ever met. I'm not taking any chances. You need to wear the shirt."

By this time there was no one in the office except us and Walter Jackson. We waited while Doyle stripped down. I noticed a number of scars and at least three bullet wounds on his torso. I didn't ask about them right now. But I was curious how much combat he had seen.

I raced ahead to check out the restaurant, and I found a table where I could sit in the back of Mama Rosa's near a three-piece band. I could tell by looking at the serving staff and probably one or two members of the band that it really was all one big family here. A pillar with plaster effigies of Cupid and a chariot laced across the top stood next to my table. I didn't know whether that was good or bad. The pillar would hide me but would also block my view.

We were using our phones for communication. No need to make this operation obvious over the radio. I let Trilling know I was set up. The plan was simple. I was far enough away that hopefully Cantor wouldn't notice me. Trilling would wear a Mets cap and sit at the bar in sight of the booth where Kevin Doyle would sit, since Cantor didn't know Trilling well. We had already decided that Dennis Wu would be our outside surveillance member. Part of it was because Cantor might notice the Internal Affairs detective sergeant. Part of it was just me being a little bit of an ass to him. I sort of liked the feeling.

CHAPTER 113

I ORDERED A Chicken Parmesan so as not to seem suspicious to the surly waiter. He looked like he was probably related to the family who ran the place. It was something about his deep-set dark eyes and Roman nose. I guessed it was his sister or cousin playing guitar in the band. The drummer and bass player had crooked noses and healthier complexions.

A young man, around sixteen years old, joined the group with a handheld microphone. As the band started playing the opening to "Crimson and Clover," the teen with a microphone strayed too close to the speaker and caused a horrendous feedback squelch. This seemed to be a pretty common occurrence. None of the staff even acknowledged it. That's what clinched it for me that the band was part of the family. No restaurant owner would put up with that otherwise.

I got a text from Wu saying Doyle and Trilling were headed

into the restaurant. At almost the same time, the front door opened, and Doyle spoke to the hostess for a moment. When she led him to a booth, I saw Trilling move on to the bar and take the last stool. I felt confident there was no way anyone would notice me in the corner. I decided that the cover the column provided was a plus as well.

About fifteen minutes later, right on schedule, Wu texted me from the outside that Inspector Celeste Cantor had just parked her car down the street and was walking toward the restaurant. Until that exact moment, I had doubts that Doyle had been telling us the truth. Something inside me wanted Cantor to *not* be involved. But that's not how real life happens.

Cantor walked directly to the booth, leaned down, and kissed her cousin on the cheek. Then she slid into the booth across from him.

It was a shock to see my friend of twenty years strolling into the restaurant to meet a hit man she'd hired to kill numerous former colleagues. It didn't matter that the two of them were related. Cantor was part of this scheme, and there was no way I was going to let her get out of this restaurant unless she was under arrest. I felt like I had to make this right for all the dead retired cops.

I casually slipped an earpiece into my right ear. I could hear everything that was said in the booth. So could Trilling and Dennis Wu. We had a small transmitter in Doyle's front pocket. The others would key off of whatever I did. When I made my move toward the booth, Trilling was to join me from the bar. Wu's job was to secure the outside in case Cantor tried to run. It was a simple plan. But every cop knows a plan can go sideways awfully fast. Or as the old saying goes, everyone has a plan until they get punched in the face. I was hoping to avoid anything like that.

CHAPTER 114

I HAD A good position behind the column. I was tucked away but could still see Celeste Cantor and Kevin Doyle at their booth. I had an earpiece to listen in. Any time someone's conversation is being monitored and recorded, I get anxious, waiting to hear if the suspect will incriminate themselves. It was no different tonight. Even with the distracting band a few feet from me, I could hear the conversation clearly over my earpiece.

I listened to them chat for a minute, catching up about family and their childhood memories. It was like any normal conversation between two adult cousins. Then Doyle switched the conversation to business. He said, "I'm done with the job you gave me. All the retirees as well as the drug runners."

Cantor didn't answer immediately. Finally, she said, "What happened with Bennett?"

"We never really got a chance with him."

"I haven't heard from Joe. He's not answering his phone. How was it working with him?"

Doyle shrugged. "I haven't seen him since we bailed on catching Bennett at his office. But I gotta tell ya, you shouldn't associate with those kinds of guys. He's a disgrace."

"Because of what he does for a living?"

"Because of what comes out of his mouth."

That seemed to satisfy her. The waiter came over, but Cantor dismissed him quickly, telling him to bring two waters and two glasses of house red.

Out of the blue, Doyle mumbled, "I didn't like killing cops."

Cantor reached across and patted his arm. "I know. I didn't like it either. But we have to look toward the greater good. Think what I can accomplish on the City Council. Think where that might lead. We both grew up here. It's not the same city that we knew. I can change that."

"That doesn't make it right."

"No, no, it doesn't. But it was necessary. I'm sorry you had to be involved, but you're the only one I could trust." She looked at Doyle for a moment, then said, "Is there any chance Bennett knows anything?"

Doyle shrugged. "How would I know?"

"When, exactly, did you plan on leaving the city?"

"Like I said, tomorrow morning."

Cantor didn't say anything for a moment. She was thinking. Then she said, "I know Bennett. He won't give up. I think you need to wait a few days before you leave. Maybe try again."

"You want me to try again to kill Detective Bennett? That's going to take more planning and time. And my costs go up too."

I glanced through the restaurant, sensing that things might be coming to a head. I was particularly satisfied that Doyle had used the word "kill" instead of some euphemism. It would help when the case went to court.

Cantor feigned a frown like she was actually sad. She reached across the table to tenderly touch Doyle's shoulder. Then she pinched his cheek. It looked like a doting aunt harassing a young nephew.

I was trying not to be obvious as I leaned forward slightly to look past the pillar in front of me. Thankfully, the band took a break. There was no one to really see me tucked away in the corner, so I shifted my seat to where I could have a better angle on Doyle and Cantor's booth. There were maybe thirty people in the place. I wondered how we could do this without anyone noticing.

When I looked past Cantor, I noticed the wide window facing the street. And leaning on a car just outside was Dennis Wu. I didn't know if he thought he was invisible or just assumed no one would bother to look out the giant window. Like a guy in a suit just waiting around doesn't stand out. Wu might as well have been looking in the window with his hands cupped at the sides of his head.

I reached for my phone to tell him to back away. Then I looked up and saw it was too late.

CHAPTER 115

I COULD SEE Celeste Cantor do a double take when she glanced out the window and recognized Dennis Wu. She was smart and had real street experience. She didn't hesitate to reach across and pat Doyle's chest. Then she reached into his pocket. She pulled out the tiny microphone that was transmitting to us. She stared at the tiny mic but didn't jerk it out of Doyle's pocket.

Cantor flopped back in the booth like she was exhausted. She was silent for a moment. Then she said, "Kevin, what have you done?"

"I had to. This whole thing just wasn't right. I've made my peace with my decision." He couldn't look his cousin in the eye. He stared down at the table and fumbled with the microphone, trying to stick it back into his pocket. He was as disoriented as Cantor.

I glanced over at the bar to get Trilling's attention. He was already looking at me for direction. I waited, still mostly out of sight of Cantor. The pillar gave me great comfort. I just hoped it was solid if things went bad. I kept my earpiece in. Cantor was burying herself on the recording.

Then she let out a sob. I could see her face flushed red from all the way across the restaurant. Right now, no one was noticing anything out of the ordinary. The soft clink of dishes and conversation drifted over the restaurant.

Cantor muttered something and stood up. Doyle stayed seated in the booth. She stuck her right hand into her purse. I knew what she was reaching for. Hell, everyone in this situation would know what she was reaching for.

Doyle saw her motion and started to move. I reflexively drew my Glock even as I calculated outcomes in my head. Would it escalate things? Could I talk Cantor out of it? How many civilians were left exposed? I knew I'd be too slow to react, but I managed to shout, "No!"

Then Cantor pulled out a small semiautomatic pistol.

Doyle froze in place, the gray gunmetal attracting all of his attention.

She pointed the pistol toward Doyle. He didn't flinch. He sat back down completely and kept looking at the barrel of the gun. That was experience. Clearly he'd had guns pointed at him in the past.

Cantor hesitated for a moment.

Doyle started to speak. "Celeste, I—" He was cut off.

Cantor fired off three quick shots. Doyle was knocked back against the booth, then fell onto the seat. I couldn't see him at all.

I was still in shock. But I had to think about all the civilians in the room. I grabbed the microphone that had been left onstage, turned it on, and tossed it toward the speaker, causing a loud and immediate feedback squelch.

I wanted Cantor to focus on me while she held a gun in her hand. And that's exactly what I got. She turned toward the noise quickly, even as patrons were falling over one another to get out of the way. She saw me standing next to the pillar.

I motioned for her to drop the gun. I was hoping she'd come to her senses and think about all the years she'd spent in the police department. I wanted her to do the right thing more than I could say.

Trilling slid off his barstool and ducked down to take cover as he drew his pistol.

Then Cantor raised her pistol and pointed it at my face.

There was nothing I could do.

CHAPTER 116

I STARED AT the barrel of Celeste Cantor's gun for a split second. Then I ducked behind the pillar as she fired, twice. One of the bullets struck the pillar. Pieces of plaster and a shattered effigy of Cupid floated to the floor. Some plaster blew into my face.

Even blinking hard to flush out some of the dust from my eyes, I could tell the restaurant was in chaos. People were rushing into the kitchen to get out the back door. The guitar player from the band started to come onto the stage to grab her Gibson. The drummer seized her by the hips and yanked her into the kitchen.

I heard another gunshot, but it didn't seem aimed at me. I peeked around the pillar. Cantor had noticed Rob Trilling and was firing at him. I couldn't see Doyle either on the bench of the booth or on the ground.

Now Cantor refocused on me. She started shuffling toward me like a zombie with the gun held up in her right hand. I knew

I'd be in trouble as soon as she had a clear target. Though I had my own gun out of its holster, I was hesitant to shoot. I didn't want to shoot Cantor. I didn't want to accidentally shoot any patrons. I didn't want to shoot anyone.

I sucked in a breath. Made sure my Glock was seated properly in my right hand. Then I stepped from behind the column.

We stared at each other with our pistols up. She kept shuffling toward me.

I said in a loud voice, "Drop the gun, Celeste." Then I added, "Please." I tried to *will* her to drop the gun.

Cantor shook her head slowly and mumbled, "Why?"

I caught Dennis Wu out of the corner of my eye. He moved right next to the window on the outside. He fired his pistol, shattering the wide window and distracting Cantor for just a moment.

She turned to shoot at Wu. Trilling and I had no choice. We both fired our pistols at exactly the same time.

CHAPTER 117

THE GUNFIRE FROM Rob Trilling and me only made the chaotic situation worse. There were at least eight injured people in the restaurant that I could see. Most had been hurt in the stampede to get out. Hearing gunshots didn't help the people who were unable to move.

Celeste Cantor was on the floor of the restaurant. She was bleeding from her left shoulder and right side. At least that's what I gathered from my position. She looked like she was conscious, and I wasn't sure exactly where her pistol was.

I yelled to Trilling, "What do you see?"

"She's on the ground and the pistol is near her right hand." It sounded like Trilling was keeping his position by the bar.

I'd stepped out from the cover I had ducked behind as soon as I'd fired. Suddenly, the restaurant felt like the quietest place on Earth. Aside from someone crying near the front door, there was no sound at all. A piece of glass dropped from the window Wu had shot out. It fell like the blade of a guillotine and sounded like a car crash in the quiet restaurant.

An overturned chair was on the floor between Cantor and me. She made a sound, and as I stepped closer I could see the pistol just past her right hand.

Her eyes seemed to focus. She reached for the gun. I leapt over the chair and landed a couple of feet away. She grasped the pistol in her right hand and immediately stuck the barrel under her chin.

I literally fell on top of her. My free hand wrapped around her wrist. She felt remarkably strong, but I wasn't sure if it was real or I was imagining it because I was so frightened. I managed to yank the gun a few inches from her chin at the same time she pulled the trigger. The sound of the pistol firing was stunning. The fact that it was only a few inches from my face and ears compounded the effect.

I couldn't hear anything as I wrestled the gun completely away from Cantor. After reholstering my own gun, I dropped the magazine on hers and pulled back the slide, ejecting the round that was in the chamber. I secured her gun in my belt as my senses slowly started to return to normal.

Finally, I had a chance to check Cantor's wounds. The shoulder wound wasn't bleeding too badly. I immediately applied pressure to the bullet hole in her side. That one was oozing blood way too fast. I used both hands and leaned into it.

Trilling came over to check on me, but I shouted for him to help the customers on the ground.

Wu hustled in and started helping Trilling with a teenage girl who appeared to be pretty badly hurt. She was crying and her leg was bent at an awkward angle.

Cantor cleared her throat and stared up at me. I could see that her pupils were dilated. She might have been going into shock. She mumbled something. I leaned down slightly, hoping to hear her better.

She said, "Mike, Mike, what have I done? I screwed up so bad."

Blood continued to pour out of her wound. It seeped between my fingers and started pooling on the floor.

I told her to hang on, help would be on the way soon. But Celeste Cantor just started drifting off.

I looked over at Trilling and Wu. They appeared to have the young woman settled and calmed down.

At almost the same time, we all seemed to remember Kevin Doyle. I jerked my head toward the booth as Trilling's and Wu's heads snapped in that direction as well.

The booth was empty.

CHAPTER 118

THERE WAS A clear trail of blood leading from the booth to the front door. Kevin Doyle had run out of the restaurant during all the confusion.

I grabbed the first responding uniformed officer. He had a first aid kit with him and was able to put a bandage on Celeste Cantor's shoulder wound, which seemed to help stem the flow of blood, then he took over in trying to keep her worse side wound in check until EMTs arrived. Then I went to Trilling and told him we were going after Doyle.

Dennis Wu said, "I'll come with you guys."

I said, "I appreciate the attitude. I really do. But you need to direct things here, Wu. There'll be a ton of cops and paramedics rolling in here with a lot of questions."

Wu just nodded and immediately turned to help a woman who had suffered some sort of cut across her face.

I brought up the phone app for the tracker we'd sewn into the hem of the shirt I had given Doyle. It took a second to catch the signal. Trilling followed me out of the restaurant and onto the sidewalk.

I turned to Trilling and said, "Looks like he's a couple of blocks over that way." I pointed to the southwest. We jogged in the direction the tracker sent us. "Now he's staying in one place. He might be hiding behind a dumpster." I turned to look at Trilling. I wanted him to know how serious I was. "We take this one as carefully as possible. He may not have a gun, but he's still really dangerous. He might be setting up some kind of ambush for us. Or at least anyone who might be following him."

I couldn't help but notice that while I was panting a little bit during our jog, Trilling was not. He followed what I was saying and nodded.

We turned a corner and were immediately met by a crowd of young people. A haze of pot smoke covered the corner.

I slid to a stop and asked the first young man I saw, "Did you see a guy in a blue shirt run past here?" I didn't want to depend on unproven technology completely. Eyewitnesses were still pretty important.

The twentysomething man said, "Sure, man. He gave us some weed." He held a giant joint right in front of my face.

I turned and started to jog again, mumbling, "Jackass."

A girl in the group grabbed Trilling by his arm. She said in sort of a loud voice, "Hey, good-looking."

Trilling tried to squirm away. I slowed down to see if he needed help.

Then the girl leaned in and said in a quieter voice, "He ran down that way. Don't say anything to my friends."

Trilling nodded and broke into a run as soon as she let go of his arm.

The signal from the tracker showed that we were getting very close. I said to Trilling, "He's right around the corner."

We both pulled out our duty weapons, and Trilling broke off to the other side of the alley. I took a quick peek around the corner and saw that it was a wide alley with dumpsters on both sides. I used the building's wall as cover.

Across the alley from me, Trilling was carefully doing the same thing. The app on my phone told me Doyle was within fifty feet. I came around the corner, now using a dumpster to cover me.

I froze when I saw a man standing in the middle of the alley. He was talking to someone sitting on a small crate. The man was animated as he spoke to the other person. He wore an old Members Only jacket.

I stepped from behind the dumpster and said, "Police! Don't move!"

The man in the alley immediately raised his hands.

I couldn't completely see the other person. I said, "Step all the way into the alley. Let me see your hands." My heart was pounding in my chest. The other man stepped into the alley next to his friend. He wasn't Kevin Doyle either.

I holstered my pistol and motioned for the men to lower their hands. As I eased closer, I realized that under his jacket, the man wore the white T-shirt I had given Doyle.

I looked down at my tracking app on the phone. It confirmed my suspicions. I asked the man where he'd gotten the shirt. I had him open his jacket so I could see it better. There was a bullet hole in the chest that had hit the Kevlar patch. Two more holes were lower on the shirt. Both had passed through the fabric. Each was rimmed with a bloodstain.

"A dude gave it to me just a few minutes ago." He pointed in the direction Doyle had fled.

I already knew it was too late to chase him.

CHAPTER 119

I HEARD THE first media report about Celeste Cantor's arrest before I even got home that night. Every publication and TV station associated with the city was leaning in on this story. I didn't blame them — it was a big deal. But I noticed the pieces on the story had more gusto than usual. The media love to bring up police misbehavior almost as much as they like to ignore great police work.

It is something cops had to come to terms with a long time ago. Especially me.

I wondered if Harry Grissom's travel companion, Lois Frang, regretted not being in the city for this. She was a reporter for the *Brooklyn Democrat* and had proven to me on our last big case that she was a very good journalist. One I trusted and didn't mind talking to. She also tended to tell the entire story, not just the sensationalized talking points most news organizations put out.

I had texted Harry earlier to give him a brief outline of the case. He might be on vacation, but I knew he'd be upset if he read this in the paper or heard it on the news rather than hearing about it from me.

Once again, the only one still awake when I got home was Brian. My eldest son was interested in the case. He'd seen a couple of brief stories on the arrest of Inspector Cantor but with no details. It was awfully nice to sit with my son, watch the news for a little bit, and unwind before I tried to sleep.

Mary Catherine didn't stir as I slipped into bed. I even managed to get out of the bedroom the following morning without waking her. Technically, I was now on leave because of the shooting. So I made a giant breakfast for all the kids and got them all off to school without a hitch.

Dennis Wu texted to tell me that Celeste Cantor was in stable condition and expected to make a full recovery. Everyone available was looking for Kevin Doyle. I knew a guy like that was smart enough to get out of the city. He'd probably left last night. Still, I appreciated hearing from Wu. Maybe he wasn't entirely the unredeemable asshole we'd all made him out to be.

I slipped back into bed after bringing Mary Catherine some toast and juice. We cuddled for a few minutes. Then she lay across my chest and looked at my tablet.

Mary Catherine said, "So far I haven't seen your name in the news stories."

"Let's hope it stays that way. This case is a black eye for the NYPD."

We watched a video report. Someone had leaked everything about the Land Sharks. The story talked about how the group hadn't reported seized money or admitted it into evidence, though the reporter also mentioned that it was believed the Sharks had put most of the money into more elaborate investigations and ultimately even toward the building of a tremendous youth center in the Bronx. I smiled at that, thinking about the other youth center built with Richard Deason's money.

I knew most reporters would discount any of the information about what the Land Sharks did for the community. I couldn't blame them at all. No one hates a crooked cop more than another cop.

We kept watching the next few stories. One had to do with the owner of a Brooklyn diner who'd been shot behind his restaurant. His tearful niece named Tammy went on and on about how she'd miss him. Witnesses said a tattooed man who looked like a biker had just walked up and shot the diner owner. That was the kind of homicide I'd like to be on for the next few months. Something simple and direct.

The last story was a short one about a fugitive named Kevin Doyle. I was surprised they didn't associate it with the story about Celeste Cantor being arrested, but maybe no one had yet made the same connection Walter Jackson did. The same old photo of Doyle from the Department of Defense flashed on the screen.

As Mary Catherine snuggled up close to me, I wondered what had become of Kevin Doyle.

CHAPTER 120

MARY CATHERINE AND I had a Friday afternoon appointment with our fertility ob-gyn, and by then I was able to tune out most of the noise about the big case. Sure, I answered a few calls from the bigwigs at One Police Plaza, but overall it was starting to feel like a true day off. And one I'd certainly earned.

I held Mary Catherine's hand through each test and scan. She was in good spirits, chatting with each of the different techs. I never knew if it was her accent or just her pleasant personality that most attracted people to her. Mary Catherine could talk to anyone and make them feel like they were the only ones in the world at that moment.

Neither of us would admit to the butterflies in our stomachs as we waited for the doctor to meet us in an office.

Mary Catherine reached across from her chair to grasp my hand. We were sitting in identical chairs facing a small conference room table. No one had made any comments about any of the tests performed so far today. I was still nervous.

Mary Catherine's stomach gurgled so loudly I inadvertently turned my head. She shrugged and gave me that beautiful smile. "I guess I'm a little hungry, and God knows what else is going on inside this belly." She patted her stomach.

"I can fix the hungry part. And no matter what's going on inside your belly, I'm with you. I think we've proven the whole family is with you, whatever happens."

She smiled. "I'm glad Ricky got his audition. This seems like a big step for him. I hope that host isn't too tough on him. Ricky can be a little sensitive as well."

"Brian and I will be there. If it gets out of hand, I'm sure we'll be able to deal with it."

Mary Catherine was quiet for a moment. She left her hand resting on her stomach. Then she said, "Michael, no matter what happens, you and the kids have made me so happy. I'll be fine."

"You'll be fine with another kid on the way. Don't worry."

"Thank you, Dr. Bennett, but I think I'll wait to hear what our real doctor has to say."

Just then the door to the conference room opened and Dr. Christina Ashe took the chair across the table from us. I liked how direct Dr. Ashe was. At the moment, she wasn't smiling, but she didn't seem upset. That was sort of the vibe we always got from her. I didn't know if she was just focused all the time or if it was a defense mechanism she had set up for dealing with disappointed couples unable to have a child.

The doctor seemed to take her own sweet time organizing her papers before she looked up and said, "How do you feel, Mary Catherine? I mean, how do you honestly feel being out of bed?"

"I guess I hadn't really evaluated it." Mary Catherine closed her eyes for a moment like she was taking a silent inventory of her aches and pains. "The only thing I can say that has changed is that I get a little bit dizzy walking around."

The doctor said, "I'd say that you've stabilized. Things seem to be going well, and I think we can ease you off bed rest."

Mary Catherine lit up and clapped her hands.

The doctor held up her hand. "But I want to make sure you won't overdo it." She shifted her eyes to me. "I'm counting on the two of you being vigilant. No housework, no lifting, and only short walks."

Mary Catherine started talking fast. "I have a few things I'm going to do around the house. Nothing too strenuous. Plus I have to help Shawna with her history project. And I—"

The doctor's tone was much more serious this time. "Mrs. Bennett, you can either slow things way down or I'll order full-time bed rest from now until the baby comes."

Mary Catherine knew when she was beat. She nodded her head and said, "I'll slow way down on everything. I promise."

I considered getting the doctor's phone number so she could teach me how she did that. I had never seen Mary Catherine concede a point so completely.

We walked out of the doctor's office into the brisk air. Mary Catherine spun around and hugged me. Then she kissed me. "We're having a baby."

That showed me how much she had been preparing herself for bad news. She was ready and excited. And I was thrilled.

CHAPTER 121

ROB TRILLING FELT like he might need to take a moment and just breathe. The anticipation and, frankly, nerves were threatening to overwhelm him. But it was all good. He had a smile on his face. He was getting ready for an honest-to-God nighttime date. Not a lunch or ice cream or family dinner at a colleague's house but an actual date that included dinner and a movie.

This was a big deal for him. He'd had a girlfriend his last year of high school, but it was never serious, and his time in the Army hadn't given him many opportunities to date. Rob was looking forward to going on a date with no drama or ex-boyfriends showing up. At least that's what he hoped.

So did his roommates. They were always encouraging him to get out and meet a nice woman. This was a big deal to them too.

Sabiha had done a good job on his hair. She'd used just the

right amount of gel and given his short bangs a little flare up into the air. When she was done, she'd pinched his cheek like he was a kid in a barber's chair.

Katie had picked out his clothes. Like the American-sounding name she'd selected, her fashion choices were simple. His best pair of blue khakis and a white button-down shirt. He liked the look. It almost made him feel like an adult for a change.

Rob caught some of the news stories on Celeste Cantor's arrest. He'd also gotten some texts from his few friends at the NYPD. Rob tried to downplay his role, but everyone wanted the inside scoop. It didn't take much for people to figure out that if Trilling was on leave, he'd probably been one of the officers involved.

Rob appreciated one of the local TV stories about the incident, which used eyewitness testimony to describe how Detective Michael Bennett had purposely stood up to draw fire away from patrons at the restaurant. The other stories on the news were about a Brooklyn diner owner being shot and, lastly, the possibility of a cold snap approaching.

Rob realized he'd been focusing on the TV because he was nervous. Just a step from actually being scared. He didn't know why. It was just a movie and dinner. He'd even made reservations at a sushi place a few blocks away. His grandpa always called sushi "bait," but Rob had really developed a taste for it.

His roommates scurried around the apartment, cleaning up any mess, no matter how small. He appreciated their interest in him having a good evening.

Katie said, "We wait in bedroom, no?"

"No, this is your apartment too. We're done hiding." Then he looked around at all five of the women. "Except for hiding from

Mr. Kazanjian. I don't want us to lose the apartment." That earned smiles and giggles all around.

There was a knock at the door.

Rob took a moment to check himself in the only mirror in the living room. He glanced over at his roommates. A couple of them gave him a thumbs-up. Then Sylvia slapped him on the butt and pushed him toward the door. Rob took a deep breath, turned the knob, and opened the door.

The smile on Juliana Bennett's face made his knees go weak. It also erased every last concern he had about dating his boss's daughter. She stepped right past him with two bags in her arms. She greeted each of his roommates by name. That was impressive, considering she'd only met them once. Then she started handing out clothes from the bags.

Juliana said, "A nice clothing store in Midtown gave us some clothes for a show. All we had to do was mention the shop's name in our printed program. These are some of the extras we're not using. I can bring more when the show closes. The way things have been going around the playhouse, that might be next week." She'd said it with a smile.

Rob watched as the girls absolutely flipped over the new clothes. Rob was glad he had told Mariah, the paramedic, that he couldn't see her anymore. She seemed to take it okay. She understood. She even said, "I saw how your partner's daughter looked at you." Rob didn't admit to anything.

Once the clothes were distributed, Juliana came over, gave Rob a peck on the cheek, and said, "You ready? I'm starving."

Rob Trilling was going on a date!

CHAPTER 122

ALTHOUGH INITIALLY I hadn't been in favor of Ricky trying out for this crazy cooking show *Rising Chefs,* I appreciated driving into Brooklyn with Ricky and Brian on Saturday for his audition. It got me away from what had turned into the near constant news coverage of Celeste Cantor's arrest and the revelations about the Land Sharks.

Ricky hadn't said much on the drive over. The normally personable and chatty teenager gazed out at the cityscape and kept his thoughts to himself. I'd already given him the "I'm proud of you no matter what" speech. I just wanted him to have some fun.

The studio was in a new five-story building in Brooklyn Heights, not far from the bridge. The lobby alone was awe-inspiring, with forty-foot ceilings, enormous potted trees, and modern art placed strategically around the atrium.

As we signed in at the security desk and walked back toward

the studio, I realized what a big deal this was. There was a huge staff and things were busy. I would have said things were "cooking," but I didn't want to become Walter Jackson with the puns.

A production assistant led us to the studio where *Rising Chefs* would be filmed. The lighting immediately caught my eye. It was soothing but also illuminated everything well. I wished I could replicate it in our apartment. Nearly a dozen workers scurried around the set, making sure everything was just right.

As soon as we stepped into the studio, I noticed that the other participants had their mothers with them. Mostly younger mothers. All of them attractive mothers. The actual participants were a mix of male and female.

I turned to the young woman who'd led us to the studio. "Think I missed the memo that said no dads or big brothers allowed?"

She smiled. Then she cut her eyes back and forth to make sure no one was listening before she said, "Chef Gino appreciates pretty women. Sometimes when these young chefs miss out on their first auditions, they and their mothers get invited back to try again." She smiled, but I sensed she wasn't happy with the situation. That might've been why she'd confessed it to me. As far as I was concerned, it made Chef Gino sound creepy.

Luckily, we'd been out of earshot of Ricky. He was still excited and interested in starting the show.

After a while, the stage manager clapped his hands and got everyone's attention. Each teen chef was given ingredients and told to make a simple Italian red sauce using any of the vegetables at their workstations.

Brian and I were allowed to stand near Ricky while he put his sauce together. The filming wouldn't start until after this exercise. The stage manager said something about first making sure each of the young chefs knew how to use spices and the ingredients to the best effect.

I noticed other kids using their phones to check recipes. Some were even clearly getting coached by their moms, which we'd been told was against the rules, but no one from the staff seemed to really care. Ricky just jumped in. He used a sharp knife to chop onions, tomatoes, green peppers, and fresh garlic at a speed that worried me. When he was done, I glanced over to make sure all of his fingers were still attached.

After about forty-five minutes, he let Brian and me have a taste of his sauce. It was fantastic. I gave him a thumbs-up and hoped he'd make it again for Sunday dinner.

Everyone knew when Chef Gino stepped into the studio. The larger-than-life TV star tasted several of the sauces as he made his way down the line. I noticed he did tend to linger near pretty moms. I still didn't think it would be an issue.

Ricky stepped up and introduced himself to Chef Gino. Gino shook his hand, glanced at me and Brian, then tasted the sauce. He smacked his lips and acted like he was a sommelier sampling a rare red wine.

Gino looked at Ricky and said, "Where'd you learn to cook?"

"At home."

"You never went to any schools or took any classes?"

"No, sir."

"It shows."

That shocked me. I figured out he was an overcritical ass, but this was too much. All three of us just stared at the overweight chef. I was at a loss for words.

Gino said, "You clearly have only a rudimentary understanding of spices. Plus you used way too many onions. The sauce has an acid taste, and the tomato-to-salt ratio is way off. You really think you'll be able to compete on a show like this?"

Now Ricky looked a little shaky. "I…I…I guess so."

Gino raised his voice. "You *guess* so? You know how many kids want to come on this show? You just wasted a spot for some promising young chef."

I was about to intervene when Brian took the lead. He stepped forward and stiff-armed Gino. Even though the chef was almost twice my son's girth, Brian backed him up a few paces.

Brian kept his voice low and even but stern. He didn't want to attract attention. "Who the hell do you think you are? You're supposed to build kids' confidence, not shatter their dreams. That sauce is outstanding. Ricky is outstanding. You're just a fat blowhard with some kind of complex. You apologize to my brother right now."

It wasn't lost on me that none of the staff had rushed to help Gino. Either it had happened before or they all felt he deserved it. The other kids—and moms—were all looking on silently. For his part, Gino looked scared, but he didn't say anything.

Brian repeated, "Apologize to my brother. You better do it right now."

Gino gave Brian a little nod. He turned to Ricky and said, "Your brother is right. I shouldn't have been so harsh."

It wasn't much of an apology. Brian forced the big chef back another step. Gino stumbled over a step stool and hit the carpeted floor with a profound thud. He just sat there like his bulk was balancing him on the floor.

Brian looked at me and said, "We should probably leave."

I said, "I agree."

Ricky slipped off his apron and casually tossed it onto his workstation. Brian and I followed him out of the building silently. Once we were outside, Ricky turned to Brian and said, "Thanks, Brian. I needed you to stand up for me so I could stand up for myself. I know now that that guy's full of crap. I'd rather the family like my cooking than the whole world."

The smile that spread across my face was so wide it physically hurt for a moment.

CHAPTER 123

THE BEACH, ABOUT fifteen miles from La Ceiba, Honduras, was perfect: low-key but with a decent restaurant and bar close by. The waters of the Caribbean barely made a sound as the tiny waves rolled onto the white sand.

Kevin Doyle stretched his whole body as he lay on the lounger under an oversized umbrella. When he moved a certain way, he felt a twinge of pain in his left side. Under his lightweight shirt, Doyle still wore bandages to cover the wounds of the bullet that had entered the side of his abdomen and exited through his back. A second, superficial hole sat near his belly button. The bullet must have clipped part of the Kevlar and fallen out as he was running away from the restaurant. He also still had a giant bruise from the bullet that had been stopped by the Kevlar in the shirt Bennett had given him.

His friend Amir had said Doyle was lucky the more damaging

bullet hadn't hit any vital organs. Amir had been the one to provide Doyle with first aid the night his cousin shot him. Then the shady Israeli had helped Doyle get out of the city safely.

Doyle had taken a circuitous route to Honduras. He decided, while he was here, to treat it like an extended vacation. He had rented a room through Airbnb under the name Douglas Mauser. So far, he'd spent most mornings sitting in the same lounger, gazing out at the beautiful water.

Doyle had no interest in resuming his former profession. He had money stashed all over the world. And he was shocked at how cheaply he could live well here.

He smiled at the pretty waitress from the little hotel bar. She knew to bring him a Coke Zero every hour or so.

She said in broken English, "You like a rum runner?"

Doyle smiled and shook his head. He didn't think he needed to tell her that he couldn't drink alcohol for a few more weeks because the antibiotics and pain pills probably wouldn't mix well with rum.

She winked at him, and he couldn't help but watch her walk across the sand to the small tiki bar.

He had a wild thought as he watched her walk away. Could she be a better Tammy? As long as she didn't want him to murder anybody. He'd have to tell her he didn't do that sort of thing. Anymore.

ABOUT THE AUTHORS

James Patterson is one of the best-known and biggest-selling writers of all time. Among his creations are some of the world's most popular series, including Alex Cross, the Women's Murder Club, Michael Bennett and the Private novels. He has written many other number one bestsellers including collaborations with President Bill Clinton and Dolly Parton, stand-alone thrillers and non-fiction. James has donated millions in grants to independent bookshops and has been the most borrowed adult author in UK libraries for the past fourteen years in a row. He lives in Florida with his family.

James O. Born is an award-winning crime and science-fiction novelist as well as a career law-enforcement agent. A native Floridian, he still lives in the Sunshine State.

Have You Read Them All?

STEP ON A CRACK
(with Michael Ledwidge)

The most powerful people in the world have gathered for a funeral in New York City. They don't know it's a trap devised by a ruthless mastermind, and it's up to Michael Bennett to save every last hostage.

RUN FOR YOUR LIFE
(with Michael Ledwidge)

The Teacher is giving New York a lesson it will never forget, slaughtering the powerful and the arrogant. Michael Bennett discovers a vital pattern, but has only a few hours to save the city.

WORST CASE
(with Michael Ledwidge)

Children from wealthy families are being abducted. But the captor isn't demanding money. He's quizzing his hostages on the price others pay for their luxurious lives, and one wrong answer is fatal.

TICK TOCK
(with Michael Ledwidge)

New York is in chaos as a rash of horrifying copycat crimes tears through the city. Michael Bennett investigates, but not even he could predict the earth-shattering enormity of this killer's plan.

I, MICHAEL BENNETT
(with Michael Ledwidge)

Bennett arrests infamous South American crime lord Manuel Perrine. From jail, Perrine vows to rain terror down upon New York City – and to get revenge on Michael Bennett.

GONE
(with Michael Ledwidge)

Perrine is back and deadlier than ever. Bennett must make an impossible decision: stay and protect his family, or hunt down the man who is their biggest threat.

BURN
(with Michael Ledwidge)

A group of well-dressed men enter a condemned building. Later, a charred body is found. Michael Bennett is about to enter a secret underground world of terrifying depravity.

ALERT
(with Michael Ledwidge)

Two devastating catastrophes hit New York in quick succession, putting everyone on edge. Bennett is given the near impossible task of hunting down the shadowy terror group responsible.

BULLSEYE
(with Michael Ledwidge)

As the most powerful men on earth gather for a meeting of the UN, Bennett receives shocking intelligence that there will be an assassination attempt on the US president. Are the Russian government behind the plot?

HAUNTED
(with James O. Born)

Michael Bennett is ready for a vacation after a series of crises push him, and his family, to the brink. But when he gets pulled into a shocking case, Bennett is fighting to protect a town, the law, and the family that he loves.

AMBUSH
(with James O. Born)

When an anonymous tip proves to be a trap, Michael Bennett believes he personally is being targetted. And not just him, but his family too.

BLINDSIDE
(with James O. Born)

The mayor of New York has a daughter who's missing. Detective Michael Bennett has a son who's in prison. Can one father help the other?

THE RUSSIAN
(with James O. Born)

As Michael Bennett's wedding day approaches, a killer has a vow of his own to fulfil . . .

SHATTERED
(with James O. Born)

After returning from his honeymoon, Michael Bennett discovers that his former partner is missing. After everything they've been through, he will never give up hope of finding her – he owes her that much.

OBSESSED
(with James O. Born)

Detective Michael Bennett must discover who's murdering young women in New York – before his eldest daughter is targeted.

CROSSHAIRS
(with James O. Born)

Michael Bennett must uncover a sniper who is taking out impossible targets around NYC. But the killer may be even closer than he thinks . . .

Read on for a sneak peek at an intriguing
New York City detective case . . .

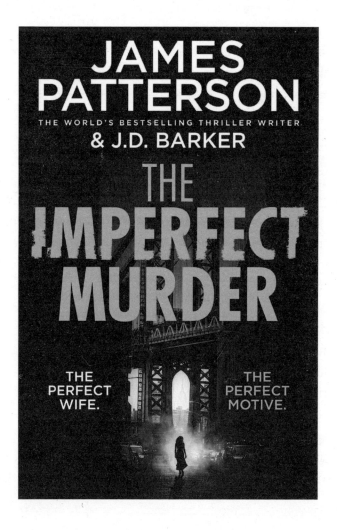

STUDYING THE SMALL observation monitor two doors down from the precinct interview room, assistant district attorney Carmen Saffi taps the end of her pen against her lips. Declan, next to her, nurses a cup of tar-black coffee from the break room. On the screen, Denise Morrow is sitting at the aluminum table, her hands in her lap; her attorney is in the chair beside her. He keeps looking up at the camera. When he speaks to her, he does so in whispers.

"Geller Hoffman just happened to show up?" ADA Saffi asks Declan.

Although it's approaching midnight, Saffi looks as sharp as she does in the courtroom — gray pantsuit, hair and makeup perfect. She's the same as Cordova, married to the job. It's like the two of them sleep standing up in their Sunday best, ready to roll at a moment's notice. Like they wait for it. Unlike Declan, who knows he still stinks of subway and despair. "The Morrows' alarm was tripped. He said the monitoring company called him," he tells her.

"Seems odd to have a defense attorney on the call list, doesn't it?"

"Said he's a family friend."

"What do you make of their body language?" she asks. "Something seem off to you?"

Declan has picked up on that too.

Denise Morrow is an attractive woman — a bit on the odd side, but attractive. She has that mousy thing going on. With the black-rimmed glasses and her hair swept up, she makes you think of a sexy librarian or a teacher from some '90s rock video. It's like she knows she's attractive and purposely tries to dial it back. Even now, sitting in an interrogation room wearing borrowed scrubs, she's striking. Every guy who passed her in the precinct hallway

1

turned to get a second look. Declan flashes back to Geller walking in on Denise Morrow naked when she was being processed—*he didn't give her a second look. He didn't give her a first look. He went out of his way not to,* Declan thinks. *Not out of respect—that squirrelly fucker doesn't know from respect. It was something else.* Declan got the feeling that seeing Denise Morrow naked was nothing new to Geller. He got the feeling that Geller and Morrow were intimate and going out of their way to conceal it. Her husband was just found dead. *She's traumatized,* Geller said, yet he didn't do a damn thing to comfort her. For her part, Morrow gave no indication she needed or wanted comforting. None of this was typical. While it might mean nothing, it also might mean something.

Cordova knocks twice on the door frame and steps into the small room; he's clutching a computer printout. "We've got life insurance, but not exactly what I was expecting."

ADA Saffi frowns. "What does it say?"

"Joint policy. They took it out three years ago. Pays out five million for natural death, eight million for accidental."

Declan whistles. "There's your motive."

"I agree. It would have been a fantastic motive if Denise Morrow hadn't canceled the payouts on David six weeks ago. Would have been one hell of a motive."

"What?" Declan snatches the paper from him and scans the text. "Says here she terminated all coverage related to David but left hers."

"That's what I just said."

Saffi's frown deepens. "So she dies in a home invasion, he gets eight million, but he dies, she gets zero?"

Cordova nods.

"And she changed that six weeks back?"

"When she paid the premiums for the year."

"You saw that apartment," Declan says. "She doesn't need the insurance money. This woman is smart. She knows we'd see insurance as motive, so she took it off the board. Don't forget, she writes about this sort of thing for a living."

"Oh, I didn't forget." Cordova smirks. "I've been looking at that too. There's something I want you to watch, an interview she did for her second book, *A Mother's Burden*. The book's about Michelle Bacot. Remember that case?"

Saffi does. "Bacot killed her husband when she learned he was molesting their thirteen-year-old daughter. Made it look like an accident—pulled the ladder out from under him when he was cleaning gutters around the house. Jersey City, right?"

Cordova nods. "I found this interview on YouTube. I'm skipping the preamble nonsense and starting at the eight-minute mark." Holding his phone between them, he plays the video.

"The jury didn't take any pity on her, though, right? I mean, Bacot is serving twelve years. Hardly the perfect crime," the interviewer says.

The camera flashes to Denise Morrow. She looks a little younger, and her hair is longer, but she's otherwise the same. "She didn't get caught; she turned herself in. It wasn't the police that got her, it was the guilt. She had saved her daughter, but she couldn't live with what she'd done. Even with the understanding her daughter would be raised by someone other than her if she surrendered, the guilt ate her up until it outweighed everything else."

"So you take guilt out of the equation, and Bacot is a free woman today."

"Exactly."

"The perfect crime," says the interviewer.

"There were no witnesses. People fall from ladders all the time."

"Not once did she report her husband's activity to the police. That's why the jury convicted. Maybe if she'd filed a complaint, gone on the record, and proved the system failed her, the jury would have shown some leniency."

"If she had filed a report, created that paper trail, the police would have had reason to suspect her when her husband died. The fact that she didn't report the crime is the reason she would have gotten away with it," Denise says.

"If not for the guilt."

"If not for the guilt."

"Why do I get the feeling that if you were in Michelle Bacot's shoes, you'd be a free woman today?" the interviewer says.

"If I had been in Michelle Bacot's shoes, not only would I be free, my daughter would be sitting here next to me, not an ounce of guilt between us."

Cordova stops the video, and a heavy silence falls over the room. He slips his phone into the breast pocket of his jacket. "I checked with Murdock at CSU. They covered every inch of that apartment and found no sign of an intruder. The only prints on the main bedroom's terrace door belong to the Morrows. No unknowns in or out on security footage. Neighbors and doorman saw nothing. Break-in appears staged. Sometimes you gotta call it what it is."

Saffi's gaze goes back to the monitor as she takes this all in. Finally she says to Declan, "Remember how I told you to handle this with kid gloves?"

"Yeah."

"Be ready to take the gloves off."

Also By James Patterson

ALEX CROSS NOVELS

Along Came a Spider • Kiss the Girls • Jack and Jill • Cat and Mouse • Pop Goes the Weasel • Roses are Red • Violets are Blue • Four Blind Mice • The Big Bad Wolf • London Bridges • Mary, Mary • Cross • Double Cross • Cross Country • Alex Cross's Trial (*with Richard DiLallo*) • I, Alex Cross • Cross Fire • Kill Alex Cross • Merry Christmas, Alex Cross • Alex Cross, Run • Cross My Heart • Hope to Die • Cross Justice • Cross the Line • The People vs. Alex Cross • Target: Alex Cross • Criss Cross • Deadly Cross • Fear No Evil • Triple Cross • Alex Cross Must Die • The House of Cross

THE WOMEN'S MURDER CLUB SERIES

1st to Die (*with Andrew Gross*) • 2nd Chance (*with Andrew Gross*) • 3rd Degree (*with Andrew Gross*) • 4th of July (*with Maxine Paetro*) • The 5th Horseman (*with Maxine Paetro*) • The 6th Target (*with Maxine Paetro*) • 7th Heaven (*with Maxine Paetro*) • 8th Confession (*with Maxine Paetro*) • 9th Judgement (*with Maxine Paetro*) • 10th Anniversary (*with Maxine Paetro*) • 11th Hour (*with Maxine Paetro*) • 12th of Never (*with Maxine Paetro*) • Unlucky 13 (*with Maxine Paetro*) • 14th Deadly Sin (*with Maxine Paetro*) • 15th Affair (*with Maxine Paetro*) • 16th Seduction (*with Maxine Paetro*) • 17th Suspect (*with Maxine Paetro*) • 18th Abduction (*with Maxine Paetro*) • 19th Christmas (*with Maxine Paetro*) • 20th Victim (*with Maxine Paetro*) • 21st Birthday (*with Maxine Paetro*) • 22 Seconds (*with Maxine Paetro*) • 23rd Midnight (*with Maxine Paetro*) • The 24th Hour (*with Maxine Paetro*)

DETECTIVE MICHAEL BENNETT SERIES

Step on a Crack (*with Michael Ledwidge*) • Run for Your Life (*with Michael Ledwidge*) • Worst Case (*with Michael Ledwidge*) • Tick Tock (*with Michael Ledwidge*) • I, Michael Bennett (*with Michael Ledwidge*) • Gone (*with Michael Ledwidge*) • Burn (*with Michael Ledwidge*) • Alert (*with Michael Ledwidge*) • Bullseye (*with Michael Ledwidge*) •

Haunted (*with James O. Born*) • Ambush (*with James O. Born*) • Blindside (*with James O. Born*) • The Russian (*with James O. Born*) • Shattered (*with James O. Born*) • Obsessed (*with James O. Born*) • Crosshairs (*with James O. Born*)

PRIVATE NOVELS

Private (*with Maxine Paetro*) • Private London (*with Mark Pearson*) • Private Games (*with Mark Sullivan*) • Private: No. 1 Suspect (*with Maxine Paetro*) • Private Berlin (*with Mark Sullivan*) • Private Down Under (*with Michael White*) • Private L.A. (*with Mark Sullivan*) • Private India (*with Ashwin Sanghi*) • Private Vegas (*with Maxine Paetro*) • Private Sydney (*with Kathryn Fox*) • Private Paris (*with Mark Sullivan*) • The Games (*with Mark Sullivan*) • Private Delhi (*with Ashwin Sanghi*) • Private Princess (*with Rees Jones*) • Private Moscow (*with Adam Hamdy*) • Private Rogue (*with Adam Hamdy*) • Private Beijing (*with Adam Hamdy*) • Private Rome (*with Adam Hamdy*) • Private Monaco (*with Adam Hamdy*)

NYPD RED SERIES

NYPD Red (*with Marshall Karp*) • NYPD Red 2 (*with Marshall Karp*) • NYPD Red 3 (*with Marshall Karp*) • NYPD Red 4 (*with Marshall Karp*) • NYPD Red 5 (*with Marshall Karp*) • NYPD Red 6 (*with Marshall Karp*)

DETECTIVE HARRIET BLUE SERIES

Never Never (*with Candice Fox*) • Fifty Fifty (*with Candice Fox*) • Liar Liar (*with Candice Fox*) • Hush Hush (*with Candice Fox*)

INSTINCT SERIES

Instinct (*with Howard Roughan, previously published as* Murder Games) • Killer Instinct (*with Howard Roughan*) • Steal (*with Howard Roughan*)

THE BLACK BOOK SERIES

The Black Book (*with David Ellis*) • The Red Book (*with David Ellis*) • Escape (*with David Ellis*)